# UNICORN PRECINCT

Also by Keith R.A. DeCandido,
from eSpec Books

**The Precinct Series**
**DRAGON PRECINCT**
**UNICORN PRECINCT**
**GRYPHON PRECINCT**
**TALES FROM DRAGON PRECINCT**

**Coming Soon**
**MERMAID PRECINCT**

**Forthcoming Titles**
**PHOENIX PRECINCT**
**MANTICORE PRECINCT**
**MORE TALES FROM DRAGON PRECINCT**

**Other Titles**
**WITHOUT A LICENSE**

# UNICORN PRECINCT

## Keith R.A. DeCandido

eSpec Books

Pennsville, NJ

PUBLISHED BY
eSpec Books LLC
Danielle McPhail, Publisher
PO Box 242,
Pennsville, New Jersey 08070
www.especbooks.com



ISBN: 978-1-942990-84-0
ISBN (ebook): 978-1-942990-83-3



All persons, places, and events in this book are fictitious
and any resemblance to actual persons, places, or events is purely co-
incidental.

Interior Design: Danielle McPhail
Sidhe na Daire Multimedia
www.sidhenadaire.com

Cover Design: Mike McPhail
Current Design based on previous cover design by Jenn Reese
www.tigerbrightstudios.com

Art Credits - www.Shutterstock.com
Unicorn Medallion © Marina Yakutsenya
Sword handle isolated © O.V.D.

*This book is dedicated to all the wonderful people
who asked me when I was gonna
write a sequel to Dragon Precinct —
it only took seven years . . .*

# ACKNOWLEDGMENTS

FOR THE NEW EDITION

Hugely massively amazingly big thanks to Danielle Ackley-McPhail Mike McPhail, and Greg Schauer of eSpec for giving the series a new home.

Also special thanks to the following for their help with "When the Magick Goes Away": JD Adams, Ben Adler, Lorraine Anderson, Lance Roger Axt, Tom B., Em Baisch, Mark Beaulieu, Bonnie Beck, Diane Bellomo, Mo Blaner, Jeremy Bottroff, Buzzy Multimedia, Karen Mitchell Carothers, Danny Chamberlain, Joseph Charpak, Mike Crate, Jim Crider, Alan Danziger, Dwight Davis, GraceAnne Andreassi DeCandido, John S. Drew, Michael Dougherty, Cormac Dullaghan, Heather Eberhardt, Michael & Rosalyn Falkner, Richard Fine, Dave Finnerty, "Finny," Lydia Fithian, Will Frank, Tony & Becky Glinka, Rich Gonzalez, Robert Greenberger, Elektra Hammond, Julie Harris, Shael Hawman, Solomon Jones, Andrew Kaplan, David "Handlebar" Kingsley, William Leisner, Jeff Linder, Shira Lipkin, Stephanie Lucas, Maryjean Lugo, Siannan MacDuff, Ken Mars, Kelsey Mayer, Ian Mond, Tiffany Newell, Meg Nuge, Mitch Obrecht, Julio Angel Ortiz, Thomas Pesso, Kalley Powell, Aaron Rosenberg, Zan Rosin, "Scantrontb," Jeff Schultz, Wrenn Simms, Tina Sorrentino, Mark Squire, Ann Stolinsky, Scott Thede, Ronnie Virga, Ariel Vitali, Josh Ward, Audrey Zarr, and Mike Zipser.

FROM THE ORIGINAL EDITION

Primary thanks have to go to the lord and master of Dark Quest Books, Neal Levin, who took an orphaned series and agreed to publish it.

Secondary thanks to John J. Ordover, the editor who acquired *Dragon Precinct* for Pocket Books, to Rosemary Edghill, Patrick Thomas, C.J. Henderson, Danielle Ackley-McPhail, L. Jagi Lamplighter, Lee Hillman, Jeff Lyman, Jean Rabe, Martin H. Greenberg, and Jennifer Ross, editors who bought *Dragon Precinct* short stories over the years; and to Elektra Hammond, who did such a fine job copyediting this one.

Tertiary thanks to the Forebearance, especially The Mom, for invaluable reading assistance, and for never giving up on me. Also to the various people in my life who have continued to be supportive and loving and who keep believing in me — you know who you are.

Finally, thanks to all those that live with me — human, feline, and canine — for everything.

# PROLOGUE

Vaspar had been thinking about how much he'd been enjoying the calm and quiet of the past five weeks when he found the dead body.

He'd been serving in the Cynnis household for his entire life, as his father had before him, and his father before him, all the way back to the founding of Cliff's End. Then when his father, along with Sir Wilt and Madam Marva, died at sea during a hurricane, Vaspar had been made head butler.

The first few years were wonderful, as the only person he was responsible for was sir and madam's teenaged boy, Malik Cynnis. Upon turning sixteen, he was made Sir Malik, and was quickly married to the wealthy Hassa Trinnek, such a link doing much to restore the Cynnis family's affairs.

For Vaspar, it was a most satisfactory situation. Sir Malik and Madam Hassa were fine people who treated the household staff very well — not an attitude often seen in the young — and bringing two rich families together meant they could hire more staff. A bigger staff meant Vaspar could delegate some of the more unpleasant tasks to less senior servants.

Everything was fine until Madam Hassa had children.

To begin with, madam's entire personality warped when she was with child to the point where the cook quit and the dressing girl almost did likewise. Vaspar had solved both problems by finding a better cook and convincing the dressing girl to stay, but it was a near thing.

And then there were the children. Awful creatures, each one was more annoying than the last. Jared, who slept with any woman he could find, a problem that only worsened after he married; Blan, with his predilection for thievery; and Crilla, who treated everyone horribly and then complained that nobody liked her.

Then came the youngest, Arra, who was a beautiful, sweet-tempered child that, if she didn't have madam's eyes and sir's nose, Vaspar would have been hard-pressed to believe she came from the same parents as the other three.

Arra was just sixteen and betrothed, and her preparations for the wedding were at too advanced a state for her to accompany her siblings to Iaron to visit friends, a journey that had taken up most of the past five weeks, and had kept the house magnificently quiet.

Sadly, Jared, Blan, and Crilla were due back in a few days, so Vaspar was reveling in the peace while he still could.

He was downstairs on the servants' floor, located just below ground level, heading toward the kitchen to fix himself a quick lunch. When he went by the sewing room, he was surprised to see two of Arra's dress girls giggling and laughing.

"What is going on?" Vaspar asked with an iron tone. These two—along with a third, oddly not present—were supposed to be hard at work on Arra's wedding gown. In fact, if he recalled correctly, she was supposed to be trying it on this afternoon.

Both girls straightened and stopped laughing at the sight of the head butler. One said in a subdued voice, "Apologies, but we're waitin' for Biroa t' get back."

Vaspar frowned. "Get back from where?"

"Seamstress down on Sandy Brook Way. We're short on fabric, y'see, an' Biroa went t' get more."

"Was Arra informed of this?"

The girls exchanged nervous glances. "Dunno. Thought Biroa told 'er."

With a heavy sigh, Vaspar said, "I will inform Arra of this delay." He had no faith in Biroa's having done so. Of the three dress girls, Biroa was by far the cheekiest, always talking back. She would never have spoken so respectfully to the head butler. She barely was deferential to sir and madam, truth be told.

The delay was not much of a concern. At first, Vaspar had been worried that the female staff had not left enough time for all the preparations. However, Vaspar's only experience with preparing a girl for marriage had been the endless nightmare that was Crilla's engagement, which had involved a great deal of shouting, revising, and starting over. Arra was far more even-tempered and, indeed, she was already ahead of schedule when compared to her older sister.

Still, Vaspar felt that Arra should at least be informed that one of her dress girls had left the mansion—without so much as *mentioning* it to the head butler—and that her fitting would be a few hours later than expected.

Climbing the spiral wooden staircase to the third floor, Vaspar then walked down the wide hallway, covered with portraits of Cynnis family members from throughout the decades. Blan had always complained that walking down this hallway made him feel as if he was being spied on by his ancestors—which, to Vaspar's mind, was reason enough to keep them there.

Most of the doors were open, since their occupants weren't home. Sir and madam were both out of the mansion—Renna, one of the chambermaids, was in their bedroom dusting the furnishings. Vaspar nodded to her as he went by, and Renna curtsied back.

At the far end of the hall was the one closed door: Arra's room. Vaspar rapped on the door three times, as was custom. "It's Vaspar," he added.

To his surprise, there was no reply.

Vaspar knocked two more times, and still no reply. She could have been asleep, but she rarely took naps at this hour. However, the pressure of the impending wedding might have taken its toll on her.

He knocked again, much louder this time. "It's Vaspar!"

Nothing.

Dashing down the hallway to sir and madam's bedroom, he said to Renna, "Arra is not answering her door. I'm concerned. Please go in and check on her."

Nodding demurely, Renna curtsied and followed him down the hallway.

Vaspar stood at a respectful distance, so that he could not see inside the room when Renna opened the door. It wouldn't do to see Arra in an indecent state, after all.

Renna turned the latch and pushed the door open.

Then she put her hands to her mouth and screamed loud enough to wake the dead.

Vaspar quickly moved to her side, saw what she saw, and realized that she wasn't screaming quite *that* loud.

Because Arra lay unmoving on the floor, blood pooling on the carpeted floor beneath her.

Grabbing Renna by the shoulders, Vaspar quickly guided her away from the doorway and down the hall.

As he did, he heard the footfalls of several people coming from the end of the hall, as various servants ran upstairs to learn the reason for Renna's piercing scream. The first to arrive at the landing was one of the footmen, a bearded youth.

"Andres," Vaspar barked, "something horrible has happened. Send for sir and madam *immediately*."

Nodding, Andres turned to go back downstairs.

"And Andres!" Vaspar said after a moment, realizing what else needed to be done.

The footman stopped and turned around.

"After that, go to Unicorn Precinct. We'll need the Castle Guard."

# ONE

LIEUTENANT TORIN BAN WYVALD OF THE CLIFF'S END CASTLE GUARD STOOD
with the sun on his face and smiled.

The heat wave that came as part of midsummer had broken, and now they had the warmth of the sun without the concomitant sodden moisture content in the air. Torin knew that this was fleeting—humidity never stayed away for long in a port city like Cliff's End—so he intended to enjoy it for as long as he could.

Seven chimes had magickally rung in the hour that started Torin's shift several minutes earlier. Around the same time as Torin's arrival in Cliff's End a decade ago, the Brotherhood of Wizards set up a spell to ring out each hour. This system had proven far more reliable than looking up at the sun and guessing, especially since the sun wasn't always visible. Amidst the mansions of Unicorn Precinct just beyond the castle, not to mention in the Forest of Nimvale on the other side of it, trees tended to obscure the sun's warm light. As one traversed the distance between the castle and the banks of the Garamin Sea—the middle-class region of Dragon Precinct, the slums of Goblin Precinct, and finally the docklands of Mermaid Precinct—the structures of the city-state itself kept the sun from hitting your face.

Indeed, the pathway that led to the castle of Lord Albin and Lady Meerka—rulers of the demesne for King Marcus and Queen Marta—had the best exposure to sunlight in all of Cliff's End. And on a warm, pleasant day such as this, Torin fully intended to enjoy it. Besides, he was *already* tardy, so he had no reason to rush. Sergeant Jonas would look disapprovingly at him in exactly the same manner whether he was ten or fifteen minutes late.

Eventually, Torin would stop standing on the pathway to the castle gates and continue inside, heading to the eastern wing of the castle where the Castle Guard's main headquarters were located.

But for now, he reveled in the sunlight, closing his eyes and smiling.

"There you are!"

His smile fell at the sound of that voice. It was his half-elf partner, Lieutenant Danthres Tresyllione, staring at him with what others might think was a sour expression, but a decade of partnership had taught Torin that that was simply her normal look.

"Sorry I'm late," he said.

"Hardly," Danthres said, putting her hands on her hips. She wore the same leather armor he did, with the gryphon crest on the chest symbolizing that they worked in Guard HQ here at the castle, and the brown cloak of their rank. "If you were sorry, you'd stop doing it, but you've come in on time perhaps thrice in ten years."

Torin grinned. "Perhaps that many, yes. I was simply enjoying the sun while it was pleasant."

Danthres frowned, making her unfortunately constructed face, a combination of the worst aspects of her dual heritage, look even more sour. "The sun is never pleasant. Anyhow, Jonas is bouncing in his boots to give us the morning rundown."

Letting out a long sigh, Torin said, "Very well," and followed Danthres through the portcullis.

Within minutes they were in the large squadroom, with three desks, a large picture window that presented a beautiful view of the forest, and several doors.

One led to the pantry, and Sergeant Jonas came zipping out of it, his green cloak billowing behind him. He was swallowing what Torin assumed to be the last of the pastries his wife sent him to the squadroom with every morning, and of which Torin rarely got to partake.

"About time you arrived, ban Wyvald. I know you don't have a good excuse for being late, so I'll save you the trouble of having to come up with a bad one."

Torin chuckled. "Very generous of you, Jonas. My gratitude."

Jonas just shook his head, then bellowed: "Attention, everyone!"

Around the squadroom Lieutenant Iaian was sitting on the edge of the desk belonging to Lieutenants Dru and Hawk. Iaian's partner, Lieutenant Amilar Grovis, sat alone with some paperwork.

The former three stopped their conversation while Torin and Danthres each hung their cloaks on the pegboard provided for same.

Jonas shuffled parchments in his hands. "Iaian, Grovis, we've gotten official word from the Lord and Lady that the corruption that you uncovered in Mermaid Precinct must be *fully* investigated."

Both detectives' eyes widened, but their expressions were diametrically opposed. Iaian looked stunned and hurt while Grovis looked thrilled. For his part, Torin winced.

A twenty-three-year veteran of the Guard who was counting the hours to his twenty-fifth year and longed-for retirement, Iaian stared at Jonas with rheumy eyes. "Are you outta your *mind*, Jonas?"

"Me? No, I'm completely sane. Can't speak to the Lord and Lady, and *they're* the ones who cut the orders. Now if you want to talk to *them* about it . . ."

Before Iaian could respond to that—and Torin knew he was cranky enough to do so in a manner that might get him into trouble—Grovis spoke up. "That will not be necessary, Sergeant. Believe you me, I will be thrilled to ferret out these miscreants. It's long past time we received this particular assignment, if you ask me."

"Nobody *did* ask you, shitbrain!" Iaian snarled. "Look, we did our bit before midsummer—we proved that Sergeant Gaffni was behind the bad glamours, he resigned, he paid a fine, and he's moved outta town. We wrote up a whole report and every-damn-thing. What the hell else are we supposed to do?"

"Apparently," Jonas said, "the western wing of the castle was less than impressed with your report, Iaian, and they want more."

Iaian folded his arms over the gryphon on his armor's chestplate. "Dammit, guards shouldn't investigate other guards."

"For heaven's sake, why not?" Grovis had his hands out, an expression of shock on his fish-like face.

Iaian rolled his eyes, something Torin had seen him do fairly often when in his partner's presence. "Because some day you're gonna be on the docks, and there's gonna be some lunatic shitbrain with a sword that's bigger than he is who just murdered his entire family and you're gonna need to bring him down, and you're gonna *need* the guards from Mermaid to have your back."

"Yes, naturally," Grovis said. "I fail to see your point."

"You always do."

Before Iaian could excoriate his partner some more, Torin inserted himself into the conversation. "If the guards become subject to an inquiry from their fellows, it erodes the trust between them. They will be far less likely to come to your aid in such an instance."

Grovis snorted in a manner typical of the upper classes to which he belonged. The son of a banker, he had been inserted into the Castle Guard by his father, who wanted to "make a man of him." When they'd first been told that, Iaian's comment was that Grovis didn't have the materials available for such a manufacture.

"Don't snort at Torin, boy," Iaian said. "He's right. Look, Gaffni was dumped in our laps, and we did our due diligence. We try to do more than that, and we'll be nailed right up the ass."

"If they're the type to deny aid to a fellow guard just because that guard did as he was ordered by the Lord and Lady, then I do not *wish* to have their assistance."

"Yeah," Hawk said, "an' when you die at the end'a that sword, you'll expire knowin' you was right."

"But you'll still be dead," Dru added.

Danthres shook her head. "Much as it pains me to say this, I agree with Grovis. If there are guards who are committing crimes, then we need to be rid of them."

"Look," Iaian said, "it's one thing if a guard's going around slitting throats or something. Yeah, that one's gotta be put away, but we're talking about making a little extra money on the side."

"Which is a crime in this city-state," Grovis said tartly.

"In Mermaid? It's just daily life down there."

"Besides," Dru asked, "why's it have to be *us* who do it? Last time there was trouble in Mermaid, it was some noblemen who found out about it and took care of it."

Jonas shuffled some more parchments. "And that's the problem. Everyone got all pissed because we couldn't police our own."

Torin felt the need to add to the conversation, even though it seemed as if they would never get off this track and continue with the morning rundown. "So what, precisely, are we to accomplish? The last round of corruption in Mermaid was exposed, Sergeant Victro was removed from his position—and all it did was pave the way for Sergeant Gaffni. Now, no doubt, the new sergeant will pick up where they left off."

# Keith R.A. DeCandido

Sounding outraged, Grovis said, "Are you saying that we should not prosecute crimes because there are other criminals?"

"I'm saying that there is too much money to be made via graft in Mermaid. As Iaian said, it's the coin of the realm on the docks. To expect else is to deny nature."

Hawk smiled. "Can tell *he* comes from where the philosophers live."

Torin smiled right back. He was born and raised in Myverin, a verdant land filled with intellectuals and artisans and philosophers. Many considered it a paradise, but Torin had been miserable there, wanting more from life than something so contemplative.

Grovis asked, "And I repeat, what is the alternative? We cannot simply ignore the criminals."

"No," Torin said, "but perhaps our attention would be better placed toward eliminating the reasons for graft on the docks in the first place."

Iaian let out a snort at that. "Yeah, but the Lord and Lady don't wanna change the way *they* do things—they'd rather make a show by having us make asses of ourselves. Throw a few perfectly good guards in the hole and pretend like they did something."

"It's not *pretending* at all," Grovis said.

But before he could continue, Jonas said, "Regardless, the order comes directly from the Lord and Lady." And then he handed a piece of parchment to Iaian.

Again, Iaian's eyes widened. "Shit."

He handed the parchment to Grovis, who went similarly goggle-eyed.

Usually, whenever the Guard received orders "from the Lord and Lady," it was really from a member of their court, speaking (supposedly) for them. Torin couldn't remember the last time he saw orders for the Castle Guard that actually contained the Lord and Lady's seal on it, as the parchment Jonas had just handed them did.

"So this isn't one of the shitbrains on the other end of the castle who's trying to fellate the Lord and Lady by doing his bit for law and order in the demesne?" Danthres asked.

"No, it's a genuine order from the two people who actually run the city-state." Jonas stared at Iaian. "If you actually want to *get* that bonus that hits when you reach twenty-five years in service, Lieutenant, you'd do well to follow their orders."

"Yeah." Iaian sounded like someone had killed his wife. Torin amended that thought quickly, however—it was more accurate to say that he sounded like someone had killed a person about whom he actually cared. Torin had never understood why Iaian didn't just divorce the woman and have done with it . . .

"In any case," Jonas said, "that's what you two are on. Dru, Hawk, we've got reports from Goblin and Dragon Precincts about a Temisan priest who's apparently talking to the dead."

Dru frowned. "What's the problem?"

"He's charging quite a bit for the privilege, and the people complaining don't think he's legitimate. Look into it." Jonas placed another parchment on their desk. "Tresyllione, ban Wyvald, are you back at the magistrate's today?"

Sitting across from Torin, Danthres shook her head. "We've dealt with the last of the stragglers from midsummer." The midsummer celebration had turned ugly when the dragon that usually circled the city-state and then disappeared for a year instead swooped down onto Oak Way and burned a mansion to the ground, along with two of its occupants. That, on top of all the usual rioters, ne'er-do-wells, cutpurses, and drunken idiots who came out at midsummer had meant a busy time for the lieutenants of the Castle Guard, but they finally seemed to be done with it.

"Good, so the next case up—"

"Tresyllione, ban Wyvald!"

That was Osric, the captain in charge of the Castle Guard, and Torin was surprised, as his voice came, not from his office to Torin's right, but from the entryway to the squadroom on the left.

Looking over, Torin saw Osric standing alongside Sir Rommett, one of the Lord and Lady's chamberlains. Torin noticed Danthres tense— she'd had a run-in with Rommett during the Brightblade case.

At the best of times, Osric looked annoyed. The silk patch that covered his left eye—lost in the elven wars while Torin served under him—and the stubble that he cultivated on his cheeks saw to that. The scowl currently on his face meant that these were far from the best of times. But that was hardly a surprise if he was being followed around by the chamberlain.

"There's been a murder in Unicorn Precinct," Osric said. "Arra Cynnis."

Before Torin could respond, Grovis stood up, goggle-eyed. "Arra's dead?"

"You know her?" Osric asked.

Grovis nodded. "She's engaged to be married to my cousin, Cam."

"Not anymore, she isn't," Osric said.

Rommett stared right at Danthres, who scowled back, then glanced at Osric. "Perhaps Lieutenant Grovis should—"

"No, it needs to be Tresyllione and ban Wyvald."

"But this case is very important because the Cynnises are very important to the—" Rommett started.

"We need our best detectives on this."

Going back to staring at Danthres, Rommett said, "If you say so. But if Grovis knows the family, he might sooner—"

"The Lord and Lady assigned Grovis and Iaian to Mermaid Precinct," Osric barked. "If you want Grovis on this case, take it up with them."

That shut Rommett up, and he turned and left. Danthres visibly breathed a sigh of relief at that.

Osric fixed Torin and Danthres with his nasty one-eyed gaze. "Get to the Cynnis mansion immediately."

Torin looked at Danthres, and they both exhaled, got up, and went to the pegboard to retrieve their cloaks.

"Another case involving friends of the Lord and Lady," Danthres said in a dull voice. "Thanks ever so much, Captain."

"I told you, I need my best detectives." Then Osric smiled. It wasn't a very pleasant expression, and Torin rather wished he'd stop. "If it makes you feel any better, though, the Lord and Lady can't stand the Cynnises." The smile dropped. "But they are important to the city-state, as Rommett said. So get a move on and find out who killed their youngest daughter."

Torin nodded as he whirled the cloak around his neck and fastened it. Danthres did likewise while snarling.

"Look on the bright side," Torin said as they headed out the door.

"There's a bright side?" Danthres sounded dubious as she asked the question.

"We've both seen that the most common guilty party in a murder is a loved one."

"So?"

Grinning, Torin said, "So it's possible that Grovis's cousin is the murderer."

Danthres, who had been walking with slumped shoulders, suddenly straightened, and even almost smiled.

She had a spring in her step all the way to Unicorn Precinct.

# TWO

Danthres stared down at the sight of a once-attractive young woman with her head caved in and tried not to throw up.

Torin looked over at her, his green eyes oozing with concern. "Are you all right, Danthres?"

"I'm fine," she lied. "It's just . . . even her name is similar."

At first, Torin frowned, then recognition spread across his face. "Treemark."

Danthres nodded. She'd only recently shared her experiences in Treemark with Torin and the others. "At least Arra here is a girl of noble birth, not a servant whose death will be brushed under the carpet, the perpetrator sent away to avoid justice."

"Indeed."

Torin knelt down to take a closer look at the body, thus saving Danthres from having to. She wasn't normally squeamish, but she wanted as few reminders of Treemark as possible.

Instead, she turned to the guard whom Unicorn Precinct had sent to secure the mansion until her and Torin's arrival, a young idiot named Garis. "Have you called the M.E.?"

"Yes, ma'am," Garis said quickly. "His mage-bird came just before you and Lieutenant ban Wyvald arrived. Said he'd be here—"

"Right now," came a cantankerous voice from behind Garis. The guard stepped aside to let in Boneen, the mage sent by the Brotherhood of Wizards to serve as the magickal examiner for the Castle Guard. He was dressed in a tunic and pants that looked as if they'd been thrown hastily on when the wizard was awakened from a nap, which Danthres considered to be a likely turn of events. Boneen waddled into the room carrying a bag filled with spell components that was even riper than usual.

Wrinkling her nose, Danthres asked, "What have you *got* in there?"

"Something I'm working on," Boneen said testily. "Didn't have time to clean the bag out before I came down here. Damn nobility rousting a man out of a sound sleep. Getting so a wizard can't get any rest in this wretched city-state."

Torin stood upright. "Definitely appears that she was bludgeoned with a heavy object. No blood-stained object in the room that I can see, save for the floor and the area rug, so the killer probably took it away after doing the deed."

"I'll be able to tell you that for sure," Boneen said as he unshouldered his bag, "when I cast the peel-back, which I can't do until you get yourselves out of the room."

"Of course," Torin said far more politely than Danthres would have.

The Inanimate Residue Spell, more commonly known as a "peel-back," allowed a mage to view what happened to a particular object or in a location in the recent past. It had proven very beneficial to the Guard in solving crimes.

However, the spell required that there be no living creatures aside from the spellcaster within range of it, so Torin and Danthres departed, with Garis closing the door behind them.

"He'll be at least half an hour," Danthres said to Garis, "so stay on this door until he's done."

Garis frowned. "'At least'? I thought the peel-back only took that long."

"In the normal course of things, yes," Torin said, "but whenever the M.E. has been awakened from sleep and rushed, he tends to take longer."

"I have to say," Danthres said, as they walked down the hallway toward the stairwell that led back downstairs, "the one good thing about this case involving the nobility is that Boneen is being harassed as much as we will be. No sense in us being the only miserable ones."

"Another possible bright note is that we might get overtime."

Danthres scowled. "I wouldn't count on it. Between the Brightblade case and midsummer, I'm sure that the coin-counters are blanching at the thought of giving the Guard any more gold than they already have."

Another guard from Unicorn, Manfred, was waiting for them. "Hello, Lieutenant," he said to Danthres with a smile.

Refusing to return the smile, Danthres instead snapped, "What do *you* want?"

Recoiling as if Danthres had struck him, Manfred said, "Uhm, well, none of the Cynnises are home. Sir Malik and Madam Hassa are en route, but won't arrive until this afternoon. The other children are returning from a trip to Iaron."

Glancing at Danthres and smiling at her from under his thick, red beard, Torin said, "They have alibis, at least."

"I gathered the household staff downstairs in the kitchen. There's a sitting room down there, also, which the servants use as a place to relax on their breaks. There are chairs in there, so I figured you'd want to talk to them there."

Danthres sighed. Every word a chore, she said, "Well done, Manfred. Stay up here and let us know if anyone arrives."

"Thank you, ma'am, I will." Manfred's smile was so bright it practically lit the room. Danthres had to resist the urge to vomit on his boots.

Heading down to the lower level, Torin asked, "Why are you being so cruel to Manfred? I thought you two were getting on?"

"We were—in a manner of speaking."

"What happened?"

Danthres sighed. In addition to being partners, she and Torin were also occasional lovers, and while he had never had any difficulty speaking of his other liaisons, male or female, to her, she had a harder time talking about hers with him. His were, of course, far more frequent than hers, which didn't help matters.

"I don't want to talk about it," she finally said.

They arrived downstairs, where a third guard from Unicorn was waiting. This one was roughly the size of a troll, and had to stoop down in order to stand in the hallway. Danthres didn't know this one's name, and didn't really care to learn it. "Where's the sitting room?"

The guard pointed a large, meaty finger at one door.

Unsurprised that this one didn't even have the power of speech— and finding herself oddly grateful—Danthres said, "Send in one—any one, it doesn't matter which—and wait until we send that person back out, then send another. Understood?"

The guard nodded.

As they went into the sitting room—a small room with a few cushions, one couch and very little else—Danthres said, "I like him."

Torin chuckled. "That's Zayl. He broke up a fight in the Ogre's Breath during midsummer and got his throat slit. He no longer can speak."

Danthres gaped. "He *broke up* a fight in the OB?"

"Yes. First person to even try in a decade."

"And all he lost was his voice? I'm impressed." Danthres had come up as a guard in Goblin Precinct, and the first thing you learned was to stay away from the Ogre's Breath. If a fight broke out, you were to wait until it ended and cart the survivors to the hole.

"They rewarded him by transferring him to Unicorn."

As Danthres nodded acknowledgment, the first of the servants entered.

Danthres took a very deep breath. This was the part of the process that was the most tedious, as she and Torin knew very little about the people involved—and, of course, in murders, unlike most other crimes, they couldn't talk to the victim. But it was also critical for the same reason.

First was Renna, the chambermaid who first saw the body.

"It was awful, it was, the poor girl just lyin' on the floor like that, it was terrible, it was, just lyin' there, her pretty head all bashed in and the blood was just everywhere, it was horrible, it was, and her about to be married an' everything, it was so very sad, it was . . ."

At no point did Renna provide any useful information about Arra Cynnis that they didn't already know, so they finally excused her.

After that was Vaspar, the butler who was with Renna when she found the body.

"She was such a wonderful girl. I was so sorry that she was going to be married off to that Grovis boy. He's a nice boy, don't get me wrong, from a good family, but it meant she would leave. Why she has to go when Crilla has to keep living here with that mindless behemoth she married is beyond me, I can tell you. This was a good house before the children came along, or at least the first three, but Arra? She made it all so much nicer. Everyone loved her. Ever since Jared was born, it was like there was a curse. All those vicious rumors about sir's business dealings, and those meetings with wizards, but what of it? He had such meetings before the children, and no one said a word. Now, though, it's fodder for gossip, which I do *not* truck with. In any event, I don't understand why anyone would hurt *Arra* of all people. In fact, the honest truth is that she's the only one of the four children who I would *not* expect to be bludgeoned to death."

He was followed by a maid.

"Well, I don't like to gossip, but I've seen Sir Malik with some *very* suspicious characters over the past few years. I think there's something strange going on. Honestly, why else marry poor Arra into that awful family of bankers? I don't think those two even get along very well. I mean, I don't like to gossip, but I've heard stories of another man in her life . . ."

Next was a pageboy who stared at the floor most of the time.

"Yeah, Miss Arra was real sweet'n'all. I honestly thought she's the most beautiful woman'n all Flingaria. Wish 'twas me she was havin' the affair with."

Then one of Arra's dressing girls, who was one of three responsible for assembling Arra's wedding gown.

"It's just *awful*. She was so *happy* all the time. I don't believe none'a that stuff about her havin' an affair nor nothin'. She was *so* lookin' forward to the weddin'! She felt like she was a princess marryin' her prince!"

Next was a second dressing girl — the third having gone to Dragon Precinct earlier in the morning to fetch material that would no longer be needed.

"She didn't care for that Grovis boy, not at all, y'ask me. She was just goin' through the motions. Me, I wanna know who the boy is she was takin' up with. I mean, I ain't got no proof or nothin' like that, but it stands t'reason, y'ask me. After all, ain't nobody who's *that* unhappy 'bout who she's marryin's *that* happy the rest of the time, y'ask me."

And so on through the staff. They talked to all the servants save for the third dressing girl, and the kitchen staff, who were all occupied preparing the midday meal.

"It's Madam Hassa. She's actually a wizard who magicked himself to look like a woman. Part'a some scam Sir Malik's runnin'. Don't believe me, eh? Yeah, nobody does, but Sir Malik, he's consortin' with mages! He's a mage-consorter!"

"She was so very sweet. I don't see why anyone would even talk crossly to her, much less hurt her or kill her!"

"Never liked that prissy, uptight bitch. Just like all the other prissy, uptight bitches in this house. If my Da wasn't the footman, I'd be out of here so fast, it'd make your head spin, that's how fast I wanna get outta this house filled with prissy, uptight bitches. An' the worst is the mother — hear a rumor she's really a mage!"

"I tell you, it runs in the family. Jared's *never* been able to keep it in his tights, and everyone knows that Crilla is sleeping with her riding instructor. I don't know who Arra's young man is, but she's just following in the family tradition. The only one who doesn't sleep around is Blan, but what woman would have him? Especially the way he steals things. Oh, I know, they say he doesn't do that anymore, but what happened to madam's favorite brooch? They say it's one of us, but we can't get anywhere near the thing anymore. Only the children have the key to that safe—it *had* to have been Blan!"

Danthres turned to Torin after the last one left. "What do you think?"

Torin rubbed his chin through his chest-length beard. "Two things: one, we need to talk to Grovis's cousin. And two, we need to find out who Arra was having her illicit affair with."

"Yes," Danthres said with a nod, grateful that Torin's mind was like to hers. Indeed, it often was—not as often as she liked, and less often than they let on to Osric—but in this case, there was little room for doubt. "Either Grovis's cousin found out about the affair and killed her, or our mystery man realized that he was going to lose her when she married into that rather unfortunate family and decided that if he couldn't have her, no one would." Danthres shook her head. "No doubt thinking that he couldn't live without her. If that was the case, why not kill himself and make the world a better place?"

With a chuckle, Torin got up from the couch. He and Danthres had questioned the staff from there, having them sit on one of the cushions. "Come, let's see if the owners of the house have arrived yet."

# THREE

Iaian hated to admit it, but Grovis's approach to the investigation was uncharacteristically intelligent.

After Torin and Danthres went off to deal with their high-class murder, and Dru and Hawk departed to talk to the people complaining about the Temisan priest, Grovis went to the squadroom's big window.

"Ep, please provide all reported thefts in Mermaid Precinct over the past year." In response to Grovis's request, the window twisted around until it changed from a piece of glass that provided a forest view, to the face of Ep, the imp who ran the file room, an extradimensional storage space. Ep was an ugly little bugger with a huge beard that put Torin's to shame.

Several scrolls ejected from the imp's beard. Grovis only caught some of them. The others fell to the floor and rolled all around the squadroom.

Once he was done picking them up—Grovis didn't ask for Iaian's help in doing so, and Iaian sure as shit wasn't volunteering—he looked them over studiously.

Unable to stand it any longer, Iaian asked, "What, exactly, are you doing, boy?"

"Attempting to determine a pattern. There are several merchants along the northern end of the docks—fishing supply stores, eateries, boat services, and so on."

"Yeah, so?"

Grovis held up two parchments. "Of the dozen businesses along that way, only two have been robbed in the past year. They've been victimized numerous times. Yet the others remain untouched. Oh, and none of the robberies were solved."

Iaian repeated himself. "Yeah, so?"

"It's a trifle odd, don't you think?" Grovis asked impatiently. "Look, contrary to what you might think, I am *not* an idiot. I'm fully aware that protection money is often paid to guards. My guess is that these two establishments failed to pay that particular tithe, and became victimized."

Iaian shook his head. "I can think of half a dozen *other* reasons why they might've been hit. Maybe they have shitty locks on their doors. Maybe the owners pissed somebody off. Maybe they have employees that want more than their salary."

"Perhaps you're right." Grovis rose from his chair. "And the best manner in which to determine that is to investigate."

With that, he moved to the door, not looking back to see if Iaian was coming along behind him.

For about half a second, Iaian considered not following his partner. It was a fool's errand, a waste of time, and maybe—just maybe—he could avoid pariah status if he didn't actually accompany Grovis.

Then he recalled Jonas's words about his twenty-five-year bonus. If he didn't perform this duty to Albin and Meerka's satisfaction, the bonus that was the only thing that kept Iaian getting up in the morning would be taken from him. He'd have to keep working for the Guard for at least another ten years.

And he'd probably be partnered with Grovis the entire time.

Unwilling to risk that, he hauled himself to his feet, winced as his knees cracked with the effort, and then followed Grovis out the door.

The walk through the city-state was done in a silence that was by no means companionable. Still, it *was* silence, and Iaian would take whatever he could get in that regard from Grovis.

As they progressed down Meerka Way, the primary thoroughfare that led directly from the castle to the docks, Iaian watched as the people's reactions altered. Among the mansions of Unicorn Precinct, they were mostly ignored. In the middle-class region of Dragon Precinct, they got the occasional polite nod, which modulated into downright scorn as they crossed into the slums of Goblin Precinct and continued into the docklands.

With a sigh, Iaian walked along the wooden planks of the docks, trying not to gag at the smell of salt water. Iaian had always hated the waterfront. At least it was still morning, so the fishing boats hadn't returned with their day's catches yet. Coming to Mermaid after noon was usually a recipe for Iaian to be doubled over and vomiting from the stench.

The first establishment on Grovis's list was Hilbrek's Fishing Supplies, which was run by a hyperactive gnome. Two of the three customers left as soon as the detectives entered.

"Oh yeah," Hilbrek said, as he was adjusting items on the shelves, "the robberies, yeah, that was no problem, nothing to worry the Guard about."

"Sir," Grovis said, "I want you to know that anything you tell us will be in the strictest confidence, with no consequences to you."

The gnome paused in his straightening up to stare at Grovis. "I'm sorry?"

"I mean that you need not fear reprisal if you tell us the truth."

Looking now at Iaian, Hilbrek asked, "What's he talkin' 'bout?"

"I rarely know," Iaian said with a sigh.

"Look, my good gnome," Grovis said, putting his gloved hands palms-down on the countertop. "I know that you were robbed because you failed to pay the protection money—"

"What're you, dense?" Hilbrek walked up to Grovis and peered at the seams of his leather armor. "That crap you're wearing on too tight or somethin'?"

Grovis backed off. "Sir, *please*, if you'll just—"

"I got robbed 'cause my cousin's a thievin' little bastard!"

Iaian tried very hard not to laugh.

"Your—your cousin, you say?"

"Of *course*, my cousin! Caught the little shitbrain red-handed!"

"According to the Castle Guard's files on the subject, the robbery of your store remains unsolved."

The gnome went back to arranging bait on the shelves. "Yeah, well, that's 'cause the Guard ain't solved it. I did when I caught my shitbrain cousin."

Archly, Grovis asked, "And *why* did you not report that the perpetrator was captured?"

"He's my *cousin*." Hilbrek looked at Grovis as if he'd grown a second head. "You really *are* dense. I ain't about to let my own cousin go into the hole."

That didn't seem to make any sense to Grovis, who seemed even more goggle-eyed than usual. "But your cousin committed a *crime*. The Lord and Lady's law specifies that criminals be punished."

"Listen you." Hilbrek walked back up to Grovis and pointed a tiny finger at the gryphon crest on his chest. "I ain't bein' reseponsible for no member of my family bein' imprisoned. You get me?"

Before Grovis could say anything else stupid, Iaian grabbed him by the arm. "C'mon, boy, we've wasted enough of this man's time."

"But—"

"If he won't report it officially, then it didn't happen. Let's *move*."

"But—"

Iaian had to drag Grovis out of the store. Iaian noticed that the third customer had also departed, and was now moving away from them at a brisk pace.

"But—"

"What'd I tell you?" Iaian asked, as they continued down the docks toward their second—and, Iaian hoped, final—destination. "There's about fifty reasons why these guys might've been hit and the cases are still open. We shouldn't even waste our time with the other one."

"Nonsense." Grovis pointed at the façade. "It's right there."

Entering Smogan's Boat Repair, Iaian found himself in a small area filled floor-to-ceiling with large pieces of wood, intimidating tools, and huge pieces of canvas. A narrow path was cleared right in the center of the space, leading to a small desk.

An elf sat behind it. Like most elves, he had perfect posture, a haughty expression, and pearly skin. Unlike most elves, he had a full beard—blond, like his hair.

"What can I do for you, gentlemen?" the elf asked.

"You can't be Smogan," Iaian said. That was a dwarven name.

The elf chuckled. "No. Smogan used to own this place. He had a great many virtues, Smogan did, but skill at dice was *not* one of them. He lost the deed to this repair place to me a few months ago."

"So why'd you keep the name?" Iaian didn't know a single elf who'd have been caught dead owning a place with a dwarven name. Then again, he didn't know a single elf who didn't shave his cheeks every day.

"Reputation," the elf said with a shrug. "People trust the name."

"All of this is very fascinating," Grovis said, "but we are here on official business."

The elf's face fell into a scowl. "Look, I told the last guards who came in here, and the ones before them, I will *not* be paying you."

Iaian sighed.

Grovis's eyes widened. "What's that you say?"

"I said I will *not* be paying that ridiculous fee you insist upon. Yes, I've been robbed, and I'm sure I'll be robbed again, but honestly, the so-called 'protection' costs me more than the thievery."

"Sir, I'll have you know that we are *not* here to collect any bribes. In fact, we are investigating just such practices here in Mermaid Precinct."

The elf frowned "Mermaid, which now?"

"This precinct, in which you live — it's called Mermaid Precinct. The officers who serve there have a mermaid crest." Grovis pointed at his own chest.

"That's a gryphon, not a mermaid."

"Yes," Grovis said slowly, "because I do not work in this precinct."

"Then what're you doing here?"

Iaian had to admit to some amusement at Grovis's frustration with this elf, who was obviously new in town, but it was tempered by the fact that the shitbrain was actually getting somewhere with this lunacy.

"My partner and I are lieutenants, working directly for the Lord and Lady."

"And who're they?"

Grovis put his head in his hands. Iaian covered his laugh with a cough and an intent study of some of the boat parts.

"The Lord and Lady *rule* this city-state, and they have entrusted us with rooting out corruption in Mermaid Precinct — such as the charging of protection money to local businesses."

"Right, okay, and I didn't pay that," the elf said, "so there's no sense in talking to me."

"Actually, there's quite a bit of sense in speaking to you, my good elf, as you can identify the miscreants who attempted to extort coin from you."

The elf shook his head. "I'm afraid not. I mean, they were humans, and they wore leather armor like yours — except, I guess, with that mermaid crest, I honestly didn't notice — but, to be honest with you, all you humans look alike."

Grovis threw up his hands in frustration, and again Iaian had to keep himself from laughing. "Look —"

Finally, Iaian decided to end this. "We've taken up enough of your time." Again, he grabbed Grovis by the arm, dragging him out of the store. "Thanks for your help."

Once they were back out on the docks, Grovis's mood brightened. "Well, that worked out better than I'd hoped."

"Really?" Iaian regarded Grovis with something like pity. "You're gonna bring *that* guy before a magistrate?"

"Why ever not? He *is* a witness."

"Right, and what he witnessed was some human he can't identify wearing a suit of leather armor he can't describe trying to get him to pay protection money he doesn't have. And once he does *that*, who do we arrest, exactly? All humans look alike, remember?"

"Still, it's proof that there's *something* going on in Mermaid!"

Pointing at the doorway to the boat repair shop, Iaian said, "He couldn't even confirm the guard he *thinks* he saw *was* from Mermaid!"

"Excuse me?"

The voice sounded behind Iaian before Grovis could reply, and he turned around to see a guard from Mermaid that he recognized as Kass. He was short and squat, with small eyes, a round head, and a massive nose. His head was shaved, but he also had a day's beard growth. Kass was a relatively new recruit whom Iaian knew from his days as a sailor. His knowledge of the docklands made him a natural for Mermaid.

"Kass! How're you doing?"

"Not s'bad, Lieutenant, not s'bad," Kass said with a smile. "Like workin' somewhere where the floor don't move under m'feet, y'know?"

"I assume," Grovis said, with eyebrow raised, "that you two know each other."

"You'll be a detective yet, boy," Iaian said, shaking his head. "Yeah, I knew Kass when he was a sailor under Captain Javis on the *White Cap*."

"Oh? What led you to give up a life on the sea for the Castle Guard?"

Kass grinned, showing very few teeth. "My knees decided they liked solid ground better. 'Sides, the cap'n went an' sold the *White Cap* for spare parts an' retired to Barlin. I figgered it was time f'r a change'a scenery."

"Indeed. Well then, how may we help you?" Grovis asked.

"Act'ly, I think maybe I can help *you*. See, I heard whatcher inna middle of, an' I think I can help y'out."

Grovis frowned. "How's that?"

"One'a the youth squad was inna store with you guys. Tol' me whatcher doin'. An' I'm tellin' ya, that ain't how things're done no more."

"What do you mean?"

"I mean, you're workin' on old information. See, you guys put away Sergeant Gaffni, an' now we don't do that stuff no more. We ain't doin' protection collection—now, mind you, we *are* collectin' coin from the local businesses, but that ain't what we're doin'. See, lotsa businesses're hurtin', plus there's lotsa kids that need help. So we been collectin' for a kinda community fund thing. Folks that *do* contribute to the charity, we make sure that the local shitbrains know *that* place is off-limits. They *do* get hit, we nail their asses. Ain't no arrests, we just beat the shit out of 'em."

Iaian let out a long breath. "So that's why we didn't see any records of robberies beyond those two places."

"Yup."

"Fascinating." Grovis sounded a bit more subdued. "I don't suppose you keep records of these donations?"

"Act'ly, we do. S'with the Cliff's End Bank."

Iaian smiled. "Well, Kass, you're in luck, because the youngest son of the owner of Cliff's End Bank is standing right in front of you."

"That right?" Kass's tiny eyes got slightly wider. "Well, then, Lieutenant, y'oughtta be able t'confirm this your own self with y'r old man."

"You may rest assured that I will do that very thing. Come along, Iaian, let us verify this man's account."

Not appreciating being ordered around, and wanting to test a theory, Iaian said, "I'll catch up. I need to ask Kass something personal."

"Very well." Grovis sounded nonplussed, but he turned and went on his way.

"So, you hear from Javis much lately?"

Kass chuckled. "Nah, I think he wanted t'start over, y'know?"

Once he knew Grovis was out of earshot, Iaian asked in a more hushed tone, "Seriously? Donating to the community?"

"Oh, it's legit, Lieutenant. We're takin' money from the shop owners, an' we're givin' money t'the bank for community stuff, jus' like I said." Another toothless grin. "But what I kinda forgot t'tell y'r partner's that the second amount's a lot smaller'n the first amount."

Iaian nodded. "Gee, I guess I'll have to forget to tell him that."

With a smile, Kass said, "Great."

After exchanging a few more pleasantries with Kass, Iaian moved to catch up with his partner. In the past, he'd lamented the fact that the existence of the Castle Guard had forced the criminals to become smarter in order to stay ahead of the detectives.

For once, Iaian was grateful that it was the case. The new sergeant at Mermaid had figured out the perfect way to mask their graft — in a manner easy to verify with the lieutenant put in charge of investigating it, since it involved his father's bank — and actually do some good at the same time. He wouldn't be surprised if the Lord and Lady publicly supported this new community initiative, never knowing that it masked the same old corruption.

Iaian had to admit he admired the simplicity of it. He just hoped that that was the end of this nonsense, and that he and Grovis could get back to *real* duties.

That hope proved a forlorn one, as he saw Grovis chatting with another of the youth squad, a curly-haired little girl.

"Iaian — give this kind girl a copper, would you please? I'm afraid that I've neglected to bring any coins with me today."

For a moment, Iaian simply stared. "Are you kidding me? You've got more money than I'll ever *see*, and you can't squeeze a copper out of your money purse to pay this kid?"

"As I said —"

"Yeah, yeah." Yanking his own purse off his belt, Iaian liberated a copper from it with a gloved hand and tossed it to the girl.

She caught it unerringly and, without another word, ran off.

"You're welcome!" he called after her. Then he stared at his partner. "So why'd I just pay her?"

Grovis sounded almost giddy. "That young lass informs me that there is a sailor who has information about bribes paid to Mermaid Precinct guards from one of the ships in port! He's waiting for us at the Dancing Seagull!"

Clapping his hands, his gloves' impact with each other echoing off the wood of the docks, Grovis strode toward the far northern end of the docks.

"Great. Just great." Iaian had thought that "breaking" the protection racket would have done the trick, but it seemed nothing was going to deter Amilar Grovis from completely ruining Iaian's career.

With a heavy sigh, Iaian ran to catch up with his partner.

# FOUR

all the way to her jaw.

When the Cynnises arrived home, both Torin and Danthres had agreed to each taking the matching sex. Madam Hassa would probably be more receptive to a female interrogator, and likewise Sir Malik was far more likely to take a male interrogator seriously than a halfbreed female.

Unfortunately, Hassa's entire response to the death of her daughter was to cry like a banshee.

When she finally calmed down enough to be questioned, Danthres asked, "Did your daughter have any enemies, anyone who would wish her harm?"

"No," Hassa said, wiping her eyes with an embroidered hand-kerchief. "She was the most wonderful — wonderful — wonderful child, she — "

Then she burst into tears again.

Danthres sighed and waited for the latest crying jag to end. Then she repeated the question.

"No, no, everyone loved her. She was the sweetest child. Why, just yesterday, she was telling me about how wonderful the wedding plans were — were going, and — "

That led to yet more crying.

After a few more attempts, Danthres finally gave up. On those rare occasions when Madam Hassa wasn't sobbing, she was spouting platitudes about her daughter that were very maternal, and also useless to a murder investigation.

She finally excused herself, allowing Hassa's attendants to descend upon her like maggots over a corpse, undoing the many pins that held her giant blond wig in place, unfastening the various bits that held her overly complicated dress together, and so on.

With a shudder, Danthres recalled watching a serving girl named Harra perform similar rituals for the ladies of the house back in Treemark. If one of these attendants had been the one to die, she doubted that Hassa would've shed a single tear. Or even known her name.

Just like Danthres's aunt.

Her mood and headache both worsening in proportion to each other, she walked down a hallway filled with ugly paintings and approached the door to Malik's office.

Inside, she found Torin sitting on an ottoman across from a large leather couch. On the latter sat a well-dressed man whose silk clothing, perfect teeth, clean-shaven face, and manicure indicated that he just had to be Sir Malik.

Just as Danthres walked in, Malik stood up, causing the leather to make an unfortunate noise. "That is *enough!*"

"Sir Malik, I simply wish to know with whom you were meeting when—" Torin started, but the nobleman wasn't interested.

"Why are you wasting time with these *inane* questions when you could be out there finding the person who *killed my daughter*?" Malik was holding a glass that had a bit of green liquid still in the bottom.

Speaking with a patience that Danthres had never in her life felt, Torin replied: "I'm afraid, sir, that asking these inane questions is critical to *how* we find your daughter's killer."

"Don't be ridiculous." Malik walked over to a sideboard that had several crystal bottles filled with liquids of various colors. "I know exactly how it works—some mage from the brotherhood comes and casts a peel-back. I assume he's in there now, which is why one of your thugs is blocking access to my daughter's body." Malik poured himself more of the green stuff and slugged it back.

Danthres noted that Torin didn't have a glass.

"The peel-backs are not always definitive, and just because we know what the person who perpetrated the crime looks like doesn't always mean we know who that person is, nor how to find them." Torin rose so he was face to face with Malik again. "The questions we ask—"

Malik unfurled one finger from the glass and pointed at Torin. "Are personal, and not your business."

"—are *necessary*, and there's nothing more personal than murder."

Noticing Danthres for the first time, Malik asked, "Who're you?"

"I'm Lieutenant ban Wyvald's partner, Lieutenant Tresyllione."

"Good, then you may remove him and yourself from my presence. I will not stand here and listen to calumnies about my daughter. She was to marry Cam Grovis, and her only interest was in him. Anyone who says otherwise is a liar. And my meetings *certainly* have nothing to do with this. Now kindly leave and find out who killed my dear Arra!"

Torin bowed his head politely and said, "Please, Sir Malik, if you find yourself recalling anything of use to our investigation, kindly send one of your staff to Unicorn Precinct and we will be summoned."

"In that unlikely event, I will. However, I prefer that you do your own jobs, rather than relying on me to do it for you."

Malik then turned his back on Torin and Danthres.

Torin gave Danthres a look and shook his head as they both exited the well-appointed office.

"Please tell me," Torin said as they went back upstairs to the bedroom, in the hopes that Boneen had finished his work, "that the wife was more cooperative?"

"Cooperative, yes. Useful, no. She spent the entire time crying. If she *is* a wizard, as some of the staff thought, she's a damn fine actor."

"Let's hope the peel-back was useful."

As they got upstairs, Danthres saw Boneen waddling out of Arra's bedroom, pushing past Garis. "It's never a good idea to hope for things, ban Wyvald. It will just lead you to disappointment."

Torin grinned, white teeth showing through red facial hair. "In this job, Boneen, I'm already quite used to that feeling."

"Then be prepared to encounter it again." He let out a sigh and wiped his forehead with fingers that were stained from the herbs and other spell components. Danthres had to swallow a laugh at the black streaks over the wizard's eyes.

"Always with you, Boneen," Danthres said.

The mage scowled. "There is *some* good news. I can confirm that the girl was murdered at half-past twenty-two last night by a person who wielded a large, blunt object."

"All right," Danthres said. "Can you tell us anything about who did the wielding?"

"That, I'm afraid, is the bad news. Whoever it was used magick to hide his identity. It wasn't a magick-user, I can tell you that much.

Probably used a store-bought spell to hide from the peel-back." He shook his head. "They really need to stop making those kinds of spells available on the open market. Just causes problems. Anyhow, I'm done here."

With that, Boneen gestured, muttered something, threw some spices into the air, and then disappeared in a flash of light.

Danthres stared at Torin. "I hate when he does that."

"Why? It gets rid of him quicker."

"True, but between the peel-back and the teleporting, he'll be exhausted and will nap for the next day at least. I wanted to ask some more questions."

Torin nodded. "We'll get the chance. In any event, be grateful that he's already said it isn't a magick-user."

"Oh yes." Danthres shuddered. If it had been a mage who committed the crime—or was involved in it in any way—the Brotherhood of Wizards would take over the investigation. That never ended well.

"It's only a pity we couldn't get more out of the parents."

"Not really," Danthres said. "If I learned nothing else from Treemark, it's that the servants notice far more than the upper classes give them credit for, and that the upper classes don't notice anything that makes them uncomfortable."

"Excuse me?"

Danthres turned to see Vaspar, the head butler, standing in the doorway.

Torin smiled. "Yes, Vaspar, what may we do for you?"

"The kitchen staff has prepared the midday meal, and sir and madam are now dining. So the cook and her minions are now free to speak to you."

Inclining his head, Torin said, "Thank you, Vaspar." He looked at Danthres. "Shall we?"

"I suppose. I can't imagine they'll tell us anything we didn't hear from the rest of the servants. Kitchen staff tend to be more separated from the rest of the household."

"Yes, but there might be some food in it for us," Torin said with a grin.

Danthres was about to point out that she didn't care about that, but before she could voice that thought, her stomach started to growl.

"Excellent point." She looked at Vaspar. "Lead the way."

# FIVE

There were days when Osric really thought he should simply retire and have done with it.

The only thing that stopped him was the need to keep feeding and clothing himself.

Not that it was his fault. The money that had supposedly been put aside for a pension for all the soldiers that fought in the elven wars had instead been put right back into the war effort. By the time the war was over, and the Elf Queen deposed, the army that Osric had joined was completely broke. And, of course, he hadn't saved any of what he did earn, which was only eighty percent of his stated wages, because that other twenty percent was supposedly being put aside for him to spend after the war ended.

Everyone knew that there was a chance that they'd never live to spend the money, and that said coin would go back into the army's coffers. What came as a shock was that the money had gone back before the soldiers died, causing issues if they were so rude as to have survived the war.

In the short term, it meant Osric had to find someone to employ a one-eyed ex-soldier. In the long term, he had to spend his days putting up with nonsense from the nobility.

This morning, it had started with the pageboy who met him at the castle gates on his way to his office and handed him a document with the Lord and Lady's seal on it, meaning orders directly from them. After passing that on to Jonas, who would pass it on to Iaian and Grovis, he went to his office — only to have *another* pageboy come to bring him to Sir Rommett's office in the western wing of the castle to tell him about the murder of Arra Cynnis and how important it was.

Now, his day had calmed down. The day-shift lieutenants were all out of the castle, working on their cases. An empty squadroom was a happy squadroom, as far as Osric was concerned, because it showed that his detectives were working. As long as they were working, it meant that the Lord and Lady's desire to keep the Castle Guard as an investigatory agency of the city-state was justified, and they would continue to employ Osric.

He wasn't sure what he would do without this particular job.

The guard whom he'd posted at Boneen's doorstep had just reported back when a third pageboy arrived in his office. After letting the guard finish his report from the M.E., Osric saw the young man.

"Excuse me, sir," the boy said, "but Lord Albin wishes to see you, sir."

Osric closed his eye and let out a long breath.

Then he stood up. "Of course."

The last time he was in Lord Albin's chambers, it was during the Brightblade case. The victim there had been a close, personal friend of Albin's, and he wanted to make sure that the Castle Guard was doing everything in its power to solve his murder. Albin pressed his case with all the urgency of a person who could absolutely destroy Osric's life if he so desired, and he made sure to remind Osric of that.

Osric had a suspicion that the conversation he was about to have would be of a similar tenor.

The pageboy led him through the opulent corridors of the castle, lined as they were with busts of people whose identity Osric neither knew nor cared about. At the end of one corridor was a huge wooden double door. The pageboy ran ahead and opened them both to reveal a long sitting room. On the left was a fireplace, currently unlit, since it was midday in the summertime. Shelves lined the wall opposite the fireplace, covered with tiny sculptures, and on the wall facing the door was a huge window with a view of the city-state. It being a clear day, you could see all the way to the Garamin Sea. Cliff's End looked rather majestic from this angle. It was a nice illusion . . . .

Lord Albin was seated on one of the couches, holding a goblet of wine near his face, as if he wanted to be ready to drink it at a moment's notice. He was in a lord's version of casual wear: a simple silk shirt, ordinary tights, plain black boots. His mustache had been trimmed back recently so it no longer overwhelmed his upper lip.

A clean-shaven man was pacing back and forth in front of the couch. He was obviously a member of the nobility, but not one Osric had encountered before.

"Ah, Captain," Albin said, rising to his feet. "Sir Malik, I thought it best to continue this conversation with the relevant party present, since Captain Osric here is in charge of the Castle Guard."

Malik turned to stare at Osric with a hard expression that probably intimidated his household staff. It took all of Osric's self-control—which, thankfully, was considerable—not to laugh in the nobleman's face.

Besides, he *had* just lost his daughter.

"Then you're the man I wish to speak to! I *skipped lunch* to have this conversation."

The noble said those last words gravely, as if that were a massive sacrifice. Osric was, again, less than impressed. In the worst days of the elven wars, Osric was lucky to get one meal a day, and he'd yet to get back in the habit of having more than that since. He often had to remind himself that most people ate a meal at midday.

"I want you to fire the two incompetents you sent to my house this morning!"

"I'm sorry?" Osric looked helplessly at Albin. He had to follow the Lord's lead on this, but he really hoped that this imbecile couldn't exert the pressure he wanted to bring to bear.

"The half-elf woman and the man with the huge beard—I want them removed from the Castle Guard's ranks *immediately*!"

"May I ask," Osric started, when no comment was forthcoming from Albin, "what offense Lieutenants ban Wyvald and Tresyllione have committed to warrant this request?"

"Instead of trying to find out who killed my daughter, they're wandering around the house spreading gossip and asking *useless* questions! Why aren't they out trying to find the person?"

"Because, Sir Malik," Osric said patiently, "asking those questions is how they know where to look. The two lieutenants are our best investigators, and—"

Malik snorted. "If that is true, then it is a sad commentary on the state of the Castle Guard."

Albin finally spoke, having gulped down some wine. "Malik, these *are* the same detectives whom Osric here put on Gan Brightblade's murder."

"And a fine mess they made of that!" Malik threw up his hands. "Three more of Brightblade's people died, including Olthar loth Sirhans!"

"However, they did find the murderer before he could kill the rest of them," Osric said through gritted teeth. "They're the best I have, and the best chance of finding your daughter's killer. From what you've described, what they've done so far is their job. Any other detective I sent would do the exact same thing, only they wouldn't do it as well."

Malik pointed a finger at Osric. "You'd best be correct. I will withdraw my request for now, but if they do *not* find my daughter's killer in very short order, we *will* be revisiting this conversation."

With that, the nobleman stormed out of the sitting room.

Sighing heavily, Albin sat back down on the couch, draining the rest of his wine.

Then he threw the goblet forcibly into the fireplace. "Damn him!"

"My Lord?" Osric prompted, raising an eyebrow.

"My apologies, Captain, for putting you in the dragon's mouth like that. Unfortunately, I am relying upon Sir Malik's investment in some projects for the city-state, and he's been balking. I've done everything I can to mollify that shitbrained popinjay, but he keeps coming up with reasons to delay agreeing, and now *this*!"

Osric was too well trained to talk back to the ruler of the city-state in any event, but even if he had been so inclined, Albin's use of profanity—not to mention lowering himself to apologize to someone of Osric's meager station—spoke volumes as to the man's position. Albin had only cursed in Osric's hearing once before, and it involved something being dropped on his foot.

"We've stalled him for now, but we *must* have results, and soon."

"Unfortunately, just before your pageboy arrived, I received the M.E.'s report. The killer hid his identity with a store-bought spell. Tresyllione and ban Wyvald are still interviewing people, and once they return, we'll have a clearer notion of what's happening."

Albin nodded. "Good. Keep me posted, please. I know that you prefer a certain level of autonomy, and normally I'm more than happy to grant it. But we must have a swift end to this case, and a good one, besides."

"Of course, my Lord." Osric bowed. "Is there anything else?"

"No, that'll be all." Albin blew out a long breath. "You're a good man, Osric. The city-state is much safer because of your good work. But it just makes things like this all the more frustrating. Get it done, Captain."

"Absolutely." With that, Osric turned and left, hoping that ban Wyvald and Tresyllione would have something solid for him when they got back.

# SIX

Lieutenant Dru shuddered as they approached the Church of Temisa on Axe Lane.

His partner noticed right away. "What's wrong with you?"

"Just don't like churches," he muttered. "Let's do this."

Hawk opened the large wooden door that had relief carvings of images of Temisa from the sacred texts. It swung open with a frightening creak that went right up Dru's spine.

They had spent the morning talking to the victims in the case. Or, rather, the relatives of the victims, since the victims themselves seemed to have no problem with what was going on.

Their first meeting had been on the top floor of a boarding house that smelled like rotten vegetables.

"Look," the woman was saying, "I love my sister, really, I do, and I feel for her that she lost her husband, really, I do, but we're tryin' to get out of this shithole we're livin' in into a *real* house, but instead, she's spendin' money on that damn priest! He says he can talk to him!"

"Who?" Dru asked.

"Her husband, y'idjit, who'd you think? He's always carryin' on about talkin' to dead folks, and him not even a necromancer or nothin'!"

Dru frowned. "Who, the husband?"

"The priest, y'idjit, who'd you think?"

The next group were staying at rooms in the Dog and Duck Inn.

"We can't *afford* this place for much longer, and we *want* to leave Cliff's End already, but he *won't* go because he's just *so* desperate to talk to Triana, so he keeps going *back*."

"How'd his daughter die?"

"Boating accident. She fell overboard and he blames himself, so he keeps going *back*."

Both families cited a Brother Mantos at the church on Axe Lane as the one who had been taking ten gold each in exchange for speaking to the dead.

So their next step was to talk to the priest.

Dru walked in behind his partner — after steeling himself to the ordeal — and saw a typical Temisan church. Wooden benches were on either side of a main pathway down the center. There were no windows — Temisa apparently preached that there should be no outside distractions when praying to her — and torches lined wooden walls that were decorated with frescoes of some of Temisa's great works.

Standing at the surprisingly plain wooden altar at the front of the church — most of the Temisan churches Dru had entered in his time had a more ornate centerpiece — was a man in the bright red robe that was typical of his calling. His head was shaved, and he had a braided-chin beard with no mustache.

Dru noticed that his skin was tanned from exposure to sunlight, but his pate was lighter than the rest of him.

"You Brother Mantos?" Hawk asked.

Looking up, the priest stepped out from behind the altar and approached them, walking down the aisle. "I am Mantos, and I have the honor of being deemed a brother in service to the great Temisa, yes."

They met halfway. Dru looked up and down and saw that the robes were brand new, the chin-beard very short.

"How may I help the Cliff's End Castle Guard this fine afternoon?" he asked.

Hawk said, "You ain't been a priest long, have you?"

"I have served Temisa for many years, Lieutenants. It is a calling I am proud to have dedicated my life to." He smiled. "However, I am new to Cliff's End. My arrival is very recent."

"How recent?" Dru asked.

"I began my service here just prior to midsummer."

Hawk asked, "Where you been servin' before that?"

"Barlin, mostly." Now Mantos frowned. "I'm sorry, Lieutenants, but — well, I'm happy to answer any questions you might have, as my life is completely open to all who enter these walls. However, I fail to see the purpose of these queries."

Dru nodded. "Fair enough. We've had some complaints about your claimed ability to speak to the dead."

Mantos's toothy smile came back. "I do not 'claim' anything, Lieutenants. I *do* speak to the dead — or, more accurately, the dead speak through me."

Hawk regarded the priest. "And you chargin' ten gold a pop for this?"

"The spell is a very difficult one to cast, and I am exhausted for several hours afterward. My time is valuable, Lieutenants." Again, the smile. "As is yours. I don't understand why you're wasting time on such trivial complaints as this. Besides which, who is doing the complaining? As far as I know, my services have been welcomed. Certainly I have heard no issue with my work."

"The complainants are relatives of Jenn Bradis and Kal Hann."

Mantos snorted. "'Relatives,' you say? Are Jenn or Kal complaining? Because if it isn't them, than I don't really see what right these so-called 'relatives' have to stick their faces into this."

"Fraud be fraud, Brother Mantos," Hawk said, "and it don't matter who tells us about it."

The priest put a hand to his heart. "Fraud? Lieutenants, I am aghast. There is no fraud here. If you wish, you may attend my next session — I'll be meeting with Kal later this afternoon at around fifteen."

Dru looked at Hawk, who shrugged. "All right, fine, we'll be here."

"I look forward to seeing you both." Mantos smiled again before he turned and headed back to the altar.

Once they walked back out onto Axe Lane, Dru let out another shudder.

Hawk stared at him. "What is *with* you, Dru?"

"I just hate going into churches."

"What, were you beat up by a Temisan priest when you were a kid?"

Shaking his head, Dru said, "Nah, it isn't just Temisan churches." He sighed as they walked toward Meerka Way. "My parents couldn't decide who they wanted to worship. Temisa, Ghandurha, Mitre, Wiate, Xinf — you name it, they tried it, and they dragged me to every damn church they could find. Made me crazy, especially since each priest preached something completely different from the last one. I used to be scared to death of the next church."

Hawk grinned. "Was wonderin' why you weren't much for religions."

"Yeah." Dru sighed. "Anyhow, let's get some lunch. And let's find one'a the youth squad."

The grin became a frown. "What for?"

"Brother Mantos there's expecting two detectives to come back. He ain't expecting two detectives *and* a wizard. I'm betting Boneen'll see right through whatever shit he's pulling."

"Yeah. An' after we get us some lunch, I wanna talk to the bishop over on Shade Way. See what he has to say about Mantos."

"Good idea." Dru slapped his partner on the back. This was why he liked being partnered with Hawk — he always thought of stuff that never occurred to Dru. And it went the other way, since Hawk would never have come up with the idea of bringing Boneen along. That was mainly because Boneen always insulted Hawk. Of course, he always insulted Dru, too, but Dru never let it get to him.

"So, where you wanna go for lunch? Sanra's?"

Dru winced. "Seriously? Last time I was there, the food *moved*. Let's go to Drick's."

Hawk made a face and stuck out his tongue. "Please — last time *I* ate *there*, I was sick for a week."

"Wasn't that the week that your father cooked fish for the first time in his life?"

"No, it wasn't!" Hawk scratched his chin. "Least, I don't think it was. All right, fine, we'll go to Drick's, but if I get sick, *you* gotta explain to Jonas and Osric why I ain't in."

"I promise I will, partner," Dru said with a chuckle, as he and Hawk turned onto Meerka Way and headed to Drick's.

# SEVEN

Torin let out a very long sigh as he entered the squadroom to the not-so-dulcet tones of Captain Osric's voice. After bellowing across the room, he retreated to his office, expecting the pair of them to follow in very short order.

The use of that particular aggravated tone usually meant that, if he and Danthres didn't have good news for him, their lives were going to be hell. Either that or *he* had bad news for *them*. Neither option particularly bore thinking about.

Danthres stared at him and rolled her eyes before removing her earth-colored cloak and hanging it on one of the pegs. Torin did likewise and girded himself for whatever Osric had planned.

Torin was not encouraged by his entry into Osric's office, finding the captain seated behind his desk and sharpening his dagger. Since the first days of the elven wars when Torin served under Osric, that act was the signal of an unpleasant conversation.

As soon as Torin sat down in one of the guest chairs, Danthres falling more than sitting in the one next to him, Osric put the dagger down. "Where are we on the Cynnis murder?"

"We really only have two realistic suspects," Torin said.

Osric blinked. "That's good."

"Not as good as you think," Danthres said with a sigh. "We don't know who the second suspect *is*."

Quickly, Danthres filled in Osric on what Boneen told them about the manner of death.

"Are we sure it wasn't just an accident?" Osric asked.

"If we could see the face of the attacker, then we'd have to consider it," Danthres said, "but Boneen said that the murderer's identity was deliberately hidden by a store-bought spell."

"That indicates premeditation," Torin added.

"So it could be any of the staff." Osric picked the dagger back up.

Danthres shook her head. "I doubt it. That is *not* a cheap spell. Even if we're talking about an unlicensed one, if it's good enough that Boneen couldn't punch through it, we're talking *at least* ten gold."

Torin added, "Perhaps one of the longer-tenured staff — that butler Vaspar, for example — could have done it."

"Yeah, they *might've* scraped the money together, but we're talking the life savings of someone in that job."

"So, who are your two suspects?" Osric then scowled. "Assuming it's *not* one of the staff?"

"Probably not," Torin said. "But while it's worth looking into the staff's finances just to be sure, we're better off looking at Arra's love life."

Danthres smiled one of her more unpleasant smiles. "She is engaged to Cam Grovis. Meanwhile, half the people belowstairs in that house had a story about the torrid affair Arra was having."

"But," Torin put in, "no one knows who the man in question is."

"That is a problem." Osric leaned back in his chair. "All right, talk to the fiancé. And take Grovis with you."

Immediately, Torin read the expression on his partner's face, and he spoke up quickly before she could say something impolitic. "That may not be the wisest course."

"And why is that?"

"He's a shitbrained imbecile, for starters!" Danthres cried before Torin could say anything.

"Yes, but he's a shitbrained imbecile who speaks these people's language."

Danthres snarled. "I lived with people just like this for over a year, and —"

Osric pointed at Danthres with his dagger. "It was barely a year, it was a decade ago, you hated every moment of it, and it was such an edifying experience that nobody knew about it until recently."

Torin started to speak, but Osric cut him off.

"And *your* experiences back in Myverin are of even *less* import, since your disdain has deeper roots and it's been even longer since you were there."

"My point," Danthres said slowly, "is that we're both perfectly capable of speaking to the upper-class morons without Grovis's help."

"Allow me a certain degree of skepticism."

"Why?" Danthres sounded defensive.

"Well, your calling them 'morons' for a start."

Through clenched teeth, Danthres said, "We've done fine before."

Torin winced, knowing what was coming.

"Would that be when you refused to apologize to Sir Rommett during the Brightblade case? Or the Jaros family, whom you pissed off when that spell caused muck to explode in their house? How about the Grabodliks? The Wains? Sir Lio?"

Danthres closed her eyes and let out something that was either a groan or a sigh or a snarl—Torin honestly couldn't tell which.

Going back to sharpening the dagger, Osric continued: "Besides which, even if *I* was naïve enough to believe that you two've changed your ways and are now the friends of aristocrats everywhere, there's the matter of the aristocrats themselves."

And then Osric told the two of them about his meeting with Lord Albin and Sir Malik.

"Ah," Torin said.

"Ah, is right," Osric said. "Had Albin been in a worse mood today—or had Sir Malik been someone he actually *liked*—you two would be looking for work in the stables outside the city-state right now."

"Point taken," Torin said. "We'll have Grovis summoned from Mermaid."

"Excellent." Osric put the dagger down. "Besides, it gives me just the excuse I need to take Grovis and Iaian off that ridiculous dragon-hunt."

Torin nodded. Osric had been playing his feelings very close to his armor with regards to the Mermaid investigation, but somehow he wasn't surprised that Osric was against it, and only kept quiet because it came straight from the top of the castle.

Aloud, he asked, "Are you sure it's wise to risk incurring Lord Albin's wrath in such a manner?"

Osric snorted. "Let *me* worry about that. Just solve the case.If we're lucky, Grovis's cousin did it, he'll confess after a few moments since he's probably never killed anyone before, and we can get on with our lives."

"That's unlikely," Danthres said.

"What do you mean?" Osric asked.

"Arra from all accounts was a sweet girl, who was dutiful and pleasant and obedient."

Torin added, "Which, from what we gathered from the staff, made her unique among Sir Malik and Madam Hassa's offspring."

Danthres nodded an acknowledgment of Torin's interjection, and then went on. "Given that Sir Malik can get a last-minute audience with Lord Albin during lunch, he strikes me as a man who does not take well to not getting his way."

Seeing where she was going, Torin asked, "You think she was going through with the wedding despite the affair?"

"Absolutely. Girls like that have their romantic notions, and sometimes they'll even act on them, but in the end, they do what their Daddy tells them to do. I'd bet a copper that the other man found out that Arra was going through with the wedding and killed her out of revenge."

"No bet." That was what Torin always said whenever Danthres made such a wager offer in front of Osric, because the pair of them generally preferred to show a united front to the captain. That didn't always work in practice, of course . . .

"You spoke to the entire staff?" Osric asked.

"All but one," Torin replied. "One of her dressing girls."

Danthres shrugged. "I doubt she'll say anything different from the other two."

At that, Osric did something Torin rarely saw him do: he gaped. "She has *three* dressing girls?"

"It's a high-class wedding, Captain," Danthres said with a snort. "It takes three of them just to carry the damn dress."

Osric performed another rarity then, by chuckling. "Fair point."

Torin rose. "We'll speak with her when we go back to question the other siblings when they come back from their trip to Iaron. Should be in a day or two."

"Fine. Send for Grovis and go talk to his cousin."

Danthres got up as well. "Whatever you say, Captain."

"Hah!" Osric barked. "If that were truly the case, Tresyllione, I wouldn't have to keep convincing the entire nobility of Cliff's End that you shouldn't be fired."

To Torin's relief, Danthres's only reply to that was to grunt and leave the captain's office.

A guard named Micah was talking with Sergeant Jonas. "Micah," Torin said, "when you're done with the sergeant, could you send one of the youth squad down to Mermaid to fetch Lieutenant Grovis and have him meet us at his home? Make sure Grovis knows that this order comes directly from Captain Osric, and supersedes any other orders he might have."

The entire Grovis family—the lieutenant's father, Harcort, who owned the Cliff's End Bank; his brother and business partner, Fentin, who was Cam's father; their sister, Magda; as well as their spouses and other children—lived in a mansion on the end of Oak Way.

Micah nodded, "Sure thing, Lieutenant." He said a few more words to Jonas, who also nodded, then he moved off.

It would take at least an hour for the message to make its way to Grovis in Mermaid and for the lieutenant to walk back to Unicorn. Since it was only a quarter-hour walk from the castle, Torin went to sit at his desk. There were some scrolls that required his and Danthres's signatures. He looked over at Jonas. "So nice of you to provide us with more paperwork to occupy us while we wait."

Jonas gave a mock bow. "I am but a humble servant."

"Hardly," Danthres said with a smile, as she sat down at her place opposite Torin. "If he was humble, he wouldn't take so much joy in it."

"Indeed." Torin looked over the scrolls—magisterial records for the various drunks, imbeciles, malcontents, troublemakers, and thieves they had rounded up during midsummer—and signed them all, handing each to Danthres when he was done.

As the last one was signed, Danthres went over to the window and said, "Midsummer."

The window contorted into the face of Ep, who stared annoyedly at Danthres. "You need to be more specific."

"Why? You're just going to misfile them, anyhow." She dropped the scrolls into his beard, and turned her back on him.

Torin chuckled, then heard the sound of Micah's voice. "Uh, Lieutenant ban Wyvald?"

Without turning around, Torin asked, "Couldn't find any of the youth squad?" One or two of the children who ran errands for the Castle Guard were almost always hanging around the castle gates, looking for something to do for a copper or two.

"Er, no, sir, I found one. There's, ah, someone here to see you."

"Oh, really, who—"

Torin cut himself off as he whirled around toward the door, and the blood drained from his face.

He had last seen the tall man standing next to Micah more than a decade-and-a-half ago. The shoulder-length hair and chest-length beard had gone completely white in those fifteen-plus years, and there were many more lines around the ice-blue eyes.

"Hello, Torin."

His voice hadn't changed a bit since that last time, either, when he begged Torin not to leave Myverin.

"Hello, Father."

# EIGHT

Back in the old days, you didn't have to deal with magick unless you had an *actual* wizard around. But then they went and formed themselves that stupid Brotherhood of Wizards, and they got it in their crazy wizard heads that they could cast a spell and then sell it to just anyone to use.

Now lousy magick was everywhere. And he meant that literally, as there were plenty of wizards who didn't play by the brotherhood's rules, not to mention charlatans who couldn't actually cast a spell, but still sold scrolls with fancy words on them pretending to be real magick.

But he was getting his revenge. He'd heard about the Castle Guard looking into what was going on in Mermaid Precinct. Not that you really *needed* the Castle Guard for that. Hell, *everyone* knew what went on hereabouts. On the docks, you did what you had to do.

He was sitting now in the Dancing Seagull, which was pretty well empty this time of day. Well, any time of the day, it was empty — this place didn't come alive until night, when it was overrun with sailors and merchants who wanted to spend the day's wages on drink and camaraderie.

Jahno hadn't been able to stand seeing that, so he preferred to come to the Seagull when the sailors were all off on their boats. Right now, his only company consisted of a dwarf slumped over the bar and the bartender. For his part, Jahno was sitting at one of the wooden tables that faced the bar, waiting for the detectives to show up.

Just as he was about to give up and threaten death upon the curly-haired girl he'd given the copper to, the door swung open and the midday sun splashed into the room, blinding Jahno. Putting a hand over his eyes, he saw two backlit figures in leather armor approach.

As the door slammed shut behind him, Jahno blinked the spots out of his eyes, and saw a young, fish-faced man walk in with an older, taller, rheumy-eyed man behind him. The second one looked nauseated and moved as if he had the weight of the world on his shoulders, while the fish-faced one seemed to have a spring in his step.

"Greetings," said fish-face, "I'm Lieutenant Amilar Grovis. I believe you wished to speak to me?"

"Are you the one that's investigating Mermaid?"

"That is, in fact, myself, yes."

The older one rolled his eyes. Jahno frowned, as the old man looked familiar, but he couldn't place him.

"Well, yeah, okay, then you're the one I wanna talk to. Take a seat."

Fish-face—or, rather, Lieutenant Grovis—sat down on the bench opposite Jahno, but the older one closed his eyes and wrinkled his nose.

"I need some air," he said.

Looking up at the older one, Grovis said, "I thought you hated the smell of fish—it's far worse outside than in here."

The older one just sneered at Grovis and then walked out.

Looking behind him until the door closed, Grovis then turned back to look at Jahno. "Very well, my good man, tell me what information you have for me."

"I ain't a 'good man,' Lieutenant, I'll tell you that much for free. Name's Jahno, and I've been a whole lot of things in my time, but I can't say I've always been good. But I honestly think that I'm a product of my environment."

Grovis looked confused. "Your environment?"

"Oh right, sorry—I suppose I should explain. You see, I'm a sailor. Or, at least, I *was* a sailor. Served on the *Amarilla* for almost ten years. Made my way up to third mate, I did."

"What happened?"

To Jahno's surprise, Grovis seemed genuinely curious as to the answer to that question. Like he actually cared or something.

"Honestly? I blame the wizards."

"I'm sorry?" Grovis's fish-face was out-and-out goggling by now.

"See, in the old days, you had to hire experienced hands on deck. You needed someone who knew his way around a boat. But not anymore, no, they can just buy a spell that does it all for 'em. Then they turn around and hire some snot-nosed kids who don't know a mainsail from a rudder, pay them a little fraction of what someone with *my* experience'd get, and they maximize profit."

"Maximizing profit *is* important," Grovis admitted, "but it shouldn't come at the expense of a good sailor such as yourself."

"Exactly! You understand me!" This was going far more smoothly than Jahno had expected. "You see, they don't appreciate what I can bring. And magick isn't exactly the most reliable thing in the world, if you know what I mean."

Now Grovis sat up straighter. "The Brotherhood of Wizards regulates magick quite skillfully, Jahno, and I don't believe you should impugn them."

Jahno had to tread carefully here. "Oh, I'm not talking about the brotherhood, Lieutenant. I'm talking about the charlatans who sell unlicensed magick."

"Oh yes, well, of course — those are criminals and mendicants who *must* be stopped."

Nodding, Jahno said, "I agree with you completely, Lieutenant — and they're not the only ones. Now, I didn't want to say anything while I was serving on the *Amarilla* because — Well, honestly, I think loyalty should mean something in this day and age, don't you?"

"I don't follow you."

Jahno made a show of looking around the tavern, even though the dwarf was still unconscious at the bar, and no one else was present except for the very uninterested-seeming bartender.

Then he leaned forward. Grovis did likewise.

"You see," Jahno whispered, "Captain Bridgers has paid *bribes* to guards."

Grovis shot up straight again. "Which guards?"

"Not sure which ones, but they all had the Mermaid crest on their armor."

"This is outrageous! I knew that there was — "

Again, Jahno found himself blinded by the sun blaring into the tavern when someone opened the door. This was probably the most traffic the Seagull had gotten during midday in years.

The older one — and Jahno really wished he could remember where he'd seen him before — was back with a little blond-haired girl.

"Pack it in, boy," the old one said. "You've been summoned back to the castle."

"What?"

The blond girl stared at some indeterminate point on the wall. "Micah tol' me to tell 'tenant Grovis that he's t'meet 'tenant ban Wivvy an' 'tenant Tresilly at his house right away, an' that th'orders come from Cap'n Osric an' they are a super seed of any other orders." The girl then smiled, and looked at Grovis. "I 'membered it all!"

"I don't understand." Grovis stared up at the older one.

"Looks to me like Torin and Danthres need your help with something on their case."

"Yes, I understood *that*," Grovis said testily, "I'm not *completely* thick, thank you, but why would the captain wish me to meet them at *my* house?"

"Didn't you say that the girl in their case was engaged to your cousin?"

Grovis stroked his chin. "Mm, yes. Indeed, it would probably be best if I were to help in the questioning of poor Cam in this horrid matter." He got to his feet.

"Don't worry," the older one said, "I'll finish up with Jahno here."

"Oh, excellent. Thanks much." Grovis looked down at Jahno. "Worry not, Jahno. I'm leaving you in the rather capable hands of my partner, Lieutenant Iaian. He's a twenty-three-year veteran of the Guard, don't you know!"

And then Grovis turned to leave. The girl followed him out. "Sir! Don't I get a copper? Sir!"

The older one—Iaian—sat down and shook his head. "Poor kid's gonna be *real* disappointed. Not that it matters—she said Micah sent her down, and Micah always overpays the little bastards."

Jahno stared at him. "You knew my name."

"What?"

"I didn't give your partner my name until after you left. How'd you know it?"

Iaian sighed. "You don't remember me, do you?"

Then, suddenly, it came to him. He couldn't believe he hadn't recognized him right off. "Oh yeah, Lieutenant, I remember you. I remember you *real* well." Jahno leaned back and smiled. "Why don't you buy me a drink, and we can talk about it a little more. When we were robbed that time a buncha years ago, you're the one that found that illegal magickal seal on some other piece of cargo, am I right?"

Iaian shook his head. "Yeah, I did. And Captain Bridgers paid me five gold to look the other way. And why not—you guys were the victims, and that seal didn't have anything to do with the case we were investigating. Was just easier on the paperwork."

"Right, I understand that. But I also understand that the gentleman who just left has a burr in his armor about police corruption in Mermaid. I don't think he'd be too keen on me telling tales of six years ago."

For several moments, Iaian regarded Jahno contemptuously. Then he let out a very long breath. "Fine, how much?"

"Well, you just said you got five gold. I think that's a reasonable amount to ask you back, don't you?"

"I—" Iaian cut himself off, shook his head, and pounded a gloved fist on the wooden table. Then he muttered, "Fine." Leaning forward, he pointed a finger at Jahno. "You get five gold, and then you disappear, right? Grovis isn't gonna hear a damn thing about anybody taking bribes, *right*?"

"Sure." Jahno smiled. "I just needed some coin to get outta Cliff's End. Bridgers kicked me off the *Amarilla* just because I was gambling. Can you believe that? Apparently he found Ghanduhra at some point, and he doesn't let anybody play dice anymore. Isn't that absurd? And me having served there for ten years of my life! It's a shame. That, and the wizards, anyhow. I'll take that five gold now, if you please."

"I don't have that kind of coin on me."

Jahno didn't like that. "No coin, no deal, Lieutenant."

"Fine." Iaian grabbed a pouch off his belt, undid the string, and upended it to reveal a pile of mostly silver and copper coins. He quickly picked out several silvers and the one gold coin that was hiding under a couple of coppers. "Here's ten silvers and one gold. I'll meet you back here tonight at nineteen and give you the other three gold, all right?"

In truth, Jahno had figured he'd have to haggle the lieutenant down to two gold, so this was fine with him. He was rather shocked that Iaian had accepted five gold so quickly, and wondered why he was so eager to part with his money.

Regardless, Jahno planned to be out of Cliff's End *long* before the time-chimes rang anywhere near nineteen. Two gold would get him plenty far away—where there weren't any damned wizards!

# NINE

Danthres recoiled as if her partner's words had been a slap to her face. She'd known Torin ban Wyvald for ten years now, and she'd never once heard anything resembling this level of venom come from his mouth before. When facing murderers, crazed magick-users, drunken dock-rats, or frothing-at-the-mouth members of the nobility, Torin had always responded with a calm tone. Danthres had always envied him his ability to maintain good humor in even the worst of situations. While Danthres had never been able to emulate her partner's behavior, it had been able to keep her own excesses in check more than once.

Yet now, when confronted with a man who, but for his blue eyes, was a pretty fair image of what Torin would probably look like in twenty years—same style hair and beard, albeit white, same aquiline nose—Torin sounded as angry as Danthres on one of her bad days. Which was most days, if it came to that . . .

Torin's father smiled, with his blue eyes twinkling in very much the same manner as his son's green ones did. "A father cannot visit his only son?"

"I mean in the *castle*," Torin snapped. "We're supposed to be restricted to people with official business." That last was said with a pointed look at the guard who'd let him in—Danthres couldn't recall his name. She generally thought of him, and indeed, all the others, as "the stupid one," which simplified her life immensely.

Nervously, the guard said, "I—I didn't have a *choice*, sir."

Torin's father was wearing a large, dark green cloak, which he now threw aside to reveal a purple silk shirt, black tights, and boots. A belt looped around the shirt, and attached to it was an ornate seal. Danthres didn't recognize the exact markings, but she guessed what it was.

"I carry the Diplomatic Seal of Myverin," Torin's father said archly, confirming Danthres's supposition. "That permits me access to the castle."

"Ah, then you're on some business with the Lord and Lady? Fine, feel free to see to it. I have work to do." Torin moved to the pegboard to grab his cloak.

Danthres moved toward the older man. "It's a pleasure to meet you, sir. I'm Lieutenant Danthres Tresyllione, and I'm your son's partner."

"Wyvald ban Garin, High Magistrate of Myverin," he said, almost by rote, but didn't even look at Danthres.

However, his response got Torin's attention. "High Magistrate?"

"Yes, Torin. Your grandfather has died, and I am now High Magistrate. Which means it's time for you to end this foolishness and come back with me to Myverin so you may take your rightful place as Chief Artisan."

Torin burst out laughing, and it was the single most frightening sound Danthres had ever heard in her life. She'd heard Torin's laugh many times—indeed, usually a dozen times daily—and it was always pleasant and easy. But this laugh was bitter, and piercing, and nasty. It sounded like it should have come from the darkest recesses of Chalmraik the Foul's belly.

"'Foolishness'? Do you *truly* still cling to the delusion that my departure from Myverin was a temporary bout of adolescent rebellion?"

"What I cling to is of no consequence. From birth, you were groomed to replace me as Chief Artisan when I moved up to High Magistrate, and to replace me as High Magistrate when I die. That is the way of things."

Torin pointed at Wyvald. "No, that is the way of Myverin. I left Myverin fifteen years ago with no intention of returning. That you have wasted those years by not training someone new to take over as Chief Artisan bespeaks a rather distressing level of incompetence on your part."

Wyvald stood up straighter. "We will not have this discussion, Torin. I am taking you back to Myverin with me."

"Hardly." Torin turned his back on his father and looked at Danthres. "C'mon, we have to go meet Grovis at his home."

Danthres started to object, pointing out how long it would be before Grovis even arrived, but two things stopped her. One was that it was obvious that Torin wanted to get away from his father. And the other was that if they went there now, there was every chance that they could start interviewing Cam without Grovis present, which Danthres preferred, orders from Osric notwithstanding. So she said, "Of course." She turned to Wyvald, "It was a pleasure to meet you,"

For his part, the older man looked only at Torin, ignoring her. Danthres found that annoying. Wyvald then said, "Torin, whatever you're doing is no longer of import! The inconsequential minutiae of life in this wretched city-state are not your concern!"

Torin didn't even respond to that, but simply left the squadroom, Danthres on his heels.

Danthres waited until they walked through the castle gates and were on Meerka Way headed to the intersection with Oak Way before finally speaking. "So, do you want to talk about it?"

Tersely, Torin said, "No."

"Torin—"

"This isn't your concern, Danthres," Torin said in a low growl that Danthres wouldn't have believed him to even be capable of an hour ago, "and I'll thank you to stay out of my affairs."

"Oh no. No no no no no." She strode in front of Torin, turned around, and blocked his way, placing her hand on the gryphon crest of his armor. "Sorry, Torin, but you do *not* get to roll those dice with me. How many *dozens* of times over the past ten years have I had you harangue me about every little occasion when I'm aggravated about something, and you've kept at me until I finally gave in and talked to you? And every time, I've kicked and screamed and tried not to, and told you it wasn't any of your business, and you'd point out that it was *too* your business because we're partners and friends, and this is what we *do* for each other, and after *all that*, after all your self-righteous carryings-on, you simply do *not* get to push me aside like that."

Torin blinked once, then again.

Then he let out a breath.

Then he chuckled.

"You're right, of course, Danthres. My apologies. I just—" He shuddered. "I never expected to *ever* see my father again. And to not only *see* him, but to learn that he *still* thinks I'm just going to jump to his whim and come back to Myverin is simply—" He shook his head. "I'm disgusted. And embarrassed for him *and* for Myverin. He's left them without a High Magistrate *and* a Chief Artisan for the four months' journey here and back, and he's going home without a Chief Artisan. I'll bet he really *hasn't* trained anyone, which means it'll be *years* before—" Then he cut himself off and chuckled. "Not that it matters. The High Magistrate hears *perhaps* one case per year, and the role of Chief Artisan is entirely ceremonial. Of course," he added with a snort, "*all* of Myverin is entirely ceremonial. Enough." He waved an arm back and forth. "Let us proceed to Oak Way."

Danthres was tempted to push further, but she'd already gotten more than she'd expected. And Torin was obviously more relaxed just based on the fact that he was now walking normally down Meerka Way instead of striding purposefully the way he had been out of the squadroom.

"So what are the Chief Artisan's purely ceremonial duties, anyhow?"

Torin sighed. "Overseeing all the paintings and sculptures that are created, making sure they are up to standard, certifying that the materials are appropriate, and so on."

"Sounds exciting," Danthres deadpanned.

"Oh, you have no idea." Torin grinned. "One year, a young man mixed paints from two different plants. It was *such* a scandal!"

"I can imagine." Danthres shook her head, then spoke in an almost wistful tone. "Honestly? It sounds like paradise. I mean, a place where the *worst* problem you have to deal with is mixing improper paints? With all the shit we see every day in this filthy job, a place like that is very appealing."

"Yes, it does *sound* like paradise," Torin said. "And for many it is. But I was dying there, and you would fare far worse."

"Oh, I don't doubt that," Danthres said quickly. "But it does seem nice."

"Well, at the very least it's very nice visually. The trees and grasslands stretch for ages into the horizon. And the flower gardens...."

For the rest of the walk, Torin waxed rhapsodic on the physical beauty of his homeland. Danthres only partially paid attention. Mostly, she wanted to put Torin back in his rightful spot as the member of this partnership who had the *good* mood.

Turning down Oak Way, they saw the many mansions that were still under construction. The previous owners of the Cliff's End Bank, the Hazlar family, had owned not only the mansion at the end of the thoroughfare, but all the land from there to Meerka Way. When scandal forced them out of Cliff's End, and the Grovis family took over both bank and mansion, they only purchased the lot at the end of the road, leaving the rest of Oak Way in the Lord and Lady's hands. They sold it off in parcels, and now mansions were being built for the newest of Cliff's End's upper class—or those who wished to have newer quarters.

Danthres didn't approve, but she didn't approve of anything that made life better for the upper classes.

Upon arrival at the mansion, they knocked on the gilded, wooden double doors, and then waited.

And waited.

Finally, an obsequious servant answered. Where Vaspar had been courteous, if a bit shocked at Arra's death, this butler did nothing to conceal his disdain.

"Deliveries are to be made at the rear," the butler said, his head upraised so he could look down at them.

"We're not messengers," Danthres said tartly, "we're lieutenants in the Cliff's End Castle Guard."

"Really?" The butler didn't seem convinced. Danthres wondered how this idiot had managed to live his apparently long life—his hair was bone-white—without ever having seen a member of the Guard, especially given that one lived in this mansion. "You *look* like messengers."

Torin said, "We're here on direct authority from the Lord and Lady investigating the murder of Arra Cynnis."

"*Are* you now?"

"We *are*," Danthres said, matching his tone. "And if you don't let us in to see Cam Grovis, we shall have you arrested for impeding the investigation into the murder of Cam's fiancée."

"You expect me to believe that?"

"I couldn't give a shit if you believe me or not," Danthres said with, more calm than she'd expected herself to express. "I *can* tell you that if you do *not* let us in, we will return with two guards from Unicorn Precinct, as well as our—our associate Amilar Grovis, who is also a lieutenant in the Guard and who lives in this mansion." It pained Danthres to refer to Grovis as an associate—she would've preferred "subordinate," or "lackey"—but that wouldn't have gotten the job done.

Indeed, the only time the butler reacted with anything other than disinterest was when she mentioned Grovis's name.

"You work with young Master Amilar?"

"Yes." Danthres was suddenly much more favorably inclined toward the butler, as he had just provided her with a new nickname for Grovis.

"Very well." The butler stepped aside to let them in.

Danthres followed Torin inside to find herself in a high-ceilinged marble hallway that was several orders of magnitude more ostentatious than the Cynnis house.

There was a great winding staircase leading upstairs and several doorways leading to other rooms. Alongside the staircase was a cushioned couch, which the butler indicated with a hand.

"Please wait here; I will alert young Master Cam to your presence."

Danthres went ahead and sat on the couch. Torin, however, chose to look up at the crystal chandelier that hung from so high atop the ceiling that even a troll wouldn't be able to reach the bottom of it without going up on his tiptoes.

"I wonder," he said, "if this place was like this when the Hazlars had it, or if the Grovises gussied it up."

"I honestly don't care all that much," Danthres said. "I just hope he gets here soon. He's our most important witness right now."

"Assuming he *is* a witness."

Danthres stared at him.

Torin continued. "You yourself said that the guilty party is probably the man she was having the affair with. If that's so, he would've chosen a time when Cam was as far from the Cynnis house as possible. For that matter, none of the staff had even seen Cam in the past several days. He likely didn't witness anything."

"Unless he's the killer. And he's still a witness to Arra's behavior in the past few months. He might have noticed something." She shook her head. "Assuming he's *not* anything like his cousin."

"We can only hope," Torin said with mock gravity.

The butler shimmered back into the foyer. "Young Master Cam is currently out riding. I have sent a pageboy to summon him. He will see you upon his return."

"And how long will that be?" Torin asked.

"Since I do not have a Location Spell in my trousers," the butler said dryly, "I am unable to determine young Master Cam's precise location, and therefore am unable to estimate how long it will take the pageboy to find him, nor how long it will take him to ride back. In addition, young Master Cam may wish to change into presentable clothes that do not smell of horse in order to take this meeting, though—" He sniffed for effect. "—I will inform him that he need not make any adjustment to conform to your sensibilities, since it is somewhat obvious that you are not so encumbered."

With that, the butler turned on his heel and oozed away.

"You know," Danthres said, "if that's the sort of thing Grovis has had to listen to every day of his life, no wonder he turned into such an ass."

Torin smiled. "Indeed."

"And now you have something to thank your father for."

The smile fell and Torin's countenance darkened. "I'm sorry?"

"Well, if he hadn't arrived when he did, we would have sat around the castle for at least another hour, *then* come here to the house. At that point, I'll bet two coppers that 'young Master Cam' would *still* have been out riding, and we *still* would have had to wait for him, with the added detriment of Grovis's presence. But Wyvald's showing up moved things along quite nicely."

"Yes, well, on the off chance that I ever see him again, I'll have to thank him."

Danthres frowned. "You don't think you'll see him again? I'll be stunned if he isn't still standing in the squadroom when we get back."

"Then we'll have to avoid the squadroom for a while."

Cursing herself for being an idiot, Danthres sighed. She had been doing so well getting Torin back to himself, and then she'd gone and made him angry again.

An hour passed with neither Cam nor Amilar Grovis showing up. When the time-chimes rang fifteen, the front door flew open to reveal the latter, at least, had finally arrived.

"Greetings, fellow detectives! Good to see you're already here. Shall we speak to my cousin?"

"He's supposed to be meeting us here," Danthres said sourly. "We're still waiting."

The butler undulated back in. "Welcome home, Master Amilar."

"Thank you, Frye. I assume Cam will be out soon?"

"He was out riding, Master Amilar. I sent the pageboy to fetch him a bit over an hour ago."

Grovis's face contorted into outrage. "Over an hour? Frye, are you telling me that my colleagues, that *lieutenants* in the Castle Guard, who are here on the personal business of the Lord and Lady themselves, have been relegated to sitting in the *foyer* while awaiting an interview with my cousin?"

Danthres had seen this expression and heard this tone from Grovis plenty of times, but had never heard it while defending his fellow detectives. She couldn't help but grin, especially since Frye had now pursed his lips and was looking distinctly unhappy.

"Well, sir—"

"Don't 'well, sir' me, Frye. This is an *outrage*! You have embarrassed the Grovis family name, and you can rest assured that I *will* be speaking to Daddy about this."

At the sound of "Daddy," Danthres found herself engaged in a mighty coughing fit.

"Look at that! She's positively parched! Go and fetch some liquid refreshment for all three of us, and bring it to the sitting room, if you please."

"Of course, sir." Frye bowed and turned to depart.

"And make it snappy! This could well be the last time you do anything so noble in this house as serve drinks!" He turned toward the couch, looking stricken. "Torin, Danthres, please accept my humblest apologies. Frye should have known better."

"It's not a problem," Torin said, dismissively.

Danthres, however, couldn't resist twisting the knife a bit. "Well, he didn't *actually* let us in until we mentioned your name. Thought we were messengers."

Grovis's jaw fell open. "Well, I *never*! Daddy will *definitely* be hearing about this, believe you me!"

As Grovis led the way through another of the doorways, Torin shot a glance at Danthres. She shrugged and mouthed the words, *"Why not?"* Torin shook his head and chuckled.

At least that was more like the old Torin.

They soon arrived in a large room with a fireplace, several ugly paintings, and an amazing collection of purple furniture. Danthres had never seen so much purple in one place before.

"Please do have a seat," Grovis said. "Welcome to my home."

"This room is very—nice," Torin said. Danthres could tell that he was on the verge of saying "purple" as the last word, and obviously thought better of it.

"Yes, it's a good place to sit and have a chat." Grovis sat in one of the chairs, and Danthres, after looking around, finally decided on the couch. Torin joined her there.

"I'm impressed," Danthres said, meaning it as the couch conformed nicely to the shape of her rear end. She was used to her butt having to do all that work against wooden benches, metal seats, and hard cushions.

"I'm sure this will all be a formality in any event," Grovis said. "Then I can get back to the important work Iaian and I are doing in Mermaid. We're making *excellent* progress, I'll have you know!"

"Really?" Danthres was skeptical. Unlike most of her colleagues, she still believed that the corruption in Mermaid needed to be rooted out, but she also had no faith in the abilities of either Iaian or Grovis—let alone the pair of them working at cross-purposes—to actually do so.

"Oh yes. I was in the midst of a promising interview when I was summoned here, but I left it in Iaian's capable hands."

Danthres rolled her eyes. "Oh, good."

"Anyway, Cam couldn't *possibly* have killed Arra, he *adores* her! Besides, he's innocent as a ewe lamb—wouldn't harm a fly."

Danthres debated the efficacy of pointing out to Grovis that ewe lambs were female, but didn't get a chance to come to a conclusion when a side door next to the fireplace opened to reveal a younger version of their colleague.

Cam Grovis had the same goggle-eyed expression, brown mousy hair, and pasty white skin as his cousin. He was obviously much younger—where Amilar's face was filled out, Cam's looked as if it wasn't quite done putting itself together yet, plus he had some obvious pimples that were probably normally covered up with a glamour that he hadn't bothered with since he was off riding by himself.

Apparently Frye's advice had been taken, as he was still in his riding clothes, and Danthres's extra-sensitive nose could still make out the horse he'd been on top of.

"Hallo Amilar. It's good to see you."

All three detectives stood up.

Amilar walked over to his cousin and embraced him warmly. "I'm *so* sorry about Arra. I only found out this morning, and I've been so busy on Guard business I haven't had the chance to offer my condolences."

Cam returned the hug with equal affection. That annoyed Danthres—members of the Grovis family having actual emotions really messed with her world-view. She'd almost have to think of them as *people*.

"These are my esteemed colleagues, Lieutenants Torin ban Wyvald and Danthres Tresyllione. Now don't let Torin's strange name or Danthres's unfortunate heritage fool you. They are two of our finest detectives—"

With a smile, Cam said, "After you, of course, Amilar."

Amilar chuckled. "Yes, well, that goes without saying, naturally."

Torin shot Danthres a look, but Danthres was able to restrain herself. Truth be told, she would've been disappointed if Amilar *didn't* exaggerate his accomplishment to his family.

Now Cam was looking at Danthres. "Unfortunate heritage?"

"Yes, she's half-elf, half-human."

"Ah, of course." Cam nodded as if that explained everything.

Again Torin gave Danthres a warning look, but again Danthres was fine. The Grovis family were Ghandurha worshippers and as such thought all halfbreeds to be abominations. Then again, they thought *all* fornicating was an abomination unless it was in the marriage bed for the express purpose of procreation within one's own species.

"How far have you gotten in the investigation?" Cam asked.

"It's still ongoing," Torin said before Amilar could say something stupid. "The peel-back revealed that whoever killed Arra used a spell to hide his appearance, so we don't know who it is."

"However," Danthres added, "in cases like this, it is often the person closest to the deceased who committed the deed."

"Really?" Cam's entire face scrunched up. "That seems unlikely. I mean, don't most people get killed by strangers on the docks?"

Torin smiled. "Actually, even on the docks, most murder victims are killed by someone they know."

"That doesn't make any sense. Murderers aren't the type of people who have friends."

"Met a lot of them here at the mansion, have you?" Danthres asked tartly.

Cam stood up straight and pushed away from Amilar. "I don't appreciate your tone, halfbreed!"

# Keith R.A. DeCandido

"Erm, now, Cam, calm down." Amilar put a hand on his cousin's shoulder.

"We should all take a seat and start over," Torin said.

"Agreed," Amilar said quickly.

Torin and Danthres both retook their seats on the purple couch, with Amilar on the purple easy chair and Cam taking the purple rocking chair.

"Now then," Torin said slowly, "we have often found, particularly in cases where the victim was killed in their own home, and it was premeditated, that it is often a lover or someone else close to them."

"Well, we weren't lovers." Cam swallowed. "We were waiting until the night of our wedding as prescribed by Ghandurha." He shook his head. "And now that day will never come. It was to be the finest wedding in *all* Flingaria, *truly* it was! People were coming from all over, and everyone in Cliff's End and Iaron and Barlin and the rest of the northern city-states and *all* Flingaria would be talking about for *years*! And now it'll never happen and the most beautiful girl in *all* Flingaria won't be mine!"

"Or indeed, anyone's," Amilar said philosophically.

"Who else's would she be?" Cam asked nervously.

Danthres shot Torin a look. He shook his head—probably not the best time to bring up the affair. Better to talk around it and see if he volunteered it.

"The point is," Torin said, "we need to know where you were last night between twenty-two and twenty-three."

"Why do you need to know that?" Cam's voice was cracking now.

Danthres snarled. "We did just mention those other cases."

"Yes, but those are *other* cases, not *my* case! I would *never* harm Arra, *never*!"

Before Danthres could reply, Amilar did something Danthres had never seen him do before: be useful.

"Cam, please—listen to me. *I* know that you would never harm Arra. But I'm your cousin. In order for the Lord and Lady's law to be enforced properly, we must know the *truth*. And we gain the truth by determining facts, not opinions. I mean, what if, say, one of our bank tellers was accused of killing his wife, and his cousin testified before the magistrate and said, 'He'd never do that!' Do you think the magistrate would just take his word?"

Quietly, Cam said, "Of course not."

"There you go."

"But that's a *bank teller*! I'm a *Grovis*! We *own* the bank!"

"It doesn't matter, Cam," Amilar said in a more insistent tone. "We *must* know where you were between those two time-chimes."

Letting out a long sigh, Cam started rocking in the chair. "In bed alone."

"Good." Amilar leaned forward and patted his cousin on the knee. "And which of the staff can verify that?"

"None. I—I gave them all the night off. They didn't come back until midnight."

"That's a bit of a problem," Danthres said. "Arra was killed at half past twenty-two. The Cynnis mansion is less than half-an-hour's walk from here. You could easily have gone there, cast the Disguise Spell you bought, killed Arra, and came home before the staff returned."

Cam's lower lip was now trembling. "That's—that's absurd!"

Danthres started to provisionally get her hopes up. Cam looked as if he was about to break. Certainly the signs were there.

Torin stared at Amilar. "Surely *someone* must have been home?"

Shaking his head, Amilar said, "No, the rest of the family was at a birthday dinner for Tam Hyas, the executive vice president of the bank. He turned fifty, don't you know? We let Cam here stay home, due to his being all nervous about the wedding, but the rest of us went. Weren't back until half past one." He turned to look at Cam. "I didn't realize that you gave the staff the evening off."

"They wouldn't leave me alone." Cam was squirming in the rocker now. "They wanted to make sure I was ready for the wedding, wanted to make sure I was feeling all right, wanted to make sure I was praying at the appointed time—they just wouldn't *stop*!"

"So you let them go?" Danthres asked.

Cam snapped. "Yes!"

"Leaving you free to kill Arra."

"No! I just wanted what was *best* for Arra! I wanted to be the perfect husband!"

"By killing her?" Danthres asked.

"I would *never* harm her! Never! I *adore* Arra! It's a privilege to spend the rest of my life with her!"

"And if you couldn't have her, no one could?"

"What?" Cam seemed genuinely confused by that one. "No one else was *going* to have her! Why do you keep *saying* that?"

Amilar rose to his feet. "Cam, I'm sorry, but I'm going to have to insist now. If we do not have some proof that you were truly alone in bed last night at half past twenty-two, we shall have to arrest you in the name of the Lord and Lady and place you in our jail."

Cam's face fell. "You can't *do* that! I didn't do anything wrong!" Tears started to stream down his cheeks from both eyes. "I just wanted to be right for her on our sacred night!"

Danthres also stood. "C'mon, Torin, let's—"

But Torin was staring intently at Cam. After ten years, Danthres knew that look—Torin had thought of something.

"What do you mean by that?" he asked gently.

Swallowing and sobbing, Cam asked, "By what?"

"Being 'right' for Arra."

"I don't—I don't know what—"

Playing along with whatever Torin was getting at, Danthres walked toward Cam. "Who cares, Torin? We have our killer. He had the coin to buy the spell and the family connections to do so quietly, and he has no alibi for the time of death. The magistrate won't need but a minute to condemn him to be hanged."

"No!" Cam pulled his legs into his chest and started to try to crawl backward, as if he could lose himself in the rocker. "Please, no, not hanged. I know I should be punished for my blasphemy, but I didn't want to disappoint Arra, and—"

"Where did you get the sex-sim?" Torin asked.

Danthres whirled around to stare at Torin. Cam and Amilar both did likewise. Danthres looked over to observe their expressions.

Amilar actually started laughing. "A sex-sim? Please, Torin, don't be *absurd*. A Grovis would *never* commit such a *horrid* blasphemy against Ghandurha." As he spoke, Amilar gestured several times, the usual invocation of Ghandurha that his worshippers practiced whenever the spirit moved them.

Cam, however, was sinking even further into the chair and was now sobbing so hard his body was rocking back and forth, causing the chair to do likewise. He mumbled, "'M sorry, 'm so sorry," into his sleeve.

Danthres put her head in her hands. They had broken him, all right.

Now Amilar stared at his cousin, his jaw dropping. "You *didn't*! Cam, how *could* you!?"

"Let me guess," Danthres said before Amilar could keep going. "You sent one of the staff to get the sex-sim, since, even if you knew where to go, you wouldn't be caught dead in such a place."

"Martin," Cam said quietly.

"The stable boy?" Amilar shook his head. "I'll have him sacked *instantly*, of all the dirty, underhanded—"

"Grovis, *shut up!*"

Amilar recoiled as if slapped. So did Danthres, for it wasn't she who'd said the words, but rather Torin.

"I beg your pardon, Torin?" Amilar put his hands on his hips.

Torin ignored him, instead leaning forward on the couch. "Talk to me, Cam. You sent the stable boy, and he brought it back."

The young man nodded so hard Danthres feared his head might fly off.

"And then you used it."

"I'm—I'm honestly not sure what—what time. I was so—so *nervous*! I couldn't bear the notion that Arra might find me—well, *disappointing*. Honestly, I couldn't *bear* it!" The sobs started again.

Danthres folded her arms over her chest. "And you dismissed the serving staff so no one would report to your family what you did."

"I couldn't risk it!"

Amilar was shaking his head. "Oh, you will answer for *this*, young man, let me tell you!"

Cam cringed. "What're you gonna do to me?" he asked in a quiet voice.

Before Amilar could speak, Danthres said, "Nothing. Much as your cousin might wish it otherwise—" She stared pointedly at Amilar. "—our mandate is to service the laws of the Lord and Lady, and you haven't actually broken any of those, since the purchase of a sex-sim is perfectly legal."

Torin stood up, finally. "Religious infractions are not our concern. You'll have to take it up with one of your holy people."

"Oh, Abbot Bromleigh will *definitely* hear about *this* come the morning, you can be assured of *that!*"

"Let's go, Grovis," Torin said.

Ignoring Torin, Amilar was now towering over his cousin, who was still cringing and weeping. "When our fathers get home tonight, you will be so—"

"Grovis!" Torin snapped.

Again, Grovis recoiled, now looking frightened. "W-what?"

"We're leaving *now*." To accentuate the point, he grabbed the lieutenant's cloak of office and dragged it toward the door leading back to the foyer.

As they approached, the door opened to Frye with a tray of drinks. "Are you departing?"

"Don't be *too* disappointed," Danthres said with a mock-sweet smile, then pushed past him. To his credit, Frye didn't spill any of the drinks.

Once they got to the foyer, Grovis turned on Torin. "What was *that* all about?"

"He's given us his alibi, Grovis," Torin said. "Now we check it. Whoever sold him the sex-sim will know precisely when it dissipated."

"I'm sorry?"

Danthres closed her eyes and sighed. "When the user is done with the sex-sim, it dissipates magickally. The seller is alerted by a ping when that happens. It's how they know how much to charge, since their fee is based on time used."

"And how precisely was I to know how such filthy things work?"

Torin got right in Grovis's face. "Because you're a detective in this city-state, and you should be aware of how things *work* in it."

"I'll have you know, Torin, that I'm perfectly aware of how *illegal* things work. But, as you and Danthres so pointedly explained inside, sex-sims are *not* illegal, even if they should be."

That seemed to deflate Torin. "You're right."

"Excuse me?"

"You're right," Torin said louder, and sounding more like himself. "I apologize. It's been a—a rather difficult day."

"I know exactly what you mean." Grovis shuddered. "I need to get back to Mermaid."

"First tell us where the stables are." Torin scratched his large nose. "We need to question Martin, find out where he got the sex-sim, then speak to the dealer."

"Of course."

As Grovis directed them to the stables, Danthres let out a resigned sigh. They'd go through the motions of checking Cam's alibi, but she was pretty sure that *that* was what he was hiding, not murder.

Which meant they were back to trying to find Arra's mystery lover.

# TEN

Kellan's day improved tremendously when he found the charred corpse.

It was only his second day patrolling the streets of Goblin Precinct. He'd joined the Castle Guard just a couple of years ago, but he'd already earned the respect of Captain Osric and the sergeants he'd worked under. He spent the usual six months in Unicorn, having proven adept at serving the needs of the upper classes without actively pissing them off, and so earned a transfer to a more challenging post in Dragon. After physically subduing a serial rapist who was also dealing in unlicensed spells and saving someone during a fire on Oak Way during midsummer, he'd been transferred again, this time to Goblin.

When Osric had given him the transfer, he'd said, "This is temporary. You do good work, and we can use some *good* people in Goblin. But your name's at the top of the promotion list, too. You're the kind of person we need in the east wing of the castle."

Kellan had been quite pleased to hear that. It meant that he'd be considered for a detective position when one opened up. Of course, his friend Manfred had gotten a similar speech from Osric over a year ago, and neither of them had gotten the subsequent elevation. Probably nothing would open up until Iaian retired, but then only one of them could get it.

Unless someone finally strangled Grovis, or his family decided to take him out of the Guard. That would be a relief.

In the meantime, the two of them had laid a wager on who would make lieutenant first.

The new day-shift sergeant, Markon, had told everyone during roll call that the detectives were all busy with important cases, and that it would need to be something very serious to call them away, so to try to solve things themselves. Most of the guards groused about that—thinking wasn't really part of their job description—but Kellan beamed. Now he'd have a chance to win that bet . . .

He smelled the body before he saw it. He was on Yocane Way, approaching Haven's Lane, and smelled burning flesh. There weren't any eateries nearby—this area was mostly residential—so he turned the corner, hoping that this might be his chance.

Lying in the middle of Haven's Lane was a charred corpse, blackened and smoking. It was tiny, probably belonging to a gnome, halfling, or dwarf. Standing near him were a couple of gnomes, shaking their heads, leading Kellan to suspect that the victim was also a gnome. Like tended to stick with like, even in Cliff's End.

"What happened here?" Kellan asked the gnomes.

One of them turned and ran as fast as his little gnome legs could carry him, but the other one stood his ground.

"Stupid. Just so blessed stupid."

A member of the youth squad ran up to Kellan. "Wan' me to stop the gnome?"

"Forget it," the gnome who had stood his ground said before Kellan could answer. "Y'ain't never gonner find Alfie, he don' wanna be found. 'Sides, he didn't do this."

"Did you?" Kellan asked.

"Nah, me an' Alfie, we foun' blessed Stompy like this. But we know who done it."

Turning to the youth squadder, Kellan said, "Go to Goblin, find Sergeant Markon, tell him we found a body, and we should probably get the M.E. here."

"Shouldn't we be gettin' a Cloak?" the boy asked, using the usual slang for the detectives.

"Just the M.E. for now, okay?" Reaching into the pouch on his belt, Kellan pulled out two coppers, twice the usual, in order to make sure the boy followed instructions.

Smiling, the boy took the coppers and ran off toward Goblin.

Kellan turned back toward the gnome. He had to get this right if he was going to win his bet.

Of course, the bet was for two coppers, so the best he was going to do was break even, but it was the principle of the thing. Besides, Kellan had the noble motive of helping to make Cliff's End a better place to live. Manfred just wanted to be closer to the half-breed woman because he found her attractive, for some strange reason. Kellan didn't see it, himself, and didn't think Lieutenant Tresyllione was all that shit-hot. Anyhow, he was more qualified than Manfred.

Two more guards—Allard and Brenn—came around the corner. The former spoke. "Kid said you had a body?" Then he waved his hand past a rather bulbous nose. "Nemmind—you definitely got one." Looking down, he saw the corpse. "Shit on a stick—that's pretty badly crispy fried."

Kellan nodded and pointed at the gnome. "Keep the body safe till the M.E. gets here."

"Just the M.E.? What about the lieutenants?"

"You heard Markon this morning—we can handle this."

Allard burst out with a nasty laugh. "What, you *believed* that?"

"You ain't heard?" Brenn said. "Kellan here ain't good enough for the likes'a *us*. He wants to be a Cloak, too. Probably wants to suck off Iaian for the privilege."

Shaking his head, Kellan said, "I'm just following orders." Then he smiled. "Besides, it's Hawk you have to suck off."

Both guards laughed at that, and then turned to stand in front of the corpse.

Kellan turned to the other gnome. "So—tell me, what's your name?"

"Oram. I live over in the Swamp."

"All right." Kellan led Oram over to the wall of a building on the street, giving them something to lean against. The gnome only came up to his waist, his shock of white hair at the same level as the hilt of the sword in Kellan's belt. "Now—" He frowned. "Your dead friend's name is what, again?"

"He ain't no friend of mine, that's for blessed sure. Ain't nobody 'round here liked his blessed self, and ain't nobody gonna be sorry he got himself all burnt."

"Okay," Kellan said patiently. He seemed to remember that Oram had called the corpse "Stompy," but that couldn't have been right. "In any case, what's his name?"

"Stompy."

So he did remember correctly. "Surely that's not his given name?"

"Yeah, I think his real name's Djili, but I ain't never heard him called nothin' but Stompy. It's on account of how he walks, like he's always tryin' to kill a blessed bug or somethin'."

"All right. So what happened?"

Oram had been leaning against the wall, but now he stepped away, and Kellan feared he'd try to run the same way the other one—Alfie, was it?—did. "I ain't goin' in front of no magistrate. Last time I did that, they done put *me* in the blessed hole, an' then I got m'self beat when I got out. Ain't doin' *that* again."

Kellan hesitated. Witnesses were usually asked to testify before the magistrate when the case came to trial—*if* the case came to trial in any case. Of course, once Boneen showed up to do the peel-back, that would show who did it.

Or at least what the murderer looked like. Kellan would still need to find the person Boneen found in the peel-back, and that would require gathering information on the person in question.

So he needed to talk to Oram some more. Even if he wouldn't testify, it would be enough for Kellan to find the perpetrator. Then he would be able to confront him with the peel-back, and probably get him to confess.

Kellan let out a long breath. Now he understood *why* the lieutenants got paid more. This was a lot harder than banging heads together during a bar brawl or brokering an agreement between feuding neighbors.

"That's fine," he told Oram. "You won't have to talk to the magistrate at all, I promise."

"Better not. Ain't doin' *that* again, you can count on that with your fingers."

"So what happened?"

Oram shook his head. "Such a blessed waste. I mean, sure, beat the beard off him, like usual, that's fine, but to go out and buy a Burn Spell to use on him like that? That's just—well . . ."

"Excessive?"

Oram looked up at Kellan with something resembling admiration. "Right, yeah, that's the blessed word exactly. Excessive."

At least now Kellan knew that it wasn't a mage who committed the crime. The presence of so badly charred a body without any other burned material around pretty much guaranteed that Djili—or "Stompy," or whatever he was called—was killed by magickal means. But if it was someone who purchased the spell, as Oram had said, it wasn't a wizard. Given the annoying secretiveness of the Brotherhood of Wizards, Kellan was grateful for that. He didn't think much of Lieutenant Tresyllione, but he shared her disdain for the brotherhood.

After Oram nodded several times and just stared at Allard and Brenn, Kellan finally prompted him with yet another query of: "So what happened?"

"I know Stompy from the Swamp. He lives there, too."

Kellan nodded. "The Swamp" was the nickname for a collection of shacks on the western end of the River Walk, just on the border between Goblin and Mermaid. It was almost entirely gnomes living there because the shacks were built on a marsh, and only very tiny structures could be constructed. That meant that the residents were entirely of smaller stature, to wit, the same group that Kellan suspected the corpse of being: gnomes or dwarves or halflings. Because dwarves preferred to live underground, and the Cliff's End's halfling population was fairly small, gnomes made up the majority of the occupants.

Oram continued. "Now every week, there's an open dice game down the alley. Come one, come all, you follow me?"

Kellan nodded again.

"Well, the game dice, they're brought by Bele every week. An' every week, Stompy comes into the game, and he switches out the game dice Bele brought with some magickal dice."

"Magickal?" Kellan blinked in surprise. "What was he doing playing a weekly dice game if he could afford magick dice?"

"Oh, he stole the blessed things, I can tell you that for sure."

"All right. So Stompy did this every week?"

"As reliable as the time chimes. He'd switch the dice, he'd roll double-sixes every single blessed time, and then somebody'd beat his blessed self to a bloody mess. Usually, it was Fakor."

Kellan raised his eyebrows. "Fakor?"

"Dwarf, lives in the Swamp, too. Everybody gets pissed at Stompy, but Fakor's usually the one takin' the lead in puttin' a blessed beatin' on Stompy."

"All right, so what changed?"

Oram craned his neck to look up at Kellan. "Whaddaya mean, what changed?"

"I mean, what was different this week? I mean, if it escalated from beating him up to burning him alive, *something* had to change."

Shaking his head, Oram said, "No, that's what's so blessed insane. *Nothing* changed. Stompy came into the game, like usual. After about half an hour, when the pot got all nice and big, he changed out the dice, like usual. An' he got double sixes twice an' won the whole thing, like usual. An' everyone yelled at him for switching out the dice, and he ran away with the coins, like usual."

"Then what?"

"*Not* like usual, Fakor goes, buys a blessed Burn Spell—which cost more than he's *got*—and goes after Stompy." He pointed down at the corpse. "That's the blessed result. Just stupid, it really is."

Now Kellan had a name, and once Boneen got here, he'd be able to provide a proper description as well.

However, things still didn't entirely make sense. "Let me see if I undertstand—Fakor killed Stompy because Stompy always switched out the dice with magick ones, right?"

"Right."

"And Fakor always beat him up?"

"Oh, *lots* of people would beat his blessed ass up. Fakor was just the loudest about it."

Kellan scratched his chin. "Okay, so if he always did this, and you always beat him up for it—why'd you let him play?"

Oram frowned. "Huh?"

"Why'd you let him play in the dice game?"

Looking at him like he had grown a new head, Oram asked, "Whaddaya mean 'why'd you let him play'? We *had* to let him play."

At this point, Kellan's mind was completely boggled. "For Wiate's sake, *why*?"

"I told you before—it's an *open* dice game!"

"It's . . ." Kellan's mouth hung open for a second. Then he closed it; then he opened it again.

Then he let out a long sigh. "All right, then." He stood upright after leaning against the wall, and looked over at Allard and Brenn, who were chatting about something or other, completely uncaring that there was a charred, dead gnome who got killed for being stupid. Or maybe he was killed because someone else was being stupider. Kellan wasn't even sure.

He also wasn't entirely sure that he wanted to win his bet with Manfred anymore . . . .

# ELEVEN

As Torin walked down Oak Way with Danthres for the second time that day, he found himself thinking back to the last time he saw his father.

It wasn't a day he'd thought about all that often. The first few months after he left Myverin, he had played the day over and over again in his head — for all that he told his father that he had made up his mind, he wasn't at all sure that he could survive the world outside the protective walls, both literal and metaphorical, of his homeland. The doubts were often crippling, especially during the brutal days and cold nights on the battlefields of the elven wars.

Torin had been astride Sylvan Wye, the beautiful brown horse that had been his since he was a teenager. He had a pack on his back, the sword his uncle had given him on his belt.

Wyvald ban Garin had stood in front of Sylvan Wye on the pathway that led toward the city gates. It was a dirt path, as nobody in Myverin had even conceived of cobblestones. And indeed, the path to the city gates was among the least used paths, for why would anybody wish to *leave* Myverin?

"Where are you going, my son?"

Torin hadn't yet grown his thick red beard, but his hair had already gone past his shoulders. He had it tied into a ponytail, and that waved back and forth as he shuddered with bitter laughter. "Do you really need to ask that question, Father? What do you think I've been preparing for the past several months?"

"You've been acting like a child, but it is long past time you set childish things aside. Varin tells me you have not attended your lessons today — or yesterday."

"I will not be taking over as Chief Artisan, Father, so Varin's lessons are of little use. Please get out of the way."

"You have responsibilities, Torin. I indulged your fantasies, but I must now insist—"

Torin had sighed then, amazed that his father didn't understand. "This isn't a fantasy, Father. I've spoken of nothing else for months. Why did you not believe me?"

Wyvald had shaken his head. "You are simply being obstreperous. You've been like this since your mother died."

"No, Father, I've been 'like this' all along. Mother simply shielded it from you because she knew you'd act like an ass."

Torin had often tried to provoke an emotional response out of his father, whom one of Torin's tutors had once referred to as "the crown prince of equanimity." Usually, the only way to accomplish that goal was to speak of his late wife in any but the most worshipful tones.

Sure enough, this time he had clenched his fists, and his mouth had curled into a vicious snarl beneath his red-and-gray beard. "Do *not* speak of your mother in that manner! I will only hear you speak of her with *respect*!"

"Easily accomplished, Father," Torin had said with a mock-sweet smile. "Get out of Sylvan's way, and you'll never hear me speak ill of Mother again."

But Wyvald had stood his ground, so Torin had done the only thing he could: he maneuvered Sylvan Wye around his father and then through the gates into the world outside.

Torin had no idea how long his father had just stood there. A part of him had wondered if he'd ever move.

"You all right?" Danthres asked.

"Hm?" Torin looked up at Danthres absently. "Oh, sorry—was lost in thought."

"You've been lost there for a while now. Honestly, you needn't have bothered coming to Minar's with me."

Torin shook his head ruefully. "I do apologize, Danthres. It seems my father's arrival has, well . . ."

"Affected you?" Danthres finished for him. "That's an understatement. Usually *I'm* the one who bites Grovis's head off."

Chuckling, Torin said, "I know. It just came over me to yell at him."

"Well, if that's the result, we should have your father show up more often."

While Torin knew that Danthres was joking, the very notion made him uncharacteristically angry, and he found he had to get his temper under control before it was Danthres's head he bit off.

Obviously, though, Danthres saw the look on his face, as she quickly added, "I *am* kidding, Torin."

"I know, I know." Torin waved her off. "You know, it's funny — I thought at the time I left Myverin that my father was completely wrong about me. He told me over and over again that I was a fool and that the outside world was not what I thought it was, and that I would lose everything I had within six months. I had laughed at him and called *him* a fool. I had the same horse I'd had since I was a boy and the finest sword in Myverin — that was all I'd need."

Danthres smiled knowingly. "How long did they last?"

With a sigh, Torin said, "I lost Sylvan Wye the first winter. One cold night, he lay down and never got up again. Which actually proved handy, as my hunting skills were excellent by the standards of the game ranges in Myverin, but woefully inadequate for a winter in the Forest of Orven. Sylvan Wye kept me fed for several days."

"And the sword?" Danthres asked.

"Not long after that, I came across a team of mercenaries. They let me come along when it was revealed that I could prepare food. Their cook had died in the winter. A pack of kobolds attacked the group one night, and my sword shattered against one monster's hide. Luckily, the others had sturdier weaponry, and we all survived."

"And you learned how to prepare kobold for dinner?" Danthres smirked as she asked.

"Hardly," Torin drawled. "They're far too gamey."

The pair approached the front door to the Grovis mansion just as the time-chimes rang eighteen times. Once the chimes were finished, Danthres pounded on the door with her fist.

Moments later, Frye gently pulled the door open, and again looked down his nose at the two detectives.

"Ah. You're back."

"Try to control your enthusiasm," Danthres retorted.

Frye stepped aside, and the pair of them entered. Without a word, Frye led them back into the purple-themed sitting room.

Cam wasn't present, but a tall man wearing a silk shirt and tights was now sitting in the purple easy chair. He was holding a glass with an amber liquid in his right hand and staring blankly into the air in front of him. His hair was black and more under control than either of the younger Grovises, and he had a thick black mustache to go with it. However, the face was unmistakably the same as that of Cam and Amilar, so this had to be either Cam's father Fentin or Amilar's father Harcort.

"The lieutenants from the Castle Guard, Master Fentin," Frye said, thus informing Torin of who it was.

"I'm Lieutenant ban Wyvald," Torin said, "and this is my partner, Lieutenant Tresyllione. We're investigating the murder of your son's fiancée."

"So I've heard." Fentin distractedly indicated the couch with his free hand. "Have a seat, please." He threw back quite a bit of his drink. Torin didn't have Danthres's sensitive nose, so he wasn't sure what the beverage was, but in his experience, alcohol of that color was generally meant to be sipped. That he gulped instead bespoke a fairly predictable lack of happiness with the situation.

After Torin and Danthres sat on the purple couch, Fentin asked, "So — is it true? Did my son purchase a —" He shuddered, then took a quick sip of his drink. "A *sex-sim*?"

"I'm afraid so," Torin said, trying to be sympathetic, though in truth he wanted to chortle at the Ghandurha-worshipper's ridiculous discomfort. Sex-sims were actually quite useful in helping young men get their technique right. However, he wasn't so impolitic as to say that to the vice president of the Cliff's End Bank on the day that he found out he'd lost his prospective daughter-in-law.

Danthres continued. "We verified with the merchant that your stable boy bought the sex-sim, the stable boy verified that he did so on instructions from your son, and we also verified that the sex-sim was only used for one minute on either side of half-past twenty-two last night."

In the hopes that it would encourage Fentin, knowing full well that it probably wouldn't, Torin said, "This means that your son could not possibly have murdered Arra Cynnis, sir. The timeline doesn't match. He was here with his, ah, purchase while the murder took place."

For the first time, Fentin looked at Torin. "I'm sorry, but — is that supposed to make me feel better?"

That took Torin aback. "Well yes, actually. Your son isn't a murderer, which means he won't be condemned to be hanged.

"If he was a murderer, then this would all be much easier to deal with. He'd be jailed and hanged and that would be that. But now . . . ."

Danthres's mouth fell open, and Torin felt his own do likewise. His partner said, "Your son's *alive*, and all he's done is something completely legal."

"Legality is all well and good," Fentin snapped, leaning forward in the purple chair, "but what he has done is horribly immoral." He leaned back again, holding the drink near his mouth. "But I wouldn't expect someone like *you* to understand."

Cutting Danthres off before she began to rant at Fentin for his snide remark, Torin said, "We understand better than you might think, sir. For starters, while Arra's murderer did so out of a callous disregard for her life, Cam did what he did last night out of love."

Fentin set the thick-bottomed glass down hard on the wooden end table, causing the amber liquid to slosh and splash. "Love? Are you mad? He's proven himself to be a thoughtless fornicator, no better than the lowlifes who wander the lesser streets of this foul city-state."

Torin found himself wondering how many of those lowlifes were customers at the bank that Fentin was vice president of. But aloud, he only said, "He actually isn't—thoughtless, or a fornicator."

"I *beg* your pardon?"

Danthres was shooting Torin the *be careful!* look that he usually had to give her when she was mouthing off at the upper classes, but Torin felt he had a point to make. "He was *practicing* for his wedding night. His only desire was to be the perfect husband for Arra."

"By fornicating outside the prescribed marriage bed?"

Now Danthres joined in. "No, by making sure he'd be able to perform in that bed. Besides, pretending to perform an act is not the same as performing it. If we prosecuted on the basis of what people pretended or desired, we'd run out of room in the hole for all the prisoners."

After gulping down the remainder of his drink, Fentin rose to his feet. Torin and Danthres both did likewise. "The behavior of our lessers is of little interest to me, Lieutenants. Your investigations have shown my son to be a blasphemer. I am grateful to you for informing me, as it means I can take appropriate action."

"Sir—" Torin started, but Fentin wouldn't let him speak.

"You are both excused—with my thanks for your diligence. Rest assured, my brother and I will speak well of you to Lord Albin when next we speak."

"Thank you, sir," Torin said automatically. Danthres, predictably, seemed less than grateful. He continued: "But I should emphasize again that Cam did nothing that was against the Lord and Lady's law."

"Which is why you are excused, Lieutenant ban Wyvald. The Lord and Lady's law is your responsibility, and you have already seen to it. Cam's actions, however, were very much against the rules of this household, and that is *my* responsibility and that of my brother. We have already dealt with his accomplice."

It took Torin a moment to figure out what Fentin was talking about. "You mean Martin?"

"If that is the stable boy's name, then, yes," Fentin said dismissively. "He has been released from his duties immediately. I will not have the staff encouraging blasphemous behavior."

Throwing up his hands, Torin said, "He was doing as his employer instructed! You cannot simply fire a boy from his job for *that*!"

"I, in fact, may do as I please within the walls of the family house, Lieutenant, as long as it remains within the Lord and Lady's law. That law does not prevent me from getting rid of stable boys who do not follow our rules. Cam was *not* his employer, he was his employer's son, and he should not have followed such an instruction without consulting my brother or myself."

"In my experience—" Torin started, but Fentin again interrupted.

His voice was harder, now. "Your experience is of little concern to me, Lieutenant. You have already been excused. Leave—now."

Before Torin could say something else, he felt Danthres's hand on his shoulder. "C'mon, Torin, let's go."

He stared at her for a second, and he saw concern on her face. After a moment, he nodded and they both walked out of the sitting room.

Once they reached the outdoors, the late-summer sun setting and painting the sky many shades of orange and red, Danthres asked, "What is *wrong* with you?"

Pointing in the general direction of the stables, Torin cried, "That boy did *nothing* to deserve having his living—his *home*—taken away from him!"

Danthres actually rolled her eyes at that, to Torin's annoyance. "This city-state is full of horses and not enough people willing to wallow in horseshit—he'll find another job in no time."

Torin would not be mollfied. "But what about their horses? They'll have to get used to someone *else* taking care of them, and—"

"They're not your horses, Torin, what do you care?"

Angrily, Torin said, "Horses are *very* particular, Danthres, you can't simply change their routine and expect them to respond well!"

"And again I ask: what do you care?"

"I—" Torin came up short, actually listening to Danthres's words. "I—" Again, he hesitated. Then his shoulders slumped. "I have no idea. I guess thinking about Sylvan Wye again . . ." He trailed off. "Forgive me?"

Laughing, Danthres said, "Are you joking? It's nice to be the rational one for a change. We should do this more often."

Torin chuckled in response. "I suppose. With luck, my father will depart soon, and things may return to normal."

"Yes—with *me* doing all the mouthing off."

"That *is* the natural order of things."

They continued down Oak Way, Torin trying to not think about the Grovis horses—which truly weren't his concern—or about that awful winter when he lost Sylvan Wye.

"We still have to talk to that last dress girl," Danthres pointed out. "Surely she's back from her errand by now—especially since that errand was probably a fool's one, given that the girl she's dressing is now dead."

"Indeed," Torin said as they turned onto Meerka Way. The Cynnis mansion was on this road between Oak Way and the castle.

Vaspar answered the door after they knocked. "Oh, hello, Lieutenants."

Torin noticed that Vaspar was clutching a small leather-bound booklet. Vaspar had a bit of growth on his cheeks, a failure of grooming that Torin would not have expected from as experienced a butler as Vaspar. Obviously, he had not yet entirely come to terms with Arra's death.

"I'm sorry," he said, "but if you're here to speak to Biroa, I'm afraid she's completely beside herself."

Danthres visibly shuddered. "We can talk to her tomorrow once she's calmed down," she said quickly.

Torin held in a chuckle, barely. He was not in the least bit surprised that his partner had long since reached her quota of dealing with simpering members of the upper classes and their servants.

Then Vaspar held up the book he was clutching. "However, I— I found something that I believe will be of use to you in your investigation. At least, I *hope* it will be. I couldn't—couldn't bring myself to read it, but you might find some—some insights into poor Arra."

Torin took the book from Vaspar's hands. The leatherwork on the covers was impressive, with a lovely knotwork pattern. He opened it to a random page, which had a very flowery handwriting, which spelled out words that were not in Common.

After a moment, Torin placed it. "You might not have been able to understand it even if you had read it, I'm afraid. It's in Kaelvan."

Danthres shot Torin a look. "What language is *that*?"

"One that isn't spoken anywhere this far east," Torin said.

Vaspar seemed stunned. "I had no idea she could write in that language. But then, I was not involved in her tutoring."

"Apparently, she could." He held up the diary. "Thank you for this."

Bowing, Vaspar said, "Of course. I hope it is of help. And you may speak to Biroa tomorrow, rest assured."

"Thank you."

He went back inside. Torin looked at Danthres, and then continued up Meerka Way.

"Perhaps this will tell us who the mystery lover is," Torin said, feeling confident for the first time since they eliminated Cam Grovis as a suspect.

Danthres sounded much less sure. "Assuming we can find anyone who can read that whatever-it-is."

Torin grinned. "No need—Kaelvan is what our neighbors to the west speak in Myverin. I mastered the tongue by the time I was seven."

Staring at Torin, Danthres asked, "You mean we have an actual break in the case?"

"Assuming she actually wrote about her secret lover."

Snorting, Danthres said, "That's not a concern. An upper-class teenaged girl? I doubt she wrote about anything else . . ."

# TWELVE

the hour.

The morning was fine. He'd single-handedly solved one of the mysteries of Mermaid Precinct — and he was looking forward to reporting their charitable contributions to Captain Osric, once he verified them with his father — and he was on the cusp of breaking a bribery case.

Or, at least, he had been. By the time he returned to the Dancing Seagull from the rather grueling and heartbreaking interview with his cousin Jahno was nowhere to be found.

Iaian just shrugged when Grovis queried him about it. "He said he only wanted to talk to you. He heard you were the one cleanin' up the docks, so it hadda be you he talked to."

"Very well, then, let us find him."

"Sure." Iaian didn't sound very excited about the notion, but Grovis didn't care all that much.

Unfortunately, nobody had seen him. At least not today.

"Jahno? Yeah, tell that shitbrain he owes me three coppers when you see his shifty ass."

"You'll prolly find Jahno at the Dancin' Seagull. Only place he goes since Bridgers kicked him off the *Amarilla*."

"I don't know Jahno. And if I *did* know him, I ain't seen him today. And if I *did* see him today, it ain't been since mornin'. And if I *did* see him this mornin', it wasn't nowhere near here anyhow. But I don't know him."

"Last time I saw Jahno was at the Seagull. Should try him there."

"Jahno? He's off on the *Amarilla*. No, wait, that's right, he got hisself kicked off the *Amarilla* 'cause he's a damned thief!"

"You just missed 'im. He was over at the Dancing Seagull."

Grovis was about ready to strangle Iaian for letting him go, when they saw an elderly dwarf with a bald head and a stomach-length beard counting coins while sitting on a stool near an empty dock.

"I know this guy," Iaian said. "It's Bradlik. He sees everything down here. Hey, Bradlik!"

The dwarf continued to count coins, ignoring Iaian until the last of the coins in his hand was enumerated. Then he looked up with squinted eyes. "Who's that? Iaian? You're too late if you wanna ride. The *Flotsam* finally got themselves a full complement when the last fella signed on this afternoon, and they left an hour ago. Ain't comin' back for another year."

"Retirement's not for another *two* years, Bradlik," Iaian said with a smile. "And when it does happen, I plan to never set foot anywhere near water ever again."

"Your loss. Ask me, a sea trip'd do you some good."

"Right, because what I want to do in my golden years is spend all of it throwing up over the side."

Bradlik laughed at that. Grovis, however, was growing impatient. "Pardon me for interrupting what I'm sure you both think resembles wit, but we *do* have police business to discuss."

Iaian leaned in toward the dwarf. "You'll have to excuse my partner, he was born with a silver stick up his ass."

They both had a good laugh at that, which only upset Grovis more. "If we may please get to the issue at hand."

Looking up at Grovis, Bradlik asked, "And what might that be, L'tenant?"

"We're looking for a man named Jahno. He was going to provide us with critical information for one of our investigations, but he seems to have disappeared."

Frowning, Bradlik asked, "You mean the fella what used t'be third mate on the *Amarilla*?"

"That's the one, yes." Grovis was relieved that the dwarf at least knew Jahno, and was willing to publicly admit to the fact.

"Yeah, well, I hope he ain't the key t'yer investigation."

Grovis started to feel nauseous. "Why's that?"

"Y'know that ship I toldja ain't comin' back for a year?"

"The *Flotsam*, yes."

"Well, they wasn't leavin' till they had a final passenger, like I said. That final fella was Jahno."

Iaian's eyes went wide. "You're kidding! He *left*? This *afternoon*?"

Angrily, Grovis whirled on Iaian. "What did you *say* to him?"

"I didn't say a damn thing, boy. He said he'd only talk to you, then he left the damn bar. Believe me, he was pretty anxious to talk—just not to me. Dunno why, but looks like he's gone now."

Shaking his head, Grovis said, "I can't *believe* it."

"Happens all the time, boy," Iaian said, leading Grovis back the way they came. Looking back, he said, "Thanks, Bradlik."

"My pleasure."

"Look," Iaian said as they walked back toward solid ground, "witnesses recant all the time. You *know* that. Now c'mon, the shift's basically over. You did good work today."

Grovis shot Iaian a look. "That sounded suspiciously like a compliment."

Grinning, Iaian said, "Yeah, well, don't get used to it. You put in your day's work, now it's time to relax. I'm headed to the Chain."

"I believe I'll join you."

Now it was Iaian's turn to shoot Grovis a look. "What?"

"After the—the revelations of this afternoon, I'd just as soon *not* go home. Father and Uncle Fentin will be beside themselves, and everyone will be talking about what an awful boy Cam is, and I don't think I can bear that." He let out a long breath. "And after this day, I could use a drink."

Iaian laughed and clapped Grovis on the back. "We'll make a detective out of you yet, boy."

# THIRTEEN

Her and Torin's shift had ended, and they were now entering the Old Ball and Chain. The public house was their usual post-shift destination, and indeed that of much of the Castle Guard. It was opened six years earlier by Urgoss, a dwarf who had served for twenty-five years in the Guard. His fellows from Dragon had attended the opening, and six years later, its reputation as a Guard bar was indisputable. At this stage, it took a great deal for Urgoss to even let a civilian in.

The day-shift detectives generally sat at the big round table in the back corner, and Hawk and Dru were already there, working on their ales. She navigated through the walkways while Torin went to the bar to fetch their drinks. Urgoss was too cheap to hire waitstaff, leaving patrons to fetch their own drinks from the bar, so he had made sure that navigation through the tavern was possible.

The back wall had a lengthy bench with five six-person tables alongside it, the last of them the round one at which Hawk and Dru sat, the former on one of the stools, the latter on the bench against the wall.

As Danthres moved to sit, Hawk said, "You look like your day sucked as much as ours."

"I'd say mine sucked more," Danthres said with a wry smile, "but I'm willing to hear your argument."

Dru started by telling about their first visit to the Temisan church on Axe Lane. By the time he was done, Torin had arrived with two ales.

"I'm not exactly clear why I had to pay for this, since *I* was the one who could read the diary."

That got Hawk's attention. "You found a diary?"

Danthres stopped Torin from answering by putting her hand over his bearded mouth. "You'll get our story when you're done with yours."

"Fine," Dru said after gulping down some more ale, and wiping his mouth with the back of his glove. "So we go back at fifteen with the M.E. in tow. First off, Boneen is bitching and moaning like never before. Says this is a waste of his talents, gobby gobby gobby, just like usual, right?" Dru shook his head. "We get there, and the client—"

"Kal," Hawk provided.

"Right, Kal—he's standin' there, and he's lookin' all sad. 'Brother Mantos is gone!' he's cryin'."

Danthres shook her head. "He ran off?"

Dru nodded. "We checked the rectory, and it didn't have anything but a cot and a bare closet. The treasury box was open and empty."

"There wasn't no sign of nobody livin' there," Hawk added. "Saw himself two detectives and figured he'd get before we found out he ain't the real thing."

"Yeah, which is great," Dru said, "but now we gotta deal with Boneen bitching *more*, which he does for ten minutes before he finally does the Teleport Spell and gets outta our hair, *and* we gotta listen to Kal whine about how we scared away the priest that was lettin' him talk to his daughter. An' then the bishop showed up."

"That must've been an enlightening conversation," Torin drawled.

"Oh yeah, it was—for the bishop." Dru shook his head. "See, just after midsummer, some guy showed up claimin' to be Brother Mantos, but the bish didn't believe him, an' sent him on his way, an' then we told him that the guy who'd been claimin' t'be Brother Mantos since *before* midsummer was a fake, trying to take people's money. Didn't believe us, or Kal, but then he saw the empty treasury box, and, well . . ."

Hawk started enumerating points on his fingers. "So let's see, we got ourselves yelled at by the families of the people bein' victimized, we got ourselves yelled at by Boneen—twice—we got ourselves yelled at by the victims when Mantos was up and gone, and we got ourselves yelled at by the bishop."

Torin asked, "Why did the bishop yell at *you*?"

"Ask *him*. Ain't like it was our fault."

Dru looked at Danthres. "So, c'mon, you found the victim's diary—you *had* to have had a better day than us."

Danthres and Torin proceeded to share their own case details, including the rather entertaining elimination of Cam Grovis as a suspect, and Vaspar handing over Arra's diary.

Then Danthres's face darkened. "Unfortunately, Arra's discretion is to a degree I never would have credited an upper-class twit with having."

Torin continued. "She not only wrote the diary in a language that perhaps twelve people in all of Cliff's End speak, but she was very vague about her lover. He's only referred to as 'my dear one.'"

Danthres immediately started quoting back what Torin had read to her back at the castle: "'I saw my dear one tonight.' 'I snuck away with my dear one, and we spent many hours in blissful intercourse away from Mother and Father's bleatings.' 'My dear one said that it doesn't matter about Cam, that we will be together always, and that no matter what, my dear one will always be there for me.' And on and on and on."

"No name?" Dru asked.

"No name." Danthres punctuated her answer with a gulp of ale. "We're no better off than we were before."

"Actually, we are," Torin said. "Keep in mind, this lover was only the subject of rumor and belowstairs gossip. This diary is the first solid proof we have that such a lover even exists."

Hawk added, "An' that's gotta be your suspect."

"Whoever he is, yes," Danthres said bitterly.

"Somehow," Torin said with a glance at his partner, "this became my fault, and I had to buy the first round."

A voice from behind them said, "Good, then you can buy mine." It was Iaian, with Grovis trailing behind him.

"Well, well, well," Danthres said, looking at Iaian's partner. "What leads you to sully yourself by consorting with the underclass?"

Iaian chuckled. "Lack of desire to consort with the upper class."

"Yes, well," Danthres said, enjoying Grovis's obvious discomfort, "I can imagine that the supper table will be a bit awkward, what with Cam actually admitting to having the same desires as every other boy in Flingaria."

Everyone around the table laughed, including Iaian, who had joined Dru on the bench. Grovis, however, was standing with his gloved hands clenched into fists. "This is *not* funny!

Cam is a fornicator, and Arra is dead, and Jahno disappeared, and—" He shuddered. "I need a drink."

"Get me an ale," Iaian called after him. "He's a little disheartened, since his best lead on corruption in Mermaid sailed off on the *Flotsam* this afternoon." He grinned. "And it cost me three gold less than I thought it would to get rid of him!"

Danthres was about to ask what Iaian was talking about, then decided she did not want to know.

"Ow!"

That was Grovis's voice. Turning around, Danthres saw that two guards with mermaid crests on their armor were standing in front of Grovis, blocking his path to the bar.

Grovis himself was hopping up and down on his left foot.

"Oh, *sorry*, Lieutenant," one guard was saying. "Guess I didn't see your *foot* there. Guess that's what happens when a dumb corrupt guard from Mermaid don't watch where he's *goin'*. Ain't that right, Filbert?"

"Yeah, Jax," Filbert said. "I'm thinkin' so."

"It was just an accident," Grovis said quietly. "If you'll excuse me, I would like to get to the bar, so I can—"

"Oh, I dunno," Jax said. "Guess that *might* not be so hot an idea. After all, you might get *impaired* if you have a drink. Ain't that right, Filbert?"

"Yeah, Jax," Filbert added, "I'm thinkin' 'e might get hisself hurt. If'n 'e drinks."

Not liking the looks of this in the least, Danthres stood up. Torin did likewise. To Danthres's annoyance, the other three stayed seated.

Filbert looked over at them. "Lookee 'ere, Jax. The halfbreed bitch's steppin' up."

"Let him through, Jax, Filbert," Danthres said. She had served with these two mouth-breathers when she was assigned to Goblin as a rookie. They'd been transferred to Mermaid shortly after she'd been bumped up to lieutenant.

"Gee, guess I'd *like* to," Jax said, "but I dunno. See this is a *guard* bar. An' guards don't go after other guards. Ain't that right, Filbert?"

Filbert grinned, showing the only six teeth he had left. "Yeah, Jax. I'm thinkin' 'e ain't no *real* guard."

"He wears the uniform," Danthres said, "and he outranks you. By intelligence as well as station." She couldn't believe she was *defending*

Grovis, but, having worked with those two, she'd take Grovis's idiocy over Jax and Filbert's incompetence any day.

Torin finally spoke up. "We simply wish to relax after a day of doing our duty, as ordered by the Lord and Lady—just as you do."

Iaian even threw in his own words, though he stayed seated. "C'mon, guys, the orders came from the Lord and Lady. Not some shitbrain who wants to make a name for himself—the *actual* Lord and Lady. You think any of us *likes* this shit?"

"Guess *he* does," Jax said, pointing at Grovis.

"Enough," Grovis said. "I'm leaving. Should never have come here."

As he moved toward the exit, Filbert called after him. "An' you shouldn't never be comin' back, neither!"

Iaian shook his head. "Shit, now I gotta get my own damn ale."

Danthres looked down on him—which she continued to do metaphorically as she sat back on the stool. "Is that really all you care about? Your ale? Your *partner* just got forced out of the bar!"

"He ain't my partner by choice, Tresyllione, and honestly, I agree with Jax and Filbert. This is shit duty, and it's bad for us, bad for the Guard, and bad for everyone. It ain't gonna solve anything, and it's gonna make it hard for us to do *real* police work!" He stood up. "And now I have to get my own damn drink."

Torin also rose. "I'm leaving."

Danthres stared up at him. "What? Why?"

"The air in here has gotten oppressive."

Without another word, Torin departed the Chain. Iaian, meanwhile, ambled toward the bar.

"Dammit," Danthres muttered.

"What is with him?" Dru asked.

"His father showed up today in the squadroom. Apparently, Torin's supposed to go back to Myverin and be the Chief Artisan, whatever *that* is. Torin doesn't wish to go."

"Lord and Lady," Dru said, "there's someone from Myverin *here*? In Cliff's End?"

"There's been for a decade now, shitbrain," Hawk said.

Dru waved off his partner. "Yeah, but Torin doesn't count. He's gone native."

"As native as anyone gets around here," Danthres muttered.

"Point is, I don't think anyone from Myverin's ever come here in my lifetime. Aside from Torin, and like I said, he don't count."

"Well, this one's likely to go home unhappy," Danthres said. "I know Torin, and I can't imagine any circumstance under which he'd return with his father."

Hawk looked at Dru. "I'm thinkin' maybe Torin had the day that sucked the most."

"Yeah." Dru drank down the rest of his ale.

Danthres did likewise. She contemplated following Torin out the door to his residence. Maybe he'd appreciate the company.

Then she decided against it. He always asked first if he wanted to sleep with her—usually because she was sometimes not especially in the mood—and he hadn't done so.

Still, she considered going against their usual routine. They'd already well and truly shattered it today in any case . . .

# FOURTEEN

As he trudged up the stairs of the building that housed his rooms, Torin pulled the key out of the pouch on his belt. The uneven wooden stairs creaked under his weight and each step of his boots on them echoed through the stairwell.

He was tired and cranky, and needed a good night's sleep that he was quite sure he wouldn't get. He knew, just *knew*, that his dreams would be filled with images of Sylvan Wye and Father and freezing in the winter cold.

Part of him thought that he should have just stayed at the Chain and drunk himself into insensibility, letting Danthres carry him home, but the moment Jax and Filbert decided to harass Grovis, Torin felt his temper fraying. If he had stayed at the Chain much longer, he was going to start a fight.

With the exception of when he was a soldier and ordered to, Torin had never started a fight in his life. The fact that he had such an urge meant he needed to depart the premises posthaste.

When he turned the key, the tumbler did not move, and he realized that the door was unlocked. He cursed himself for his carelessness, allowing his father's presence to so distract him that he didn't even remember to lock his door.

And then he cursed himself again for forgetting that his father didn't show up until this morning.

Which meant that there was someone in his apartment.

Putting his hand on his sword hilt, Torin slowly opened the door.

His rooms were small but functional. There was a large sitting room with a wood-burning stove in the center, useful for both cooking and heating the place during the colder months. To the side was a water basin. Two doors on the left led to the privy and to a small bedroom. The building had four apartments, two on each floor, and the four privies were adjacent to each other, all emptying into a cesspool behind the building. When he'd first taken the place, Torin had questioned the wisdom of putting the privy that close to the bedroom, but the tubing that fed from the privy to the cesspool was well enough placed so that there was rarely any kind of smell. Certainly nothing bad enough to impair sleep, though when Danthres had slept with him here during the hottest days of summer, she had sometimes complained of the odor.

As he opened the door now, he saw that the lantern that sat atop the stove in the center of the sitting room was lit.

And his father was sitting on the small chair Danthres had gotten him for his birthday last year, reading over some scrolls.

Without preamble, Wyvald said, "*This* is where you live? This — this *hovel*?"

"You do realize, Father," Torin said through clenched teeth, "that I can arrest you right now for breaking and entering."

"Your landlady let me in. She recognized instantly that I was your father."

"I shall have to have words with her." Torin unfastened his cloak and tossed it onto the couch, too aggravated to even hang it up properly. Besides, he knew the lack of fastidiousness would annoy Wyvald.

Wyvald set the scrolls aside. "You know, Torin, I had been willing to at least discuss this with you, but seeing the appalling conditions in which you choose to live, I'm afraid that any conversation would be pointless."

"Good. Then you may leave." Torin pulled his gloves off and tossed them on top of the cloak before sitting next to both of them on the couch.

Standing up, Wyvald said, "Pack your things, Torin. We are leaving for Myverin at first light, and I will brook no argument."

Torin couldn't help but laugh at that. "Oh, I won't argue with you, Father. But I won't go with you, either."

Walking over to the couch, Wyvald stood over Torin. "You have no choice! Until your grandfather died, I was willing to indulge you, but now —"

Looking up at him, Torin's laugh modulated into a snarl. "Really? And how do you intend to enforce this lack of choice? That seal you carry allows you access to the castle as a courtesy, but I'm afraid, High Magistrate, that it gives you no actual authority within this city-state." Torin yanked off one boot, and then pulled on the other.

"I have authority over *all* citizens of Myverin, Torin. If you do not obey my command, there *will* be consequences."

"Really?" After removing the other boot and flexing his toes, which were relieved at being freed, Torin got to his feet and faced his father. "The punishment for a citizen of Myverin refusing the judgment of the High Magistrate is to be cast out and have his citizenship privileges revoked until such a time as he obeys the judgment." Torin smiled. "You see, I remember what my tutors taught me oh so long ago." The smile fell. "Even if, by some quirk, you were to actually *have* any authority over me here in Cliff's End, the absolute most that you could do to me is something I already did to myself fifteen years ago."

"Think about what you're doing, Torin," Wyvald said tightly. "If you make this decision, you'll never be welcome in Myverin again, and no citizen of Myverin will ever acknowledge your existence."

Torin shook his head in disbelief. "You truly are delusional, Father. When you rehearsed this conversation prior to arrival, did you honestly believe that I would come crawling back to Myverin, so incredibly frightened of the consequences of the rest of my life being *exactly the same as it is now*?"

Wyvald looked around. "I would think that continuing to live this wretched existence would indeed frighten you to your very core. It certainly does me." He stared back at his son with the withering gaze he had always used upon him as a boy. "You would have your own house with hectares of land all to yourself." He looked down at Torin's bare feet. "You'd have boots that actually *fit* your feet."

Torin shrugged. "I have wide feet."

"And you choose to live in a place that cannot accommodate that? This place is *that* primitive?"

"I choose to *live* in a place, Father, not simply *exist*." He turned and walked away from Wyvald, unwilling to face him anymore. "Myverin is beautiful, yes, and I would indeed have a far more luxurious residence there. But I would stagnate, Father. A life dedicated to philosophy and art is simply one that holds no interest for me."

"So you choose instead to live the life of a—a common soldier?"

"No, Father, I tried that, and it was actually *worse*. Only youthful stubbornness kept me from running back home after that first winter." He shuddered involuntarily, then turned back to face Wyvald. "But here I've found the place for me to *be*. As a citizen of Myverin I was bored, and as a soldier I was devastated, but here, I've found the perfect mix of both. I'm not just a foot-soldier, Father, I'm a *detective*. I solve crimes, using the skills your tutors taught me — but in pursuits that have a *practical* value, unlike life in Myverin."

Now it was Wyvald's turn to look away from his son. "I blame myself," he said with a sigh.

"Good," Torin said with a cheeky smile. "So do I. Accept your blame, then, and leave my home."

"This isn't a home, it's a sewer."

"Then leave my sewer. Or I *will* have you arrested."

"I did not break and enter, as you so crudely put it."

Torin put his hands on his hips. "Fair enough, but you *are* trespassing."

Wyvald regarded Torin with an expression that the latter read as pity, which only infuriated him even more. "I will not return to Myverin without a new Chief Artisan, Torin. I will use every means at my disposal."

"And I will use every means at my disposal to keep you from doing so. I believe, High Magistrate, that the means available to a lieutenant in the Castle Guard are considerably greater than those of a lone visiting dignitary from a nation that doesn't even have a standing army."

"We shall see."

With that Wyvald turned and departed.

Torin quickly locked the door behind him, and then removed the rest of his armor.

He suspected sleep would not be forthcoming any time soon.

# FIFTEEN

Danthres had been standing in front of the Cynnis mansion for the better part of an hour when Torin finally ambled up Meerka Way.

He looked surprised at her presence, and said, "Danthres? What's going on?"

Before Danthres answered, she got a good look at her partner, and her already-considerable concern grew. Torin had bags under his green eyes, and his hair and beard were both horribly unkempt.

In answer to his query, Danthres said, "It's over an hour past roll call. I made an excuse for you to Jonas, then Osric came in and told me that the other Cynnis children returned from Iaron late last night."

"So we'll be talking to them, then?" Torin asked wearily.

"Afraid so," Danthres said gravely. "Still, it's possible that Arra confided in one of her siblings about her lover. Plus, we also have the third dressing girl to speak to."

"Fine, then, let's."

He walked toward the door, but Danthres put a hand on his chest. "Torin, what happened? Even *you* aren't generally *this* late. And it doesn't look like you've slept. Was it the neighbors again, or were you thinking about your father?"

Torin snorted. "I wish it was the neighbors. I could just threaten them again. No, it was Father."

Shaking her head, Danthres put a hand on his shoulder. "Torin, you need to stop thinking about him."

"Well, that's difficult when he shows up in my sitting room unnanounced."

Danthres's eyes widened. "He did *what*?"

Torin filled her in on his father's appearance at his home.

"He *is* stubborn, isn't he?" Danthres shook her head again.

"That's one word for it. In any event, I tossed and turned all the night long. I barely heard the time chimes." He let out a very long breath. "Thank you for covering with Jonas."

She smiled. "That's what partners are for."

Danthres walked up to the large wooden door and knocked on it. Apparently, the arrival of the remaining Cynnis brood had as ill an effect on Vaspar as the arrival of Wyvald ban Garin had on Torin, as Vaspar looked almost as bad as Danthres's partner. His cheeks had gotten fuzzier — Danthres suspected he hadn't had the opportunity to shave with the return of so many, especially as it was late last night — and it looked as if he hadn't changed clothes since Danthres saw him last.

"Ah, Lieutenant Tresyllione, Lieutenant ban Wyvald, welcome back. Was —" He looked back and forth, then lowered his voice while leaning forward. "Was the evidence I provided of some use to you?"

"Some, yes." Danthres uttered those two words in a like whisper, but then raised her voice. "Are the other children ready to see us?"

"Hardly children anymore," Vaspar said in a tone that Danthres wasn't sure was wistful or aggravated. "Please, come inside."

Vaspar led them to the same office where Danthres had had to rescue Torin from his interview with Sir Malik.

"Sir is not at home today," Vaspar said, "so I took the liberty of securing his office for your interviews."

Torin actually was able to scrape together a smile for that. "Won't sir object?"

"It is the room best suited to the task," Vaspar said archly, "and that is all that matters."

Danthres suspected that that was not true, but she let it go.

Vaspar had them sit on the same couch that Torin had sat on previously, and then he brought in the oldest child, Jared. He was a very attractive specimen, Danthres thought, assuming you liked that sort of thing. He had the dark hair of his father, the ice-blue eyes of his mother, and cheekbones that he must have gotten from some other relative.

His hands were folded in front of himself as he spoke in a subdued tone. "So horrible about Arra. And so close to her wedding! This is just horrible. Horrible. Do you have any idea who did it?"

Danthres shook her head. "The peel-back revealed that the murderer hid his identity through magick. We're fairly certain it's someone who knew her and cared about her."

Jared unfolded his hands and put one over his heart. "You don't think Cam had anything—"

"No," Danthres said quickly. "He has an alibi."

"Good—I'd hate to think we were all so wrong about him." Jared shook his head. "If there's anything I can do . . ."

Torin finally spoke up. "Perhaps there is. As far as we can determine, Arra had an illicit lover."

Jared chuckled playfully. "I doubt that. Ours is a devout family, and we have been trained from birth to be true to our obligations."

"Really?" Torin asked snidely. "Is that why you purchased a house in Dragon Precinct for the express purpose of having illicit affairs there?"

At that, Jared blinked in shock. "Excuse me?"

"The house currently owned by the Grabodlik family. Their house faerie told some fascinating tales of the previous owners—including the oldest Cynnis son, who couldn't keep it in his tights."

The pleasant face became somewhat less so, and he stood up, snarling. "That filthy little milk-lover! I'll kill him!"

"Too late." Torin had a nasty grin on his face.

Danthres stared at her partner with concern, as he was taking *pleasure* from Jared's anger.

He went on: "I'm afraid we learned this when we interrogated the faerie for the accidental death of one of the residents, which he caused. The magistrate sentenced him to death."

"Good." Jared shook his head. "Fine, so you know my dirty little secret."

"Don't be too impressed," Torin said. "We spoke to your household staff and the first word is all that applies, as your affairs are neither little, nor much of a secret."

At that, Danthres winced. Torin had just gotten the entire serving staff in trouble with the eldest son of the house. He'd done them no favors by revealing them as a source.

"So perhaps," Torin continued, "Arra went to you for advice."

"I'm telling you," Jared said through clenched teeth, "that Arra did *not* have an affair. It wasn't in her nature. And if she *had* come to me seeking advice—which she most assuredly did not—I would have told her to end it as quickly as possible. Cam Grovis is a good man, and they would make a fine match. I would have urged her to stop fooling about and settle down for the good of the family."

"Advice you seem unable to take for yourself." Torin was practically sneering as he spoke.

Jared stood up and practically barked his next words. "*Yes*, Lieutenant, advice I do not take for myself! *If* Arra were to have an affair — which I *assure* you, she would *never* do — I would tell her to learn from *my* mistakes. I've done enough damage, I see no reason to encourage it to continue."

Danthres asked, "So you don't know with whom she was having the affair?"

"I'm telling you, she wasn't *having* one! Now if that's all, I just returned from a two-week journey and I have a sister to mourn."

Without waiting to be excused, Jared stormed out.

Staring angrily at her partner, Danthres asked, "What was *that*?"

Torin seemed genuinely confused. "What was what?"

Danthres pointed at the door that Jared had just left through. "*That*. Why did you set him on the defensive?"

"I didn't wish to sit through the hypocrisy."

"Yes, and that worked *so* well that he flounced out of the room before he could tell us that who she was having the affair with."

"He didn't know." Torin smirked. "Didn't you hear, she didn't *have* an affair?"

"Please tell me you're not so far gone that you took him at his word?" Danthres asked pleadingly.

"Of course not — and I'm not 'gone,'" he said testily. "He told us enough that he can still tell his parents and himself that he knew nothing of the affair, while making it clear that he cautioned her to break it off."

Danthres nodded. "It might well have been his advice that caused her to end it, thus leading to her death. Either way, though, you put him on the defensive far too quickly. We need to be more gentle with the next one, not give him reason to shut down right away. And you know how I know this?"

Torin just stared at her.

"Because it's what *you* taught me!" She shook her head. "Lord and Lady, how did it come to this? *I'm* preaching a gentle approach."

"You're right, of course, Danthres." Torin's tones had grown subdued. "You take the lead on the rest."

Vaspar came in, then. "That went rather quickly."

"But it was informative," Danthres said. "Please send in the next one?"

"Of course."

Blan entered moments later. Short where his brother was tall, blond where Jared was dark, and with his father's brown eyes instead of the blue eyes his mother passed on to the elder son, Blan carried himself with his father's arrogance as well.

"I really don't have time for this nonsense," he said without preamble.

"Your sister's death is nonsense?" Danthres asked with mock surprise.

"No, your wasting time talking to people who weren't even *here* when it happened is nonsense. You should be finding the killer, not taking up *valuable* time that could be spent in more profitable pursuits."

Danthres shot Torin a look, but he stuck to his word and let her take the lead. "In fact, we know who the killer is generally, but not specifically."

Blan's face soured. "That doesn't even make *sense*."

"The killer was able to hide his identity from the peel-back. However, we are fairly certain that the person in question is someone Arra was having an affair with."

That prompted Blan to burst out laughing. "Oh, *very* droll. *My* sister? Having an *affair*? I speak of course of Arra, not *dear* Crilla, who would sleep with a chamberpot if it bought her a drink first. But Arra? *Never*." He shook his head. "It troubles me, truly, that such imbeciles are tasked with maintaining law and order in this sewer of a city-state. We just came from Iaron—now *that* is a civilized place. Not like this vermin-infested . . . ." He shuddered, removing a handkerchief from his pocket and using it to dab his eyes for no obvious reason. "In any event, if you are attempting to seek out an illicit lover, you will *never* find my sister's killer. Not that you would, anyhow, as you're obviously completely incompetent, if you even *believe* such a thing. Where did you even *hear* such a salacious rumor?"

Danthres found herself unable to resist. "From Arra."

"I beg your pardon?" Blan was now waving the handkerchief back and forth.

"She kept a diary. In it, she makes several explicit references to her lover, to how much she adores him, and so on."

"That's—that's absurd!" Blan shook his head. "I can't believe you even *read* her diary! After all, it's in some awful language I can't even *read*, and—" Blan stopped short.

Danthres smiled. "And how would you know *that*, exactly?"

"Never mind." He turned his back on the lieutenants. "I must go."

Like his brother, he stormed out.

Torin shook his head and chuckled. "Will no one in this family sit through an entire interview?"

"Apparently not." Danthres leaned back on the couch. "At least now we know why Arra wrote her diary in such an obscure tongue."

Torin nodded. "What a pity the final entry was two months ago. I suspect that Jared's advice to his sister came shortly before the trip to Iaron six weeks ago. She broke it off some time after that, leading our killer to seek out a magickal disguise and kill her."

"It's a good theory." Danthres sighs. "We just need some evidence to back it up."

Vaspar came in and cleared his throat.

"Yes, Vaspar?" Danthres prompted.

"I'm afraid, Lieutenants, that Crilla has refused to speak with you. She says she refuses to speak with unclean thugs."

Danthres shot Torin a look. "'Unclean thugs'? That was really the best she could come up with?"

"If I may be so bold, Lieutenants," Vaspar said hesitantly, "I doubt Crilla would have been able to tell you anything. She barely acknowledged Arra's existence. She is unlikely to provide any information of any use—or indeed of any truth."

Torin chuckled. "In that case, I suppose we should see the final dressing girl."

"Of course."

Moments later, Vaspar led a very pretty young woman into the office. Danthres was impressed—she'd never really thought of humans as being particularly attractive. But this woman was perfectly put together. She had fine cheekbones that wouldn't have been out of place on an elf, lovely long dark hair, very wide and open blue eyes, and a bright smile.

"Hello," she said in a mellifluous tone that Danthres found to be incredibly soothing. "My name is Biroa."

"Lieutenant Danthres Tresyllione, and this is my partner, Lieutenant Torin ban Wyvald."

Biroa's beautiful eyes widened. "I'm impressed. I know that Cliff's End is a bit of a catch-all, but someone from Sorlin working with someone from Myverin is *very* rare."

"Now *I'm* impressed," Danthres said.

"Well, the names gave it away for both of you—and for *you*," she added to Danthres with a mischievious smile, "it's written all over your face. You're *obviously* of mixed elven and human heritage. As for *you*," she now looked at Torin, "that name is indeed a dead giveaway."

Torin smiled, and it was his first warm smile of the day, for which Danthres was grateful to Biroa. "True, but few people this far east recognize that. They just assume I have a bizarre name."

"Well, by the standards of these decadent eastern lands, you do." Biroa continued to smile pleasantly, then her face fell. "But you're not here to speak of nomenclature, but of poor Arra's death."

"Yes. We need to know about the young man she was having the affair with."

Biroa let out a small laugh. "I'm sorry, Lieutenants, I don't mean to make light of your question, but—I'm simply a dress girl. Arra never said anything to me about having an affair with any young man. Honestly, she was too busy being worried about her father."

That piqued Danthres's interest. "What about her father?"

"Well, he has all those secret meetings with that wizard. There's obviously something going on there. Arra was very concerned, to be honest, because every time she asked Sir Malik about it, he'd put her off. One time, he even denied that he was meeting with a mage, but we *both* saw the wizard right here in this office!"

Danthres was outraged. "Secret meetings with wizards? Obviously, *something* is going on there."

Torin started, "Danthres—"

"Sir Malik *was* acting secretive," Danthres pointed out. "He put you off when you asked about his odd meetings, and the entire staff mentioned them."

"True," Torin said slowly, "but wizards are private citizens like everyone else."

Danthres just stared at Torin.

He relented. "All right, not *just* like everyone else, but they are permitted to meet with whomever they wish."

However, Danthres wasn't giving up. She *knew* that there was something to this. "Yes, but why do so in secret? What would a wizard, of all people, have to hide? On those occasions when they do hobnob with the little people, they make a very big show of it. Besides, think about our theory of the case."

Torin frowned. "I'm sorry?"

Danthres leaned forward on the couch. "Think about it—we've assumed all along that it was someone who loved her, but there's someone it could have been besides a lover or fiancé. What if it was her father? He could have gotten the spell from his wizard friend and killed Arra because she was asking too many questions about his secret meetings."

Torin rubbed his bearded chin. "It's a possibility—but like our other theory, it lacks evidence to back it up."

"Well, I doubt Sir Malik would say anything," Biroa said in a soft voice, "but perhaps you could talk to the wizard. His name is Lord Ythran."

Eyes widening, Danthres turned to Torin. "Really, now?"

Biroa's head tilted to the right. "Do you know him?"

"Oh yes," Torin said. "He obfuscated our investigation into Gan Brightblade's murder. And then he inserted himself into another case during midsummer."

"It's an open question," Danthres added, "which of those was more annoying."

Then Torin sighed. "Unfortunately, getting a meeting with someone of Ythran's stature is difficult under the best of circumstances. And we don't have proper grounds for such a meeting—yet."

"What more do we need?" Danthres asked with more than a little outrage.

"I did say 'yet,' Danthres. After all, we now have something to go to Sir Malik with."

"True." Danthres turned to Biroa. "Is there anything you can recall from the time you saw Ythran and Malik together? Anything they said?"

Biroa shrugged. "I'm sorry, I don't remember." Then her face brightened. "Wait, I do recall a mention of an earth-pig—whatever that is. It's a type of animal, isn't it?"

"Not exactly," Torin said with a frown. "It's a creature from legend, particularly among some of the dark elf tribes of the southern lands. But to the best of my knowledge, such a creature doesn't actually exist."

"Well, perhaps," and now Biroa's mischeivious smile came back, "their secret is that they're trying to resurrect the beast from mythology?"

Danthres laughed. "Perhaps that is the case."

Placing her hands upon her lap, Biroa got up. "I hope that I've been of some use. I'm just sorry I can't tell you about the boy she was sleeping with—I just don't know anything about that."

"It's possible he's not even our suspect," Danthres said. "Don't worry."

With a smile, Biroa turned and left.

Leaving Torin to regard her with confusion.

"What?" she asked defensively.

"You jumped to quite a large number of conclusions, Danthres. These meetings could well have nothing to do with Arra's murder. Besides, just because you don't *like* the brotherhood doesn't mean that they're all horrible people."

"We know that Ythran's an ass."

"That doesn't make him a murderer."

Danthres nodded. "Perhaps. But, since no one seems to have the foggiest notion who Arra's mystery lover is, why not try this lead and see where it goes?"

"Oh, I don't disagree," Torin said. "However, you seem to be very eager to change our entire theory of the case based on the word of one dressing girl." He smiled. "And you're usually the one who sticks to one theory stubbornly until forced to change it."

At that, Danthres laughed. "Yes, well, I'm also usually the one who's stubborn and undiplomatic, so apparently we're changing roles for this case."

Shuddering, Torin said, "Only for as long as Father's here. I promise, once he's gone, I'll be back to my usual charming self."

"I hope so—I *hate* being the polite one."

# SIXTEEN

Just as Torin entered the squadroom with Danthres, Dru and Hawk
were walking out.

"Lucky us," Hawk said, "we got us a robbery on the docks."

Dru shook his head. "You guys in Unicorn, us, Iaian, and the fish in
Mermaid—remember when all the crime used to be in Goblin?"

"Ah, the good old days," Danthres muttered.

"Yeah. Wish us luck," Dru said as they departed.

As the other two detectives left, Jonas moved toward Torin and
Danthres.

"I've received reports from Dragon and Goblin. They canvassed all
the spell shops, and none of them remember selling an Occlude Person
spell any time in the past six months."

Torin sighed. "That just means it wasn't purchased legitimately."

"Or the shop owners don't remember," Danthres said bitterly.

Jonas shuffled some of his parchments. "Some of them did keep
records . . ."

"All in Dragon, no doubt," Torin said with a smile. "Yes, and when
we went to Minar's Emporium to check on the sex-sim, we also asked
him about it, and he showed us very detailed records. Still, that just
means we're back where we started."

Osric came out of his office. He was holding his dagger in his hand,
but not the sharpening stone, which Torin chose to view as a good sign.

"What progress are you making?"

Before Torin could answer, Danthres blurted out, "We may have a
new suspect."

"Besides the lover?" Osric asked.

"No one even knows who it is," Danthres said. "In fact, I'm starting
to come around to the notion that she made the lover up. I can't believe

that, in an entire household staff, *no one* knows who Arra was seeing clandestinely. It's just not possible that they could *all* be kept in the dark like that—unless it was just a young girl's flight of fancy."

This was Torin's first time hearing this particular theory, and he had to admit that it made a certain sense. And he wasn't about to point out the problems with it—like the lack of evidence not necessarily meaning lack of existence—but instead said, "Either way, if the lover exists, we still don't know who he is."

"But we *do* know that Sir Malik has been having secret meetings. Biroa told us all about them."

Shaking his head in obvious confusion, Osric asked, "Who's Biroa?"

"The third dressing girl," Danthres said. "She's proven to be very valuable. She told us all about Malik's clandestine meetings with Lord Ythran."

Osric noticeably deflated. "Please tell me that there's another Lord Ythran."

"Sadly, no," Torin said with a wry smile. "The very same local representative of the Brotherhood of Wizards."

"That's *all* we need." Osric shook his head. "So you think that Arra found out about the meetings and her father killed her?"

"It's something we have to look at," Danthres said. "Sir Malik wasn't home, so we re-interviewed some of the staff, and also did first interviews with the staff who took the trip to Iaron, which was very enlightening. We also sent one of the goons from Unicorn to bring Sir Malik here."

Osric's scowls were legendary in the east wing of the castle, and they had been just as much so during his time in the army when Torin served under him. Right now, he was fixing Danthres and Torin with one of his most powerful.

"You're going to bring the father of a murder victim into one of the interrogation rooms?"

"No," Danthres said, "we're bringing a suspect to be questioned in the castle, as is standard."

"Besides," Torin added, "the last time I tried to talk to him, he threw me out of his office rather than answer any questions about strange meetings that his staff noticed him having. Best not to give him that option the second time."

Twirling his dagger around in his hand, Osric let out a long breath. "All right, go ahead. But tread carefully. Do recall that this is the same nobleman who wanted you two fired, and he's unlikely to improve his opinion of the pair of you if you accuse him of a murder he didn't actually commit."

They both went to sit at their desks, waiting for Zayl to return with Malik. Danthres and Torin had both agreed to send the mute guard because his inability to speak would likely annoy and confuse Malik, and because anyone who could break up a fight in the Ogre's Breath would have no trouble convincing a nobleman to cut a meeting short in order to be interviewed by the Castle Guard.

Normally at this point, the pair of them would go over what they knew of the case, which helped them form a strategy for the interrogation. This was hindered by Danthres's focus on Biroa's interview to the exclusion of all else and Torin's unusually short temper. It was also possible that the latter was having a negative impact on Torin's interpretation of the former.

So Torin was in an even fouler mood when Zayl entered with Sir Malik, who looked quite aggravated himself.

"*What* is the meaning of this? I've been trying to ask this imbecile for the reasons why he barged into my trustee meeting, but he has been utterly silent on the subject. I want him fired! And I *still* want the two of *you* fired!"

"My apologies," Torin said with a pleasant smile. "We simply asked Unicorn Precinct to send a guard to fetch you—we did not realize they would send Zayl. He's mute, you see—wounded in the line of duty."

That deflated Sir Malik only for an instant. "Very well, he can keep his job, but I wish to know why you ordered me brought here in the first place!"

"That will become clear soon enough, Sir Malik," Torin said. "You see, some new evidence has come to light. If you'll accompany us to the interview room, we shall explain."

Malik put his hands on his hips. "*What* new evidence?"

"We will explain inside," Torin said.

"Very well." Malik let out a sigh and followed Torin into the interrogation room, Danthres right behind.

The east-wing interrogation rooms were effective spaces that looked random and thrown-together. Many interpreted them to be the rooms the architects forgot when designing the castle. In fact, they were set up with precision and care: drab, windowless walls painted in a neutral color, a single lantern casting odd shadows, and a beat-up old table, behind which was an uncomfortable stool for the interviewee to sit on, faced by the detectives, sitting in much more comfortable chairs on the other side.

Torin led Sir Malik to the stool. "Please have a seat, Sir Malik."

He looked around and shuddered. "Why must we speak in here?"

For the first time since Malik's arrival, Danthres spoke. "We thought it would be best not to air your daughter's dirty laundry in the midst of the squadroom, through which dozens of people come in and out every hour. In here, we have some privacy—I would think you'd value that."

Another sigh. "Fair enough." He sat down on the stool, and immediately squirmed. Torin doubted that he'd ever sat on anything that wasn't cushioned in his life. "Tell me of this evidence, and quickly, so I may leave and speak again to Lord Albin about removing the two of you from your posts."

"First of all, a question." Torin sat in the one of the chairs opposite Malik. "Do you know a Lord Ythran?"

Malik frowned. "I don't think so. I converse with many lords in my business, but that name doesn't ring a bell."

"This one is a mage. He's the local representative for the Brother-hood of Wizards."

Nodding, Malik said, "Ah, yes, of course, well, then I may have met him once or twice. What does this have to do with—"

Torin held up a hand. "All in good time, Sir Malik. Now, are you familiar with the Church of the Earth-Pig Born?"

Now Malik chuckled. "There is such a church? I had no idea. Isn't the Earth-Pig a creature of myth?"

Danthres was still standing, leaning against the ugly wall, her arms folded across her chest. "From the south. The Earth-Pig is a minor demon who comes forth when Flingaria is in need of spiritual cleansing."

"Ah yes," Malik said, nodding, "I recall now. The Earth-Pig rises from beneath the ground when Flingaria needs him. It's an old legend."

"So," Danthres said, deliberately changing tracks quickly, "you've never met Sir Ythran?"

"It's Lord Ythran," Malik said dismissively, "and I told you, I probably only met him once or twice."

"Yet you know him well enough to correct his title."

"You called him 'Lord' earlier," Malik said defensively.

"Yes, but we could've been mistaken the first time rather than the second." Danthres was smiling now. "Yet you already knew he was a lord, didn't you?"

"Of course not, I barely know the man." Malik started palming sweat from his forehead. "Is it hot in here?"

"Really?" Torin leaned forward in the comfortable chair. "Then how do you explain the four witnesses who saw Lord Ythran having meetings in your office—the very same one you kicked me out of yesterday. One of those witnesses is your cook, who recalled several occasions when she had to make a special meal primarily of steamed vegetables for a visiting wizard. Those are times that coincide with when the other members of your staff recall seeing someone matching Lord Ythran's description in your house."

"Look, there's nothing in the Lord and Lady's law that forbids meeting with wizards, all right?" Malik continued to squirm, though Torin doubted it had much to do with the stool.

Danthres smiled. "So you did meet with him?"

"So what if I did?" Malik's voice started to squeak. "It's not a crime!"

"Yes, but lying to the Castle Guard is a punishable offense."

"What do you mean?"

"Just now," Torin said, "you told us you didn't know Lord Ythran, and now you've admitted to meeting with him. This makes us wonder what else you've lied to us about."

"And," Danthres asked, "what those secret meetings were about."

"I—"

Torin interrupted Malik. "We were told by one of your footmen that you sent him with your children to Iaron to perform an errand—specifically to drop off some scrolls to the Church of the Earth-Pig Born in Iaron."

"I've never heard of—"

"Yes, yes," Danthres interrupted, "we know you said you never heard of it, yet you donate scrolls to them. You also 'recall' the myth of the Earth-Pig that doesn't actually exist except in that Iaron church. The actual legend from the south has nothing to do with any of that."

"How do *you* know?" Malik asked defensviely.

With a grin, Torin said, "Danthres is from Sorlin. She heard the stories of the Earth-Pig as a girl."

"And they sound nothing like the legends you parrotted just now, which are in fact from the Church of the Earth-Pig Born, which has only existed for about seven years. The footman we talked to was more than happy to provide us with one of the posters that you also sent with him to Iaron."

"Apparently," Torin added, "there were a couple that were mis-scribed and had mistakes, so he brought them back and was able to show them to us."

Danthres grinned. "Can't very well hang a sign that urges people to go to the temple on Fajril Way when it's on Fajril Lane."

Glancing back at Danthres, Torin said, "Could also be on Fajril Alley."

"Yes, they are quite fond of Fajril in Iaron, aren't they?"

Malik waved his hands back and forth. "This is madness! What does my work with the church have to do with my daughter being murdered?"

"Everything!" Danthres cried, even as Torin leaned back and smiled. She pushed herself off the wall and started walking toward the table. "Arra found out about the little scam you and Ythran were running, creating a religion in Iaron. Tell me, how many charitable donations were made to the Church of the Earth-Pig Born in the past seven years that now sit in your bank account?"

"Look, if people want to donate to a church, who am I to stop them? It is *very* hot in here!" The sweat was now almost pouring down Malik's face.

"So you admit it?" Danthres asked.

"Yes, Lord Ythran and I have had meetings about the Church of the Earth-Pig Born, of which I am a trustee. Are you satisfied?"

Danthres now leaned forward, placing her palms flat on the table. "Not even a little bit, Sir Malik, because you've already lied to us twice, and about matters that relate *directly* to your daughter's murder."

"That's absurd! I love Arra more than anything! And this has *nothing* to do with her!" He shook his head, and wiped more sweat from his brow. "Gods below, she was the only creature that sprung out of Hassa's wretched womb that I didn't want to drown at birth."

Torin frowned. This was not going quite as expected, but they had to keep pushing. "I don't believe that the Lord and Lady will think very highly of a nobleman who consorts with wizards to defraud people of money through the veneer of religion."

Malik pursed his lips. "Albin and Meerka have always been very open about religion and emphasized the freedom of anyone to worship as they see fit. We've done *nothing* wrong."

"No, actually," Torin said, "the *Lord* and *Lady* have great respect for the *actual* gods and the people who choose to worship them. They emphasize the freedom to worship whatever *actual* religion people practice."

"So we don't think they're going to look too kindly on this."

"Neither are the priests of Temisa, Ghandurha, Wiate, Mitre, Xinf, and Vides, who no doubt view you as siphoning off their legitimate acolytes."

His eyes wild, spittle flying from his mouth, sweat continuing to ooze from his pores, Malik cried, "Enough! All right, I admit, Lord Ythran and I have had these meetings of which you speak, and we are involved in this church, I admit all of that freely and without reservation! And the reason why I do that, the reason why I am willing to sacrifice the millions of gold coins and my good name and that of my family is for this reason, and this reason only: I did *not* kill my daughter."

"Really?" Danthres didn't sound convinced, despite his many repetitions of the word *reason*.

"Yes, Lieutenant, really. I wasn't even home when my daughter was killed, a fact that can be confirmed by half the nobility in this castle, up to and including Lady Meerka. I was at a dinner party here in the castle for Madam Lyssa, whose birthday was that day. I didn't leave this castle until well past midnight."

Torin looked up at Danthres, who was crestfallen. He quickly said, "We will, of course, have to verify that."

Malik threw up his hands. "Go *right* ahead! Gods below, it is disgustingly *hot* in here!"

Rising rapidly to his feet, Torin grabbed the stunned Danthres by the arm and brought her out into the squadroom.

"I don't believe it," she was muttering. "It has to be wrong. We have to check this."

"And we will," Torin said, trying to sound reassuring, but firm. "But we also have to prepare ourselves for the fact that he might not have done it."

"He could've been lying," Danthres said. "After all, he lied most of the time we were in there."

Shaking his head, Torin said, "By the time we got that far, we'd broken him." He chuckled. "Not that he was all that difficult *to* break. But he had nowehere left to go by then, and do you really think he'd use Lady Meerka as an alibi if he thought she would be anything other than completely supportive of it?"

Letting out a very familiar growl, Danthres said, "No, he wouldn't. Dammit!"

Unable to stand it anymore, Torin asked the question that had been nagging at him all day. "Why are you so committed to this theory anyhow? We didn't even think of Sir Malik as a suspect until Biroa mentioned it."

"Yes, but it all fit so perfectly!"

"No more or less than the lover did."

Osric's voice came bellowing forth from his office door. "What fit so perfectly?"

Torin and Danthres exchanged glances. Osric was not going to be happy about this. However, keeping it from him would do no good, so they provided a précis of their conversation with Sir Malik.

That naturally led to one of Osric's standard scowls. "You mean to tell me you brought him in there without even *checking* to see if he had an alibi first? That's the sort of idiotic mistake I'd expect from Grovis, not the pair of you!"

"We did expose the false-church scam he's been running with Lord Ythran," Torin said weakly.

"Honestly, we can arrest him solely on that charge," Danthres added. "And do the same for Lord Ythran."

That did not seem to mollify Osric in the least. "You do realize that we have no actual authority to arrest Lord Ythran."

Danthres frowned. "I was under the impression that we had the authority to arrest anyone within the Lord and Lady's demesne."

"Strictly speaking, he isn't within it," Osric said with a heavy sigh.

"We've been to his mansion," Danthres said, referring to their first visit to the wizard during the Brightblade case when it looked as if Chalmraik the Foul might have somehow resurrected himself, "and it was right there on Maple Path in Unicorn."

Osric shook his head. "On Maple Path, yes, but not in Unicorn. His mansion is built on soil belonging to the brotherhood."

Before Danthres could object, Torin quietly said, "He's considered a diplomat?"

"More of an emissary, but yes." Again, Osric sighed. "There's also the matter of whether or not they broke any of the Lord and Lady's laws, considering that this church is in Iaron."

"True, but Sir Malik did admit to the crime," Torin pointed out.

"If it actually *was* a crime." Osric came across as being insistent and angry at the same time. It wasn't a pleasant combination.

Abruptly, the the captain turned and went back into his office, no doubt to seek out his dagger that he might sharpen it.

"Come on," Torin said, "we have a certain amount of work to do. We have to verify Malik's alibi—and we need to talk to Boneen."

"Lord and Lady, why do we have to speak with *him*?" Danthres asked with a sour expression.

"Because we can't very well report the activities of Lord Ythran to the local representative of the brotherhood when that representative is Ythran himself. Boneen is the closest we have to a substitute."

Danthres snarled again. "Joy."

# SEVENTEEN

From the time he was a small boy, he had wanted to be a sailor just like his grandfather. Grandad spent his entire life sailing on the Garamin Sea, bringing goods back and forth between Cliff's End and the elven lands to the south. This was all before and during the elven wars, so he often risked his life facing off against boats that represented either the humans or the elves, who didn't like the idea of trading with the other species.

Of course, most of them were simply trying to pick a fight, and Grandad's usual way of dealing with them was to offer them some of those very goods. Humans may not have liked the idea of their kind trading with elves, but they were more than happy to take a bribe of linen or boots from the south.

That was why Hawk had come down on the side of *not* investigating the graft in Mermaid Precinct. From a very young age, Hawk had learned the value of bribery in getting things done without violence.

Hawk himself hadn't been sailing in years. Grandad died, and Dad said that he got seasick whenever he stepped on a boat, so he never took Hawk with him the way Grandad did. He missed it, but he had to take care of Dad in his old age, so he kept working for the Castle Guard.

Dad wouldn't live forever, though. Hawk's plan was to quit the Guard as soon as Dad died, or when his twenty-five years were up, thus vesting his pension, whichever came first. Then he'd buy a boat and become a shipping captain like Grandad. It was too risky a profession right now when he had his father to support, but his pension would take care of Dad down the line.

Dad would probably complain about it, but Hawk was used to that.

He and Dru arrived at Felspan's Fine Fish. The smell was over-powering, and Hawk was sure the piscine odor would take days to get out of his armor and dreadlocks. That would probably annoy the shit out of Iaian, which to Hawk's mind made it worthwhile all by itself.

"Haven't been back here in ages," Hawk said.

Dru looked over at him. "This one of the places you used to go with your grandfather?"

Hawk nodded. "After a nice long day at sea, we'd be gettin' our dinner here. 'Course, back then, Felspan was still alive, and it was just some crap-ass old shack that was always fallin' apart."

Looking over the solid wooden structure, Dru smirked. "Not really a problem anymore."

"Yeah, Felspan's son-in-law came in and fixed up the joint. I ain't been here since he took over, though."

Two guards from Mermaid Precinct were standing near the entry-way. Hawk also was surprised to see customers going in and out.

Dru asked one of the guards, "What's going on?"

"Whaddaya mean?"

"Why isn't the scene secure?"

The guards looked at each other. "What's to secure? We talked to the owners, they told us what happened, and they need to stay open to do business, don't they? Can't afford to stay closed waiting for *detectives* to haul their asses clear across the city-state, can they?"

The other one said, "Yeah, and kinda went and told 'em to give youze guys the details. We kinda told 'em you was the *important* ones, so don't go givin' us nothin'. We're just kinda dumb guards from Mermaid."

Hawk frowned. "What're you—"

"Forget it," Dru said quickly, putting a hand on Hawk's shoulder. "Let's go."

They went inside, Dru practically pushing Hawk in. The fish smell went from overwhelming to overpowering.

"What's wrong with you?" Hawk asked.

"Those two're pissed about Iaian and the fish snooping around down here. So they're giving us attitude, fine. Let it go, let's do our jobs."

With a sigh, Hawk said, "Yeah, okay." This was just what he needed, two surly guards messing up the scene.

Inside, you'd never know the place had been robbed. Nothing seemed out of place. There were piles of fish on tables, merchants in white aprons running back and forth to put fish into sacks, and customers bellowing requests.

Hawk grabbed one of the people in aprons. He was a blond-haired boy. "We're looking for the owner."

"You guys want some fish? We got some trout in fresh from—"

Dru interrupted. "We're lieutenants in the Castle Guard. We need to talk to the owner about the robbery this morning."

"I don't know nothin' about that. Happened before my shift started."

"Fine," Hawk said. "Where's the owner at?"

The boy looked around, then pointed at a large man with no hair and a flat nose. "That's him." With that, the boy ran off to try to find a customer to serve.

Walking over to Flat Nose, Hawk saw that he was just collecting some coins from a dwarf couple. The pair took their sack and moved slowly out of the store, chatting with each other in Dilene, the dwarven tongue. Hawk only was able to pick up a few words—they were speaking in a dialect he didn't recognize—but they seemed to be trying to decide how to prepare the fish they bought for dinner.

Flat Nose regarded Dru and Hawk disdainfully. "You two the detectives?"

Hawk nodded. "I'm Lieutenant Hawk, and this is my partn—"

"I don't give a shit what your names are, I give a shit what took you so long."

"Excuse me?"

"Guards said you'd be here in a quarter-hour."

Dru shot a look at Hawk, who just shrugged, then said, "Sir, we work in the castle. We had to walk here from there, and that takes a bit longer than a quarter-hour."

"Thought you shitbrains had a wizard on staff. Whyn't he teleport you?"

"He ain't the most reliable," Hawk said. "Look, we need to be askin' you 'bout the robbery this mornin'."

"What for? I already told everything to the guards."

Dru now had his head in his hands, muttering something.

Hawk said, "Well, that's fine, but we're needin' to be hearin' it, too."

"They said *they'd* tell you. For Wiate's sake, what kinda outfit you shitbrains runnin'?"

"Sir, we—"

"I got a business to run. The two guards were the ones who I talked to."

"Can you be tellin' us those guards' names? So we know who to be askin' for."

"How the hell should I know what their damned names are? They're guards. Don't you shitbrains all know each other?"

Hawk was debating the efficacy of explaining to this gentleman the exact size and sprawl of the Castle Guard's enrollment, and then decided that life was too short. "Thank you for your time, sir."

"You'd better find out who robbed me!" Flat Nose called out as they turned to leave.

Outside, salt water mixed back in with the fish smell. Of the two guards, there was no sign.

"Shit," Dru said.

"So let me see if I'm havin' this right," Hawk said. "We got no idea what got stolen. We got no idea when it happened. We basically got nothin'."

"And," Dru added, "the people who do know have all made it clear they won't tell us. And, as an added bonus, the owner's gonna blame you and me before he blames the two shitbrains who just wandered off."

"And all because'a Grovis and Iaian's damn stupid investigation?"

"Looks like, yeah."

Hawk sighed. Dru did likewise.

"Hell with this," Dru said, "let's get back to the castle and just tell Osric what happened. Maybe he can convince the Lord and Lady that this is screwing us up the ass."

"Yeah." Hawk shook his head. "I hate coming to the docks."

# EIGHTEEN

TORIN AND DANTHRES HAD ARRESTED SIR MALIK ON THE CHARGE OF FRAUD.
The magistrate saw him immediately — such, Danthres was reluctantly reminded by Torin, was the benefit of having the prefix "sir" — and released him on his own recognizance, on the theory that he had roots in Cliff's End, including a large family and a daughter to bury. Because he was so unlikely to depart, there was no need to incarcerate him in the hole until the magistrate could hear his case. That duration would be short in any event, as Malik's case leapfrogged the magistrate's calendar so that it would be heard in only two days' time.

They had a guard escort Sir Malik back to his mansion, then returned to the squadroom in time for Boneen to inform them that they could meet with Lord Ythran at his mansion at sunup tomorrow to discuss the situation.

Danthres frowned. "What does that *mean*, exactly?"

Sounding even more exasperated than usual, Boneen said, "It means you will sit down with the local representative of the brotherhood and discuss the situation with him."

Before Danthres could say anything, Torin spoke with more patience than Danthres could muster — well, ever, really. "Boneen, the situation directly involves the rep—"

"I *know* what it involves," Boneen snapped. "Look, just be there at sunup, all right? Now if you'll excuse me, I have to go down to the docks to do a peel-back on a fish store — assuming that Dru and Hawk can convince the owner to empty the place. Somehow, I doubt it, yet here I go to the docks for no good reason."

With that, Boneen waddled out of the squadroom.

By this point, the detectives' shift was over, so Torin went home with Danthres, on the theory that his father wasn't likely to show up at her place. They had a somewhat awkward night together — Danthres wasn't entirely in the mood for sex, and Torin's usual sensitivity seemed to be replaced by clumsiness — and then Torin tossed and turned, waking up from a nightmare more than once.

Danthres had comforted him as best she could, which wasn't all that well, truth be told. They both woke up aggravated.

Since the appointment was for sunup, they went straight to Maple Path, where they knocked on an ornate door.

"So what do you think," Danthres asked, "will the door be answered by a polite butler like Vaspar or an obsequeous shitbrain like Frye?"

"As I recall from last time, it was a sprite."

"Right." Danthres had forgotten that, mostly by virtue of wanting to put the whole experience out of her mind. She hated magick. "Well, let's see what — "

The door simply opened on its own, with a rather disconcerting creak.

Torin looked at Danthres. Danthres looked at Torin.

They both shrugged and entered. A ball of light hung in the middle of the well-appointed foyer, and it started to move up the circular staircase.

Danthres followed it, Torin right behind. It took them down a lavish hallway to the same office where they'd met with Ythran previously. As before, it had a sofa, various art objects, a scrying pool, and a plush reclining chair. A bas-relief of the brotherhood's seal — a male face with leaves and branches growing out of several orifices — decorated one wall, with a picture window on the opposite wall providing a view of the Garamin.

However, the person sitting in the plush chair, smoking a pipe with an atrocious blend of tobaccos, was *not* Lord Ythran. Like far too many mages, he had white hair and a beard, but he kept his cut much shorter than was fashionable. His robes were a surprisingly bright red, and his fingers were short and stubby as they held the pipe.

"Ah, greetings. You must be the lieutenants from the Castle Guard. My name is Gunderson."

Danthres moved toward the couch.

"Please, *don't* have a seat, as I have a great deal of work to do today. Suffice it to say that any investigation you might be making into the Church of the Earth-Pig Born is over. The brotherhood will take over from here, and you need not concern yourselves. Also, moving forward, if there are any matters that require the attention of the brotherhood, you may direct them to me. I will be providing that function and living in this mansion. You may leave now."

Torin and Danthres exchanged another glance. Torin spoke: "Sir, we—"

"I *said* you may leave now. I'm very busy, I've been casting quite a bit already this morning, and I don't have the interest in wasting any energy on teleporting you away, so kindly depart on your own."

Teleport Spells always made Danthres nauseous—Ythran had used it on her more than once—and she was more than happy to leave on foot rather than go through that, again.

Once they got back onto Maple Path, Torin said, "We need to get to Sir Malik's, *now*."

Danthres frowned. "Why?"

"Because it's obvious that the brotherhood is removing all traces of the little Earth-Pig scam, and we need to find Sir Malik before the brotherhood sends him somewhere very far away."

Nodding, Danthres immediately started heading back toward Meerka Way.

When Vaspar answered the door this time, he looked, if possible, even more harried. He also still hadn't shaved, and his cufflinks weren't in.

Which meant, to Danthres's mind, that something was horribly wrong.

"I'm sorry, Lieutenants, but things are a bit—well, hectic, here. Perhaps if you could come back this afternoon—"

A voice came from behind the butler. "Vaspar? Who's at the door?"

Vaspar called back: "The lieutenants from the Castle Guard, Sir Winthrop!"

Torin mouthed *Sir Winthrop?* at Danthres, who just shrugged. There was no such person at the house, nor had one even been mentioned at any point.

Then Danthres did recall one of the servants they interviewed, after the other three children came back, had mentioned a Sir Winthrop.

"Why is Sir Malik's brother-in-law here?" Danthres asked.

That prompted a look of confusion from Torin, reminding Danthres again that he was truly off his game.

Before Vaspar could say anything, a very tall, stick-thin man with curly black hair and a very weak beard stepped forward. "I have arrived from Iaron to take charge of the household. We intend to have all the carriages packed by week's end. I'm glad you're both here, actually, as we require that Arra's body be released to us."

"Excuse me?" Danthres asked.

"Arra's body must be returned to us so that it can be buried alongside her grandparents in the family crypt."

"Before we do that," Torin said, "we must speak with Sir Malik and Madam Hassa."

Winthrop wrinkled his nose. "Not really possible, I'm afraid. They're not here."

"When will they return?" Torin asked, though Danthres and he both knew the answer.

"Their stay away from Cliff's End is open-ended and indefinite. Please, see to the return of Arra's body posthaste? Thank you." He turned to the butler. "Come, Vaspar, there is much to do."

"Of course, Sir Winthrop." Vaspar gave the lieutenants a brief, helpless expression, then dashed after the nobleman.

Shaking his head, Torin muttered, "That happened faster than expected. And if he got here from Iaron this morning, he had to have been teleported by a mage. They really are moving to cover this up as quickly as possible."

"I hate magick." Danthres felt the urge to spit in disgust. "So now what?"

Torin shook his head. "Nothing. I was hoping to speak to Madam Hassa, since we have yet to give her a proper interview."

"We can't let them leave at week's end if we haven't solved the case."

Nodding, Torin said, "Let's deal with that when we get that far. If we're lucky, we'll put it down before then."

"Lord and Lady, where does *that* optimism come from?" Danthres was incredulous.

With a grin, Torin said, "Perhaps I'm returning to my old self."

"Good, because I don't think I can take another night like that."

His face fell. "I am sorry, Danthres. The nightmares were—"

"It's all right." She put a hand on his shoulder. "So, what next?"

"We should fulfill the request to return the body. Boneen hardly needs it, and perhaps in the act of delivering it, we might be able to ask some more questions."

Danthres nodded. "Worth a try."

It was midday by the time Boneen returned to the castle, Dru and Hawk in tow.

Jonas asked, "Any luck with the peel-back?"

Dru shook his head. "The owner wouldn't empty the damned shop. And our good friends at Mermaid wouldn't help clear the place. In fact, they told the owner that there was no need to empty the place."

Hawk was frowning. "We gotta be stoppin' this damn investigation into Mermaid, or we ain't gonna get shit done."

"In any event, the peel-back proved impossible to cast, and my valuable time was wasted," Boneen muttered. "Just a perfectly wretched day, so far." He glowered at Torin and Danthres. "Why do I suspect you two are going to make it worse?"

"Actually, no, Boneen," said Torin. "Our request is but a simple one: we wish to release one of the bodies downstairs. Arra Cynnis."

"Good, I can use the space. Come with me."

Danthres started walking behind Boneen and in front of Torin toward the west-wall doorway, which led in turn to the narrow, winding staircase that would take them to Boneen's lair in the basement. Danthres was sure to take several deep breaths before proceeding downstairs, so she would inhale as little as possible while in Boneen's sanctum.

At the bottom of the staircase was just a doorway with no other access in any direction beyond the small landing. The door itself was masssive, decorated by a knocker in the shape of a gryphon at its center.

If someone other than Boneen approached, the gryphon would animate and speak in a squeaky voice that managed the impressive feat of making Ep sound pleasant. Danthres was eminently grateful that the M.E.'s presence saved her from that.

As he reached the final stair, Boneen gestured, and the door creaked open in a manner depressingly similar to that of the front door to Ythran's — or, rather, Gunderson's — mansion.

Lit by what Danthres assumed to be a magickal source, the windowless room was filled with tables, many of which held bodies covered in the blue tinge of a Preservation Spell. Other tables held parchments, various bits and pieces, and jars containing either liquids, herbs, or both.

Boneen walked over to the body of Arra Cynnis. The right side of her face, Danthres noted, remained quite lovely thanks to the spell; the left side was marred by the broken skin, blood, sunken skull, and pulped brain matter that resulted from her fatal injury. The M.E. muttered an incantation, gestured twice, and then lightly touched the body's forehead.

The blue tinge faded.

And then her features started to melt. Danthres's stomach rumbled as she watched the entire body liquefy before her eyes. The stench, already awful, got worse to the point where Danthres's sensitive nose couldn't handle it and she ran out of the room.

Torin was right behind her, and Boneen waddled up about a minute after that.

"Well," Boneen said, "*that* was unexpected."

"What could cause that?" Danthres asked, her nose still wrinkled from the memory of the stench.

"Any number of things, all of which involve the person being killed by having their life force magickally drained. Could've been a vampire, but I didn't see any markings to indicate being bitten."

"What kind of spell can do that?" Danthres asked.

Boneen pointed at the staircase he had just come up. "What, that? There is no spell that can kill in that manner, Tresyllione. Only a creature *of* magick can do *that*."

Danthres put her hands on her hips. "You told us it was a store-bought spell that hid the killer's identity."

"No, in fact, I said no such thing. What I *did* say—and I *do* wish you'd actually *listen* when I spoke to you, it would save us *all* some trouble—"

Somehow, Danthres managed not to punch the mage in the nose.

"—what I *did* say was that it wasn't a magick-user and that it was *probably* a store-bought spell. Plenty of magickal creatures can also hide their features from a peel-back in that manner—but they are *not* magick-users."

"You mean to tell me that our killer might actually be—"

Torin finally spoke. "I know exactly who and what our killer is."

Staring at her partner, Danthres said, "What?"

"I said I know who and what our killer is. If I hadn't been so addled by my idiot father . . ." He shook his head. "Come on. We need to interview Biroa again."

# NINETEEN

BIROA DIDN'T PARTICULARLY LIKE THIS ROOM. THE ONE LANTERN WAS POORLY lit, and made it feel like it was already night-time, even though she knew daylight still shone in the Cliff's End sky.

Not that the Cliff's End sky was anything to rave about. The humidity that came of being this close to the Garamin usually meant that the sky was hazy and unpleasant to look at.

With poor Arra's death, Biroa was safe in the assumption that she wouldn't have any ties to Cliff's End anymore anyhow. After all, a corpse didn't need a dress girl, and besides, the family was now all up and moving to Iaron with that drip, Sir Winthrop.

The lieutenant with the thick red beard walked in, after she'd been sitting there for who-knew-how-long. "Where's your partner?" Biroa asked.

"Busy," the lieutenant said. Then she remembered his name was ban Wyvald. She probably would have forgotten it, but Myverin names were so wonderfully poetic . . .

"Pity." Biroa smiled. "She was fascinating. Such an interesting mix of human and elven. I could stare at her face all day."

"No doubt." Lieutenant ban Wyvald was holding a leather-bound book in his hand.

"May I ask what this is about?"

"I regret to say that it's for the same reason we spoke previously—Arra Cynnis's murder."

Biroa frowned. "I don't understand. Didn't Sir Malik . . . ?" She let the question trail off.

"Didn't Sir Malik what?" ban Wyvald asked as he sat in the chair opposite the uncomfortable stool she was sitting on.

Shaking her head, Biroa said, "Sir Malik and that awful wife of his were taken away last night. It was all very quiet and mysterious, but I assumed it was to save them the public humiliation of a murder charge. I always knew he had evil in his heart."

With a small smile, ban Wyvald said, "I'm afraid you were misinformed. Sir Malik and Madam Hassa's departure had nothing to do with Arra's death."

Again, Biroa said, "I don't understand."

"Sir Malik may have had greed in his heart, but not evil. He was consorting with a wizard to create a false church in Iaron. Very scandalous, but nothing to do with Arra's murder."

"Oh." That genuinely surprised Biroa. *Why else take Malik and Hassa away like that, if not because he killed his daughter? Surely a mere fraud wouldn't –*

Then she thought back over ban Wyvald's words. Biroa had steered clear of the Brotherhood of Wizards since its formation, so she sometimes forgot how unforgiving they could be—and how long was their reach.

"So who *did* kill poor Arra?"

"An excellent question. We've been looking for her lover."

Chuckling, Biroa said, "Are you back on that again? I told you, she never said—"

"She never said anything to you about having an affair with a young man. That is true. However, we do know that she was having an affair with *someone*."

Biroa frowned. "What do you mean?"

The lieutenant patted the top of the leather-bound book. "This is Arra's diary. She wrote it in an obscure tongue that few know this far east. Conveniently, as the man who was being groomed to one day become High Magistrate of Myverin, I learned to read Kaelvan by the time I was seven, so I'm one of those few."

"Ah."

Another smile. "An interesting language, Kaelvan. Every noun has a suffix to indicate one of three genders—one for male nouns, one for female nouns, and one for no gender at all. Obviously *man* is male and *woman* is female. Most inanimate objects are neutrally gendered, but some are made male or female. For example, *sword* is male, as is *armor*."

Biroa favored ban Wyvald with a smile of her own. "That would probably annoy your partner."

"Yes, well, the Kael are a rather traditional people when it comes to such roles. The dress you wear would be female, while the tights Sir Malik wears would be male. Other things, such as furniture, have no gender."

"While this is fascinating . . ."

Holding up a hand, ban Wyvald said, "I'm getting to the point, trust me. You see, in her diary, Arra always referred to her lover with the gender-neutral suffix. Never the male *or* the female. I didn't really notice it at first, frustrated as I was with the fact that she didn't provide a proper name, but she also kept the lover's sex a secret as well."

"Really?"

"Yes. And that's curious, because the only reason to do that at all is if the lover was something unexpected. As bad as an affianced scion of the Cynnis family having an affair with a young man would be, that's as nothing compared to the scandal if she was having an affair with a young *woman*. Especially given that her affianced is a worshipper of Ghandurha, who frowns rather on same-sex couplings."

Biroa found she had nothing to say to that.

Getting up from his chair, ban Wyvald started to pace around the room. "What's also curious is that Arra didn't die from being bludgeoned to death."

"How could she not have?" Biroa asked in a tone of incredulity.

"When Sir Winthrop asked for Arra's body to be returned to him for burial, our magickal examiner removed the Preservation Spell from her body, and it immediately liquefied. That generally happens a day or so after a magickal creature drains the life from a body—in this case, the spell delayed it. But if her head was bashed in, there wouldn't be any life to drain, so the injury had to be *after* her death. A coverup to make it look like someone angry with her struck her on the side of the head—like, say, a father outraged that his daughter learned of his secret fraud."

Biroa simply sat quietly.

"The funny thing is, you simply could have drained her and left Cliff's End. Isn't that what a succubus usually does?"

With a nasty grin, Biroa dropped the illusion of the pretty young dress-girl she'd been maintaining since her arrival in this abominable city-state, and let her true skeletal form be revealed for only the second time in recent memory, the first had been when she at last consummated her relationship with dear, sweet Arra.

A second later, tendrils of energy surrounded her arm and leg bones, and she found herself unable to move.

That prompted a wide smile beneath ban Wyvald's thick red beard. "And that proves it. I'm afraid this castle is very well warded. Any succubus who shows her true form remains imprisoned as you are right now."

Biroa snarled and spit and struggled against the magickal restraints, even though she knew it was pointless. "*How* did you know?"

"Danthres. She was *far* too amenable to your suggestions, and far too trusting of your word. She's been my partner for a decade. I'm closer to her than any person has ever been, and she doesn't trust *me* that overwhelmingly. And a succubus who preyed on women rather than men fit the evidence."

"I do not *prey*, you stupid human. I *love*! Arra was never happier than when she was with me!"

"And then you killed her."

"Of *course*!" How could this imbecile think otherwise? "That is always the ultimate end of true love!"

The door to the room opened, and the lovely half-elf came in, along with some manner of wizard.

"It seems you were wrong, ban Wyvald," the mage said. "That is not a succubus."

Turning to stare at the short, wizened human, ban Wyvald said, "What do you mean?"

The mage pointed at the magickal restraints. "See the green tinge? That means she's a hone-onna."

"Yet she acts like a succubus," ban Wyvald said.

"No, succubi sleep only with men. Hone-onna will seduce anything."

The half-elf was glowering at her. "I can't believe I let you play me like that."

"It wasn't play, Danthres," Biroa said, focusing all her emotions on the half-elf. "I must love another now that my love is gone from me."

"No, thanks."

The mage stepped forward. "I'll take care of this creature."

Biroa struggled against her shackles, but she could not move.

Long was the brotherhood's reach, and terrible their retribution. Biroa feared she would now learn just *how* long and terrible . . .

# TWENTY

Amilar Grovis stared at Iaian while Captain Osric spoke to the shift.

It was a rare situation when all six detectives were in the squadroom at the end of the day — which was fitting, since Torin and Danthres had been missing from roll call, as they had to meet with someone from the Brotherhood of Wizards.

"Grovis, Iaian," Osric was saying, "you're done. We're never going to get anymore than we've gotten from Mermaid unless someone does something stupid — and they're not gonna do anything stupid as long as they know you're poking around. Besides, the longer we keep this up, the more what happened with Dru and Hawk today will keep happening, and crime in Mermaid will skyrocket. I've already spoken with Lord Albin, and he agrees that it's best to let it lie."

"Pity." Grovis was still staring at Iaian.

"Well, I for one am grateful." Hawk put his hands on his dreadlocks-covered head. "Now maybe we can be doin' some proper crime-solvin' instead of bein' treated like shit."

"Here, here," Dru said.

"And with the Cynnis murder put down, Tresyllione and ban Wyvald are back in rotation as well. But Grovis, you and Iaian get the first call."

"What about us?" Dru asked.

"You still have a robbery to solve. Try to bring Boneen back tomorrow before the boats come in."

Hawk lowered his hands. "You're expectin' us to be bringin' Boneen down to the docks at sunup? You kiddin', right?"

"Do I look like I'm kidding, Hawk?" Osric asked.

Grovis didn't see his expression, because he was still staring daggers at his partner. However, Hawk's silence spoke volumes.

"All right, shift's over. Go home."

Torin, who'd been oddly silent, left quickly. Danthres followed soon after. Hawk and Dru were talking about heading to the Old Ball and Chain for drinks as they departed. Jonas had already gone home, and Osric retreated into his office.

That left Grovis and Iaian alone in the squadroom.

"Okay, boy, you been staring at me since we got here. What's the damn problem?"

Grovis couldn't help himself. He laughed.

"Something funny, boy?"

"Oh yes, Iaian, quite a bit in fact. Where to begin, I wonder?" Grovis shook his head. "Perhaps I should start with the revelation that my cousin is a fornicator? Or that his prospective father-in-law was defrauding hundreds of devout citizens of Iaron for profit? Or that his fiancée was in love with another woman?"

"She was a succubus, boy, she couldn't help herself."

"It was a hone-onna, apparently, not a succubus, but that hardly matters. She described that—that *thing* as her 'love.' It's disgusting."

"So that's what's funny?"

"I believe that it's the fact that I'm partnered with a criminal."

Iaian leaned forward and spoke in a very quiet tone. "Watch what you accuse people of, boy."

However, for the first time since being partnered with the older detective, Grovis was not intimidated by him. "I'm not accusing you of anything. You see, in order to do that, I must have proof, which I do not have. If I had proof, I would indeed accuse you, and then I would arrest you. But I am lacking in evidence." He stood up so he could look down on Iaian physically, since he was already doing so metaphorically. "However, you can rest assured that I know what you did."

Now Iaian leaned back in his chair and folded his arms, looking up at Grovis with his sad, old eyes. "What do you know that I did, exactly?"

"I know you paid Jahno to leave Cliff's End before he could testify as to the wrongdoing of the soldiers of Mermaid Precinct."

"And how do you know that?"

Grovis exploded. "Because I am nowhere near the fool you all imagine me to be! I spoke with him at the Dancing Seagull, Iaian, he was *ready* to speak. Then, after I leave him alone with you, he suddenly decides to take a lengthy sea journey? Tell me, how much was the integrity of the Castle Guard worth? Two gold? Three? Or was it just worth a copper piece, perhaps? Life is cheap in Mermaid, or so you keep telling me."

Unfolding his arms and spreading them, Iaian asked, "What do you want from me, Grovis? It's a shitty world. We try to make it a little better—for other people, sometimes, and sometimes for ourselves. If you don't like it, go back to Daddy's bank."

At that, Grovis snorted. "Father specifically forbade me from working in the bank. He said I had to serve in the Castle Guard in order to make a man of me. It seems that being a man means being cynical and world-weary and despicable and contrary to all the teachings of Ghandurha that I've taken to heart since I was but a boy." Turning to walk out of the squadroom, Grovis curled his lips into a sneer. "Congratulations, Iaian. You may well make a man of me, yet."

Grovis left the squadroom, realizing he had nowhere to go. The Chain was not a wise place for him to go, and the thought of facing his family nauseated him.

So he simply walked down Meerka Way, and headed into the heart of Cliff's End. Perhaps he could find someone breaking the law . . .

# TWENTY-ONE

THIS TIME WHEN HE CAME HOME, TORIN'S DOOR WAS LOCKED. HE HAD BEEN holding his breath from the moment he removed the key until it released the tumbler that allowed him to open the door.

With luck, Wyvald had gone back to Myverin empty-handed. It provided the first relief Torin had felt in quite some time. His entire walk here from the castle was emotionally confusing and annoying. He had the usual high he always had when he and Danthres put down a case. It gave him satisfaction in a way nothing else in his life ever did.

But the return of his father had put him completely out of sorts. He couldn't even properly enjoy closing the case.

As soon as he opened the door, a furry orange fist collided with his face.

Stumbling backward, Torin reached for the hilt of his sword. The right side of his face burned, and the salty taste of blood filled his mouth from a loosened tooth.

With a hiss, the hobgoblin—which had apparently been waiting in his apartment for him—leapt at him, long, orange-furred arms raised.

Realizing he wouldn't be able to draw his sword in time, he elbowed the hobgoblin in the stomach.

It collapsed to the ground, in considerably more pain than Torin would've expected from a simple elbow to the gut.

As the hobgoblin wheezed, Torin put his sword to his neck. In Heb, the creature's tongue, he asked, "Who sent you?"

Shrieking, the hobgoblin leapt to his feet and starting attacking again, just a mass of arms and legs. Torin held his hands to his face, his sword pointing upward as he did so.

The hobgoblin cut himself on the sword edge, watery green ichor spilling all over Torin's floor from the fresh wound in his arm.

That told Torin a great deal right there.

He kicked the hobgoblin in the ribs then again put the swordpoint to his neck. Again he asked, "Who sent you?"

"I did." Wyvald stepped out of the bedroom.

The hobgoblin took advantage of Torin's brief distraction to run out the front door. After mulling it over for a second, Torin decided to let him go.

Wyvald was less accepting. "Come back here!" he bellowed, albeit in Common.

Torin simply stared at his father.

"Aren't you going to go after him?" Wyvald asked incredulously.

"An elderly, bleeding hobgoblin stumbling around Dragon Precinct? He'll be picked up in no time." He made a mental note to check with Sergeant Grint on his way into the castle for his shift tomorrow.

Frowning, Wyvald said, "Elderly?"

"Yes. That was why I took him down so easily—a young hobgoblin wouldn't be so easily stopped. He also wouldn't have had such watery blood. For that matter, he wouldn't have needed to take money from a pathetic old man trying to find some way to kidnap his son."

Wyvald said nothing, merely hanging his head in what Torin sincerely hoped was shame.

"Hobgoblins are creatures of opportunity," Torin continued, walking over to the water basin and grabbing the cloth that hung from a peg in its base. "They take what they want. As a general rule, they're poor choices to hire, because the only ones desperate enough to accept a job for their services are the ones too far gone for their services to be worth paying for." He ran the cloth slowly up the blade from the hilt to the point, making sure he got all the green blood off. "If you actually *knew* anything of the world outside Myverin's walls, you might have known that, High Magistrate."

Looking back up at Torin, Wyvald said, "I had to do *something*." He let out a long breath through his teeth. "You derisively refer to me by my title, yet it is only a probationary one."

Torin frowned. "How is that possible? You said Grandfather died."

"Yes, and I repeatedly told the Council that you would return to us and take on the title of Chief Artisan, as you were born to do."

Unable to believe what he was hearing, Torin almost lost his grip on his sword. "You told them I was coming *back*?"

"I couldn't believe that you wouldn't!" Wyvald bellowed.

Torin recoiled as if Wyvald's sharpness was physical rather than verbal. He could count on the fingers of one hand the number of times his father had raised his voice. Wyvald's preferred method of communicating displeasure was quiet disappointment.

Wyvald continued. "I truly believed in my heart that you were simply acting out of childish revenge, and that once you were made aware of your responsibilities, and you learned that it was time for you to assume your duties as Chief Artisan, then you would happily return home."

"I can imagine very few circumstances under which I would return home, Father, and none of them would involve happiness." He chuckled and shook his head. "You know, I should be angry — especially since you've *once again* broken into my place of residence, and this time brought hired help to kidnap me, however incompetent that help might be. But I'm not, Father. I remain embarrassed."

"Living in a place like this, you *should* be."

Rolling his eyes, Torin said, "Of *you*, Father! I'm ashamed to even be related to you!" He shook his head. "You never did understand me, did you? Not once."

"I didn't have the same trick of it that your mother did," Wyvald said quietly.

But not quietly enough, as Torin instinctively pointed his sword at his father. "Don't you *dare* speak of her! *She* made time for me, Father! She loved me, she understood me!"

"I tried —"

"When? She was the Council Chef, her hours of work were carefully prescribed, centering around mealtimes. Yet she always managed to carve out time for me *every single day*, no matter what lavish dish some member of the Council decided he or she *had* to have. But you, whose duties were flexible, which were not tied to any particular time, you who could go *months* without having yourself called upon to act as Chief Artisan, you could not bring yourself to make time to spend with me."

"My duties were more complicated than that," Wyvald said weakly.

"No," Torin cried, "*her* duties were more complicated than that, and *she* made it work!"

A long, ugly pause followed Torin's words, which hung in the air. Torin stared at his father, wondering what next ridiculous thing he might do to get Torin to come home.

"When the blood poisoning took her after she cut herself," Wyvald said slowly, "it seems I lost both my wife *and* my son. It simply took me seventeen years to figure it out."

Snidely, Torin said, "Better late than never." He sheathed his sword. "Go back home, Father. Explain things to the Council. Tell them — tell them your son is dead. To one degree or another, it will be the truth. Either way, I will *not* come home with you."

Wyvald stared at his son with his ice-blue eyes. "You are truly happy in this hole of hell, aren't you, Torin?"

"Yes, Father. More happy than I've ever been."

"Amazing." He shook his head. "Very well." He walked toward the door, passing by Torin.

Before he got completely by him, he put a hand on his son's shoulder, looked over at him, and gave him a small smile.

"The beard looks good, son."

And with that, he departed. Torin hoped it was never to again return.

Torin turned to watch him go down the stairs. The seal he carried would guarantee him safe passage back through Iaron, Barlin, and the other northern city-states until he reached the Llanna Mountains, and thence to Myverin.

Turning back, Torin found his nose completely filled with the smell of hobgoblin blood. He wondered if the smell was really as bad as he thought it was, or if it was the memory of the events of the past several minutes that made it more intense.

Either way, it didn't matter. There was simply no way he'd be able to sleep here tonight.

Closing and locking his door, he went downstairs and out onto the crowded thoroughfares of Dragon Precinct. At one point, he swore he saw someone in a brown cloak making his way down Meerka Way, but Torin lost him in the crowds.

Within minutes, he found his way to Danthres's rooms and knocked on her door.

After a few seconds, Danthres — who had already removed her armor and was only wearing a shift — opened the door.

He smiled as he looked at her state of undress. "I could've been anyone."

"No, honestly, it couldn't have been anyone but you. Your father again?"

"My father, finally. He made his last play, but he'll be on his way back to Myverin by sunup. I promise to tell you all about it—tomorrow. For now, may I—"

Danthres stepped aside. "Always."

"Thank you. Without you—"

"Think nothing of it," Danthres said as Torin entered. "This is what we do, Torin—we help each other. I help you when your father makes you mad—in every sense. And you helped me when a succubus made a fool of me."

"It was a hone-onna." Torin corrected her automatically as he came into her sloppy sitting room, with clothes, bits of food, several half-empty cups, and other items strewn about. "Will you never clean this place?"

"My experiences with cleaning services have been poor, as you well know. Besides, I'm comfortable this way. *Happy* this way."

Torin smiled. "As am I, Danthres. As am I."

# ABOUT THE AUTHOR

KEITH R.A. DeCANDIDO IS A WHITE MALE IN HIS LATE FORTIES, approximately 200 pounds. He was last seen in the wilds of the Bronx, New York, though he is often sighted in other locales. Usually he is armed with a laptop computer, which some have classified as a deadly weapon. Through use of this laptop, he has inflicted more than fifty novels, as well as an indeterminate number of short stories, comic books, nonfiction, novellas, and anthologies on an unsuspecting reading public. Many of these are set in the milieus of television shows, movies, games, and comic books, among them Star Trek, Cars, Doctor Who, Supernatural, World of Warcraft, Orphan Black, Alien, Marvel Comics, and many more. We have received information confirming that more stories involving Torin, Danthres, and the city-state of Cliff's End can be found in the novels Dragon Precinct, Goblin Precinct, Gryphon Precinct, and the forthcoming Mermaid Precinct, Phoenix Precinct, and Manticore Precinct, as well as the short-story collection Tales from Dragon Precinct. His other recent crimes against humanity include the urban fantasy novel A Furnace Sealed; the Orphan Black coffee-table book Classified Clone Report; the Alien novel Isolation; the Tales of Asgard trilogy of prose novels featuring Marvel's Thor, Sif, and the Warriors Three; short stories in the anthologies Aliens: Bug Hunt, the two Baker Street Irregulars volumes, The Best of Bad-Ass Faeries, The Best of Defending the Future, Joe Ledger: Unstoppable, Nights of the Living Dead, The X-Files: Trust No One, among others; and writing about pop culture for Tor.com and Patreon. If you see DeCandido, do not approach him, but call for back-up immediately. He is often seen in the company of a suspicious-looking woman who goes by the street name of "Wrenn," as well as several as-yet-unidentified cats. A full dossier can be found at DeCandido.net.

# "When the Magick Goes Away"

*Danthres & Torin's First Case*

# KORT

NO MATTER HOW MANY DECADES HE LIVED AS A WIZARD, AND HE'D LIVED plenty by this point, Tam Kort never grew tired of drinking ale in a tavern.

Of late, his preferred drinking hole of choice was the Stone Kobold, located on Axe Lane in the port town of Cliff's End. One of Kort's magick shops was located in Cliff's End, and his employees had spoken highly of the place. Kort had been coming here for a few years now, ever since the people of the northern city-state of Iaron, where another of his shops was located, learned he was a wizard. That took all the fun out of it. When people knew you were a magick-user, they bowed, they scraped, they sucked up, and they generally stopped treating you like a person. Kort came to a bar so he could listen to stories and enjoy the company of people.

Wizards weren't people. Kort had spent enough time as a member of the Brotherhood of Wizards to understand that to be a fact. Indeed, he'd figured *that* little truism out after spending about an hour with the mage he was apprenticed to, the old bastard.

But, as he hoisted his third — or was it fourth? — ale, Kort didn't think about being a wizard, he just thought about having a good time.

"And then, and *then*," said a dwarf, who was sitting on the stool next to Kort, his legs swinging in the air even as he gesticulated in the energetic telling of his tale, "the stupid bastard starts *playing* the lute! Of course, it sounds like utter shit, and I finally had to grab the thing and smash it against the wall. That's when all the coins came pouring out of it and onto the floor."

A brown-haired human woman on the other side of the dwarf asked, "He thought you were paying him with a lute?"

"T'be fair," a bald, thick-bearded human next to Kort said, "in th'hands'f a great bard, a lute's of tr'mendous value."

Gava, the tall, beautiful human woman behind the bar, laughed and said, "That leaves Sam's lute out, then."

Kort also laughed. "I'll drink to that." Sam was the bard who performed at the Stone Kobold thrice weekly, and Kort endeavored mightily to make sure that his trips to the Kobold were on one of the other four days.

His imbibing in honor of Sam's awful bardistry was enough to finish his current flagon, and he placed it down on the bar and asked Gava for another. She held the flagon under the spigot of the ale barrel, then handed it back saying, "This one's on the house."

Eyes widening, Kort asked, "To what do I owe the privilege?"

"You're just about the only gentleman in here," Gava said with a bright smile. "Certainly the only regular. You always tip well, and you're the only person who's never tried to get me to sleep with them."

Were they not in Kort's current favorite bar, he might have told Gava that wizards were encouraged to tamp down their sexuality in order to focus on the magick. Strong emotions like lust and love played merry hell with spells. Not that all wizards lived up to that notion, as Kort had learned the hard way…

"Actually, lutes can be of even greater value than gold," said a deep-voiced man from the other side of the bar. He had long red hair and he either had become too lazy to shave or was in the midst of growing a beard.

The dwarf spit his ale in surprise. "Are you mad? Nothing's of more value than gold."

"Value is circumstantial," the red-haired man said. "During the war, I spent a winter in the Nemerian Wastes. Gold would, at that point, been of far less use than a lute, as a lute can be used for kindling."

Everyone chuckled at that one.

Another dwarf, who sat at a table near the bar, stared at the red-haired man. "You fought for the king and queen against the Elf Bitch, didja?"

He nodded. "I served under General Osric in the 17th Company for three years until the Elf Queen finally abdicated her throne."

The dwarf grinned. "Hah! I served in the Elmgren Regiment of the dwarven army. You must've fought at Hobgoblin's Run."

"Indeed, I did. Torin ban Wyvald." He held up his flagon.

"Zorbanig," the dwarf replied, doing likewise. "A pleasure."

"Y'know," the bearded man next to Kort said, "Osric's here'n Cliff's End now. He's runnin' th'Castle Guard."

"So I've heard," ban Wyvald said with a smile.

The other dwarf, who'd told the story about the lute, asked, "What happened at Hobgoblin's Run?"

Kort sighed. He hated war stories, but they were becoming increasingly common, as more and more ex-soldiers started pouring into Cliff's End. Some came here due to lack of work, others used Cliff's End the way so many did, as a waystation. The city-state had the busiest port in all of Flingaria.

And *all* of them had stories to tell about the elven wars. It grew tiresome.

Still, Kort gulped down his ale while trying to at least pretend to be interested in the story that ban Wyvald and Zorbanig told about their battle — thought Kort noticed that the former did most of the talking.

"You tell your story well, Torin ban Wyvald," the brunette two stools down from Kort said after he got to the part where the elves retreated. "Perhaps Gava should hire you as the new bard."

Gava shook her head. "Sadly, that's not my choice, and we're still stuck with the old bard."

"Of course," Zorbanig said, "you lot were lucky we showed up, otherwise your sorry asses would've been routed by those pointy-eared bastards."

"That is certainly possible," ban Wyvald said before sipping some more ale.

Zorbanig slammed his flagon down onto the table and stood up. "You callin' me a liar, human?"

"Not at all. As I said, it's possible you're right, and we might have lost the day without your arrival. Since you *did* show up, we shall never know."

Kort was impressed with ban Wyvald's deft but gentle attempt to defuse the situation.

Sadly, the attempt failed, as Zorbanig then stomped toward ban Wyvald angrily, elbowing the bearded human next to Kort as he strode by.

"'Ey, watchit, shorty!" The human took a clumsy swing that cleared Zorbanig's head by two handslengths, then stumbled forward into another table, spilling half a dozen drinks while doing so.

The four burly humans sitting there did not look pleased. One grabbed the human by the head.

Zorbanig yelled, "Fight! Fight!"

Kort had very little memory of what happened after that, beyond a flail of arms, legs, and ale both within and without its containers. For his part, he muttered a Shield Spell that kept him safe from harm.

Within a minute, the melee was over, as most of the Kobold's patrons were lying on the floor, breathing heavily, crying in pain, or moaning softly. The exceptions were ban Wyvald—who appeared to have comported himself well in the fight, standing over two of the large humans from the table next to Zorbanig's—and Kort himself.

Turning to the bar, Kort said, "Gava, you'd better—"

But of Gava, he saw no sign.

Ban Wyvald was peering over the bar. "I'm afraid she is unlikely to answer, sir."

Looking over, Kort saw that Gava lay prone on the floor, blood trickling from her mouth and from the wound formed by the ornate dagger lodged in her chest.

# QUANE

Lieutenant Quane struggled to throw the cloak on over his neck and in very short order found himself tangled in it. The brown cloak with the gryphon crest emblazoned on the back that symbolized his new rank as a lieutenant in the Cliff's End Castle Guard now covered his entire face. That, at least, spared him the indignity of watching his fellow detectives laugh hysterically, not to mention whatever dire look his new partner was giving him.

He could *hear* the laughter, though. Plus Nael saying, "Bravo! Well done, Quane, well done!"

Once he finally managed to disentangle himself from the cloak and place it properly, he looked over at his partner.

"Are you *quite* finished?" she asked. She stared dolefully at him. Her bizarrely constructed face was the result of a human-elven pairing, but she was much uglier than the half-elf prostitute in that place on Sandy Brook Way that he visited last year.

"Yes, Lieutenant Treslin," he said quickly.

She winced. "It's 'Tresyllione,' and will you just call me 'Danthres' and have done with it, you stupid shitbrain?"

"Sorry, Lieutenant—I mean, Danthres!" He followed her toward the exit from the squadroom, leaving the snickering of the other four detectives, as well as Sergeant Newcastle.

Quane had to follow Danthres as he still had yet to figure his way around the castle. In fact, when she made a left out of the squadroom, Quane cried, "Left?" a bit louder than he should have.

Danthres stopped, closed her eyes, and turned on her partner. "Oh, Lord and Lady, Quane, will you just *follow* me? You don't need to express surprise at everything that doesn't go as you planned. You're a detective now, and I guarantee that *nothing* will go as planned and you'll just exhaust yourself from all that shock. Don't worry, you'll learn your way around the castle eventually."

"I—I know, Lieut—I mean, Danthres." Quane shook his head. "I'm sorry, but I was assigned to Unicorn and Mermaid, and I never really got up here to the castle much, except for that ceremony, and that other—"

"Quane!"

Recoiling as if slapped, Quane stammered, "I'm—I'm sorry, I just—"

She held up a hand. "Stop talking. Now."

Quane stopped talking.

With that, Danthres turned and continued out of the castle.

They walked in silence out of the portcullis and onto Meerka Way. Exiting the castle, which was deemed Gryphon Precinct, they traversed into the city proper. Quane had always found Lord Albin and Lady Meerka's method of dividing up the city-state to be genius.

He tried to remember the borders of each precinct. From the castle to—was it Pine Path? Anyhow, that was Unicorn Precinct, where the wealthiest citizens of Cliff's End resided. That was where Quane had served as a rookie in the Guard, taking complaints from annoying rich people. Between there and Axe Way was the middle-class district of Dragon Precinct, with the slums between Axe Way and the docks serving as Goblin Precinct. The docklands themselves were Mermaid Precinct, and it was Quane's cleverness in helping figure out who hijacked the *Fool's Gold* that led to his promotion when Lieutenant Bergin quit the Guard rather suddenly.

It wasn't until his third day on the job as a lieutenant that Sergeant Newcastle informed him that Bergin had quit rather than continue to be partnered with Danthres. And that Quane was now her sixth partner since her own promotion almost half a year earlier.

As they passed Oak Way, Quane cursed himself. "Pine Path," indeed. It was Oak Way that served as the demarcation between Unicorn and Dragon. He should have remembered that.

They reached Axe Lane—not Way, dammit—and turned left until they reached the Stone Kobold.

Forbin was on guard outside the tavern. Quane nodded at him.

"Ho there, Quane," Forbin said, then said more formally to Danthres, "Ma'am."

Danthres looked back and forth from Forbin to Quane. "You two know each other?"

Nodding, Quane said, "We came up in Unicorn together. Remember that gnome that kept trying to peek into Lady Murvane's bedchamber?"

That got a chuckle out of Forbin. "Indeed. No matter how many times we cast his tiny form into the hole…"

Quane grinned. He wasn't entirely sure why the dungeons beneath the castle and the holding cells in the precincts were collectively called "the hole," but that name had been part of the Guard's lexicon since he joined, so he called them that, too, so he wouldn't look like an idiot. At least not like more of an idiot than he had been since being promoted.

Danthres snarled. "*If* you two are done with your hilarious reminiscing about your soft duty in Unicorn, we have a case."

"With respect, ma'am, that's why they put rookies there—because it is, as you say, soft."

"I wouldn't know," Danthres said. "When I first joined up, I was assigned to Goblin."

Quane watched Forbin's eyes go wide, which was the way he himself had reacted when Danthres had informed her of the same thing. That was not standard procedure for the Castle Guard.

Danthres stared at Forbin intently. "What have we got?"

"A bar brawl, much like any other bar brawl. I have not questioned any of the participants, though I overheard one person mention that a dwarf started it. There are a couple of dwarves inside, by the way. In the end, the bartender was found with a knife in her chest."

Danthres folded her arms. "I'm impressed. That's more than I usually get out of a guard. Please tell me you haven't let anyone leave."

Shaking his head so fast Quane wondered if it would turn all the way around, Forbin said, "No, ma'am. Everyone's still present and accounted for—at least, since I arrived shortly after I received word of the fight. I can't guarantee that someone didn't depart the premises before my arrival."

"Good enough." She stormed past Forbin and went into the Stone Kobold.

Forbin glanced sidelong at Quane. "She's a fun one, isn't she?"

Quane just shuddered and went inside as well.

As soon as they entered the bar itself, everyone started speaking at once. The bar was mostly populated with humans, as well as a smattering of dwarves. No elves or gnomes or halflings or any other species that Quane could see.

"Quiet!" Danthres yelled, her voice echoing off the Kobold's wooden walls.

Everyone shut up. Quane wondered if they put her on crowd control when she was a guard in Goblin.

"Everyone stay where you are. We need to look at the victim, then we will be questioning you one by one. Where's the body?"

Several of the patrons pointed to the other side of the bar, located against the back wall. Danthres strolled to it, moving past the tables that were shoved haphazardly about the floor.

Quane followed, then stumbled as he kept crashing into tables that Danthres, somehow, nimbly avoided.

They got around to the other side of the bar. Looking down, Quane saw a blond-haired human woman. Her tunic was darkened by blood, pooling beneath her from around the dagger jutting out of her chest. Her eyes just stared upward without blinking, and the blood looked like it was everywhere, and…

Suddenly, Quane's entire being was focused on the nausea that welled up from his belly into his throat. Turning, he ran toward the front door and barely made it out before throwing up right onto Forbin's boots.

"Damnation, Quane, do you know how much they charge us for a Laundry Spell on boots?"

Quane stood hunched over, hands on knees, trying to get his breathing under control. His lips were caked with puke, and his mouth tasted like something died in it. Pointedly, he ignored Forbin's question. Given what was on the ground in Cliff's End, his puke was the least of what was staining Forbin's boots in a given day.

Wiping his mouth with his glove, he stood upright, took a very deep breath, and walked back in.

Danthres was standing just on the other side of the door. "Lord and Lady, Quane, is this your first dead body?"

Swallowing down the leftover bile, Quane nodded.

"How did you — Oh, never mind, I don't even want to know." She pointed at a table. "Go sit down." She turned around and looked at the assembled multitudes before pointing at a human woman. "You, come over here."

The woman came over and sat down opposite Quane, Danthres taking a seat between them. "Tell me," she said, "what happened?"

She shrugged. "Dunno. Some dwarf and that man over yonder," she pointed at a red-haired man seated at the bar, "were tellin' war stories, and next thing I know, everyone's gone mad."

"Which dwarf?"

The woman looked about. "Dunno. Ain't here no more. Said his name was Zubering or summat."

"Did you see who killed the bartender?"

"Her name's Gava—she was a good woman."

Quane said, "I'm so sorry for your loss."

Danthres shot him a look.

The woman said, "It's everyone's loss. Other bartenders in this dump are shitbrains, but she knows how to pour. Anyhow, I didn't see who killed her. And if I did, I'd've cut him m'self."

Once they were done with her, Danthres called a human man over. He said more or less the same thing, though he had no idea what the dwarf's name was. Then a dwarf, who said that the dwarf who started the brawl was named Zorbanig. Then an older human man.

"I come in fairly regularly," the man said. "My name's Tam Kort, and I don't know who Zorbanig was—except that he was a dwarf who fought in the war—but I've never seen him before. Of course, I've never seen Mr. ban Wyvald over there before, either, but he didn't sneak out while the brawl was going on."

Danthres frowned. "You're sure he left then?"

Kort hesitated. "Not entirely, but I didn't see him at all after the fight ended. Stands to reason. Also, he and another person, a human, seemed to have some sort of prearranged movement where Zorbanig bumped him, and the man swung over his head and stumbled into a table with a bit of deliberate clumsiness."

"I can't help but notice that you're uninjured," Danthres said.

Quane shook his head. He hadn't even noticed that. Everyone else in the place had at least the beginnings of a bruise, if not a cut or two, except for this Kort gentleman.

Kort smiled sheepishly. "I'm afraid I'm of little use in a fight, and I'm a tremendous physical coward. I kept my head down and didn't engage."

Danthres then summoned the red-haired man over.

"Greetings, Lieutenants. My name is Torin ban Wyvald, and the person you wish to speak to is named Zorbanig. He's a dwarf, completely bald, with a mark on the left side of his head. His beard is brown with some gray, and very thick."

Danthres blinked. "That's—quite a bit of detail."

Ban Wyvald shrugged. "I was suspicious of him. He claimed to be from the Elmgren Regiment, which fought alongside my own 17th Company at Hobgoblin's Run. But his remembrances seemed vague at best, and when I mentioned Captain Birok's big charge, he nodded and said he remembered it well."

Danthres smirked. "I take it that Captain Birok did not charge during that battle?"

Smirking right back, ban Wyvald said, "That would be rather difficult, since he'd been dead for a month by the time Hobgoblin's Run occurred." The smirk fell. "After I finished the story, he picked a fight, despite all my attempts to defuse his anger. And then he and a compatriot appeared to deliberately provoke a table full of men."

"You seem to notice a great deal," Danthres said slowly.

"You seem suspicious of that, Lieutenant."

"Can you give me a good reason why I shouldn't be?"

Quane frowned. Danthres was talking like this man was a suspect, which was absurd, given how cooperative he was.

"I can, as it happens. I was raised in Myverin, and trained to be observant of my surroundings at all times."

"Myverin's real?" Quane blurted out. "I always thought it was a myth!"

"So did I," Danthres said. "Certainly, people who voluntarily leave Myverin are."

"An odd statement," ban Wyvald replied, "from someone who voluntarily left Sorlin."

Now Danthres smoldered. Quane found himself slowly nudging his chair away from her. Sorlin was one of those places in the south that Quane had heard stories about—something about elves experimenting on humans, maybe?—but he wasn't sure of the reality. He had no idea that Danthres was from there, or indeed if she really was. But ban Wyvald just mentioning the place obviously pissed her off.

Tightly, Danthres said, "We're not here to discuss me, Mr. ban Wyvald, but the bar brawl and the murder of a woman."

"I'm afraid two of the brawlers occupied my attention, to their detriment, so I did not witness the murder. However, you may be able to obtain assistance from the man you interviewed before me."

Quane blinked. "Mr. Kort already told us everything he knows."

"No, shitbrain, he didn't," Danthres said dismissively. "He merely answered what we asked him."

"Did he tell you that he's a wizard?" ban Wyvald asked.

Now Quane's jaw dropped. "He's not a wizard!"

"I'm afraid I must agree with my idiot partner," Danthres said. "Wizards generally announce themselves."

"I can't speak to why this Kort gentleman hid his true nature, but he spent the entire fight sitting on his stool at the bar, and was left completely untouched by it, even as all those around him were caught up in it whether they wished to or not. That could only have been accomplished by a spell he cast."

"That's amazing," Quane muttered.

Danthres gave her partner a withering look. "Hardly. He could have bought a Shield Spell."

But ban Wyvald just shook his head and pointed at the doorway to the Stone Kobold.

Turning around, Quane saw a sigil painted on the wall over the doorframe, though he had no idea what it meant.

"That symbol," ban Wyvald said, "can be found on most reputable taverns throughout—"

"Yes, yes, yes," Danthres said with a sigh.

Quane swallowed. "I've never seen it before."

"It's a ward, shitbrain." Danthres gave her another of her withering stares. Quane was already getting tired of them. "It prevents any store-bought magick from working where it's placed. But it won't stop natural magick, so wizards can still function where that ward appears."

At this point, Quane's head was swimming, as he hadn't known any of this. "All—all right then, if he *is* a wizard, how does that help us?"

"During the war, there was a court-martial of a soldier who claimed that a fellow soldier had been killed by an enemy scout, but nobody had seen this scout. There happened to be a wizard in camp, and he offered to cast a spell called Inanimate Residue. It can tell the wizard what has happened to certain inanimate objects, to peel back time on that object and reveal its past."

Frowning, Quane repeated himself. "How does that help us?"

Danthres was leaning forward. "This spell can be cast in a room?"

"He told me it could. It certainly can't hurt to ask this Kort person if he is capable of such."

"Assuming," Danthres added with a smile, "that he *is* a wizard."

Ban Wyvald smiled right back. "Assuming."

"You admit you might be wrong?" Danthres tilted her head quizzically.

"Of course," ban Wyvald replied matter-of-factly. "I'm only guessing—I might be mistaken, and Kort may simply be a *very* talented coward."

"That was, in fact, what he claimed," Danthres said. "We shall see. And I'm impressed. Most men would never admit to the possibility of being wrong."

"Then it would seem that I am not like most men."

Danthres snorted. "Doubtful. Is there anything else you wish to add?"

Shrugging, ban Wyvald said, "Only that the woman was obviously targeted, and Zorbanig's purpose was to provide a distraction that would allow him, or someone else, to kill her."

"Are you sure of that?" Quane asked.

Danthres looked to the ceiling in supplication, and Quane realized he'd screwed up yet again. "Lord and Lady, you stupid shitbrain, of *course* that's what happened! Gava was very carefully stabbed right in the chest where she'd be guaranteed to die almost instantly. That type of precision doesn't happen in a bar fight."

"I—" Quane started, but Danthres had already gotten up and walked over to Kort.

After following her progress across the tavern, ban Wyvald turned to Quane. "Is she always so—so direct?"

Quane snorted. "That's the polite way of putting it. I've only been partnered with her for a short while." And he wasn't sure he'd be partnered with her for much longer, though he didn't say that aloud. "Thank you for your cooperation," he added as he rose and went after her.

She was now standing in front of Kort. "Tell me, Mr. Kort—are you a wizard?"

Several of the other people in the tavern laughed at that. "He ain't no wizard!" "Kort ain't no more a mage than I am!" "Like a magick-slinger'd be caught dead in *this* place!"

Kort, however, just sighed. "How did you know?"

More expressions of shock and disbelief and outrage.

Quane was about to explain that ban Wyvald had figured it out, but Danthres talked over him. "That doesn't matter. What does matter is whether or not you are capable of casting an Inanimate Residue Spell."

Instead of answering directly, Kort just stared at Danthres. For her part, Danthres stared right back. Quane had to look away, but neither lieutenant nor wizard did.

Finally Kort sighed. "Now I'll have to find a new tavern—*again*."

"Is that a yes?"

"Yes, it's a yes. I'll need everyone to depart this tavern. The spell only will work if there is nothing alive in the space."

"But," Quane said, "aren't *you* alive?"

Danthres barked a laugh. "Congratulations, shitbrain, that's the first smart thing you've said in your entire life."

"The spellcaster, obviously, can be present," Kort said slowly. "If we're to do this, let's get it over with, so I can find a new tavern to patronize. I'll need half an hour to cast the spell."

Looking at Quane, Danthres said, "Let's clear the place out."

Stunned that she didn't call him "shitbrain" that time, Quane started to herd people out of the Stone Kobold. Within a few minutes, they'd cleared everyone onto Axe Lane. They were all muttering various importuning about how surprised they were that Kort was a mage.

With a sigh, Danthres looked at Forbin. "All right, I see no reason to stand around for half an hour, so you stay here, and when the wizard in there is finished, escort him to the castle."

"Uhm—" Forbin started.

"Is there a problem?" Danthres asked in a tone that made it abundantly clear that the answer to that question needed to be "no."

Forbin, however, did not catch the tone—or, more suicidally, didn't care. "Ma'am, I'm afraid I'm off-shift in a quarter-hour, and Sergeant Alvin made it abundantly clear that we cannot have over-time."

Danthres put her head in her hands. "Then send someone to Dragon and get a replacement!"

With that, Danthres stormed off. Quane gave Forbin a quick shrug, and then ran to catch up with her.

As soon as he did so, Danthres said, "You were utterly useless in there, shitbrain. Osric keeps insisting that I must have a partner, but a tree would've been more beneficial than you. At least it would provide shade."

Quane instinctively wanted to be outraged. That was the sixth time she'd called him a shitbrain today, and he was sick of it. But he couldn't muster up that outrage because in the back of his head he knew that she was absolutely right. For all that he'd been clever on the *Fool's Gold* case, he wasn't, it seemed, cut out to be a detective. That ban Wyvald fellow was of more use to the investigation than he.

# TORIN

TORIN BAN WYVALD FELT ODDLY NERVOUS AS HE APPROACHED THE CASTLE that served as the seat of Lord Albin and Lady Meerka's demesne.

He had, over the past five years, left his childhood home — the only person to voluntarily leave Myverin in recent memory, or even not-so-recent — nearly died in the Forest of Orven during a particularly brutal winter, and fought in a war. He had done more than he ever could have imagined when he departed the safe haven of home for the greater world of Flingaria outside Myverin's cloistered walls.

So why was his stomach doing backflips at the notion of simply approaching a castle door?

Steeling himself, he entered through the portcullis, traversed the grand foyer — and then had no idea where to go next.

Conveniently, there was a man in armor standing near one of the doorways. The style of leather armor was the same as the other members of the Castle Guard he saw at the tavern. This one had a gryphon insignia on his chest, just like the two lieutenants, but no cloak, like the guard who'd been standing outside.

"Excuse me," Torin said to the guard, who had been staring straight ahead until Torin approached him.

"Yeah?" the guard asked.

"My apologies, but I'm here to see General Osric."

The guard squinted. "Ain't no General Osric here. 'Less Cap'n Osric's been promoted without tellin' nobody."

At that, Torin chuckled. "My apologies. Your captain and I served in the war together, and he was a general then."

"So I heard." He stepped away from the doorway and pointed down a corridor. "Head down 'at way, then hang yourself a left at the big dragon statue, then a right at the unicorn tapestry. Right through 'ere's th'squadroom."

Inclining his head, Torin said, "My thanks, kind sir," and then followed those directions.

Once he navigated past a hideous statue of a dragon and a pretty tapestry portraying a unicorn gamboling in the woods, he found himself in a large room filled with desks. A picture window filled the north wall, providing rather a nice view of the forest outside the city-state's outskirts. The east wall had a doorway, and three more doorways ran across the south wall.

He saw three people in leather armor that had the same gryphon insignia on the chest as Tresyllione and Quane from the Stone Kobold and the corridor guard, though he saw neither detective. None were wearing cloaks, but Torin noticed a pegboard on which hung five earth-colored cloaks. The three were each sitting at desks, writing on scrolls. One got up and went to the window, saying, "The Gerrin case."

The window then shimmered and twisted, the forest view being replaced with the bearded male face of an imp. Said imp spoke in a thin, reedy voice. "You don't need to say which case, you know. I'm perfectly capable of filing the scrolls in their proper place."

"Your optimism amuses me, Ep," the lieutenant said. "Just put these with the Gerrin case."

"Fine, fine," Ep said in what Torin imagined to be a long-suffering tone.

The lieutenant placed the scrolls in the imp's beard, and it disappeared shortly thereafter, allowing the view of the forest to return.

After that, the lieutenant turned to look at Torin. "You impressed with the view or the imp?"

"Oh, I've seen imps before," Torin said with a smile. "The boat I took to Cliff's End used one for announcements to the passengers, and I encountered more than one when I served in the army."

Returning the smile, the lieutenant said, "So it's the view, then?"

"It is a very pretty forest. It's called Nimvale, if I recall the area geography, yes?"

"Yes. Surprised you didn't learn that upon arrival—no, wait, you came by sea, you said."

Torin nodded. "I'm actually here to see Captain Osric. Is he available?"

"That depends on who needs him."

"I'm Torin ban Wyvald."

Offering his gloved hand, the detective said, "I'm Lieutenant Gef Linder."

Accepting the hand, Torin added, "I served under your captain when he was a general in King Marcus and Queen Marta's army."

Linder chuckled. "Ah, took on the Elf Queen with him, didja? Well, he'll be willing to make time for you, most likely." He leaned forward. "Tell me—did he really lose the eye fighting the Elf Queen's brother?"

Glancing sidelong at Linder, Torin asked, "Is that what he told you?"

"Oh, Wiate, no, he won't tell us a damn thing. No, it something that Sir Palrik told us once."

Torin blinked. "'Sir' Palrik?"

"You know him?" Linder shook his head. "Right, of course you do, you both served under the cap'n."

"I had no idea Palrik was of the nobility. He certainly never gave any indication of it during the war."

Linder snorted. "He hasn't given much indication of it here, neither. In fact—"

He was interrupted by the east-wall door flying open and three people walking out: Quane, looking relieved, Tresyllione, looking pissed, and Osric, looking—well, looking a great deal like Osric always did. Torin couldn't remember a time when his erstwhile commander didn't scowl.

A man wearing a green cloak came in from one of the other doorways. As he did, Osric said, "Sergeant Newcastle, take Lieutenant Quane to Sir Gevlin. He'll need to be processed out, as he's resigning his commission as a member of the Castle Guard."

Newcastle, the man in the green cloak, sighed. "C'mon with me, boy." The pair of them exited through the same west-wall door that Torin had come in through. Quane had been completely out of his depth in the Stone Kobold—the half-elf woman was doing all the work—but Torin had thought he was at least trying. Quitting seemed an extreme reaction.

One of the other detectives said, "Couldn't handle it, huh? Or couldn't handle *her*? Not that anyone can handle her. What that, Danthres, ten partners?"

Osric and Tresyllione both gave that detective a nasty look. Then Osric did the scariest thing Torin had ever see him do.

He smiled.

"We'll have to see how good you are at handling, then, Iaian. As of now, you and Tresyllione are partners."

Iaian's face fell. The other two detectives chortled.

"Trust me," Tresyllione said in a low voice, "I'm as thrilled about it as you are."

"What did I do to deserve this?" Iaian asked.

"You're one of the more experienced detectives I have," Osric said, "and I want this murder solved. We have too damn many bar brawls as it is, now people are using them to shield a murder. I want it solved, and that means I need my best detective on it."

"Hey!" Linder said. "Since when is this shitbrain your best detective?"

"Thanks, partner," Iaian muttered.

Osric put his hands on his hips. "Since he closed the Gerrin case. And don't tell me you both closed it, I know for a fact that he was the one who found that gnome and interrogated him while you were taking a personal day."

Torin shook his head and chuckled. Osric hadn't changed a bit, it seemed.

At that point, Tresyllione was staring at Torin. "What are you doing here? Did you remember something else?"

Before Torin could reply, Osric also noticed him. "Lord and Lady, is that you, ban Wyvald?"

"Yes, sir. My apologies, Lieutenant Tresyllione, I'm afraid I'm not here about the incident at the Stone Kobold. Rather, I'd like to visit with my former commanding officer."

Osric looked at Tresyllione. "*He* was that witness you mentioned?"

"Yes," she said.

"Well, I'm afraid I'm going to have to disagree with your assessment of him as someone we shouldn't trust."

Torin shot Tresyllione a look. "Why not trust me?"

Iaian rolled his eyes. "Don't take it personal, mister. Danthres doesn't trust anyone."

"You needn't be concerned," Osric said. "There is no circumstance under which Torin ban Wyvald would be part of a conspiracy to commit murder. Take Iaian, go see if you can find the people the wizard found with that spell."

With a big sigh, Iaian got up from his chair and went to the pegboard. "What spell is that?"

"A damned impressive spell, actually," Tresyllione said as she headed toward the pegboard. "It peels back the events in a place and shows them to the wizard."

"Just the wizard?"

Tresyllione nodded. "It won't work if there are any other living beings around."

"So we have to take the wizard's word for it?"

"Yes, but—well, he's a wizard. They're completely trustworthy." Tresyllione spoke as if it were the most natural thing.

Iaian and Tresyllione moved toward the door as Iaian put his cloak on. "Yeah? What about Chalmraik the Foul?"

"Fine, members of the Brotherhood of Wizards are trustworthy. If they weren't, the Brotherhood wouldn't let them in, would they?"

"Hope so. Who're we looking for?"

The woman's answer was lost as they continued down the corridor and out of earshot.

"So, ban Wyvald," Osric said, "what brings you here?"

Suddenly conscious of the eyes of Linder and the other detective—not to mention the imp in the window—Torin said, "I'd be happy to answer that question—in private, if you don't mind."

Nodding, Osric said, "Of course not." He looked around the squadroom. "Linder, Karistan, I'm sure you have work you can be doing. And where the hell is Nael?"

Karistan said, "He's chatting with Jezz, that sailor friend of his, about the robberies on Sandy Brook Way."

"So why aren't you with him?"

"Jezz doesn't like me."

Osric shook his head. "All right. Don't you two need to talk to the magistrate first thing in the morning?"

"Yes, we're ready."

"You'd better be." Osric took a breath. "C'mon into my office, ban Wyvald."

Grinning, Torin followed Osric into the small office.

As the captain closed the door behind them, Torin said, "I see you still can't leave a room without shouting at each of your subordinates at least once."

"Can't let them think I'm not paying attention, now, can I?" Osric sat down behind the desk, and Torin took one of the facing guest chairs. "When did you get into Cliff's End?"

"Two days ago, on the *Stars Rising*. The boat's first mate was grumbling about how much harder it was to make an 'honest' living the last year, ever since old 'One-Eyed Osric' took over the Guard."

Osric snorted. "Good to know my reputation is preceding me."

"You definitely have been doing well for yourself. That first mate was not the only person who spoke highly of your Castle Guard." He grinned. "And you can afford a better eyepatch."

The captain's hand moved to the silk patch that covered his left eye, which was of much higher quality than the one he'd been using in the last days of the war. "Indeed. But I can't take complete credit. The Guard is entirely Lord Albin's work. I merely administrate it—though I will freely admit to doing a better job than my predecessor." He shook his head. "Then again, a dead goblin could do a better job than Brisban. I've been working to get rid of the detectives he thought were worth promoting and trying to promote up the ones who actually know their asses from their elbows."

"I suppose it's not going as well as you'd hoped, based on what just happened with young Lieutenant Quane."

Osric shrugged. "His sergeant back at Mermaid thought highly enough of him that I didn't want to just let him go." He chuckled. "So I paired him with Tresyllione, which I knew would have him quitting inside a week."

Slowly, Torin said, "She's—interesting."

"She's brilliant, is what she is, but she's also impossible. She's gone through half a dozen partners since I promoted her." He shook his head. "Brisban put her in Goblin as a rookie. Usually, we break people in by sending them to Unicorn, but—" He chuckled again. "Apologies, ban Wyvald, you don't know our system. Goblin Precinct is our poorest area, and Unicorn where all the rich bastards live."

Torin nodded. "Of course."

"Brisban kept Tresyllione in Goblin, hoping she'd wash out. He felt she wasn't Guard material." He blew out a breath. "He may have been right, to a degree. She is constantly fighting with the nobility, and irritating witnesses, and just generally being difficult. But she also has the best instincts of anyone I've ever seen." A small smile pricked up the side of his mouth. "Enough about my travails, I doubt you wish to hear them. What have you been up to?"

Leaning back in the wooden chair, Torin said, "Less than I'd like to admit. Since my pension never materialized—"

That got a small growl from Osric. The army had a policy whereby, if someone died, the money set aside for their pensions would be fed back into the army's coffers. What they neglected to mention was that they had done so for the living soldiers as well, so anyone lucky enough to live through the war did not receive their promised reward.

Torin went on. "—I've had to find work here and there. It hasn't been easy—there are far too many former soldiers and not nearly enough things for them to do."

"We've taken on several as guardsme—"

Osric was interrupted by a knock at the door. Then it opened to reveal the sergeant, Newcastle. "Sorry to interrupt, Captain, but I'm afraid Sir Gevlin needs to see you right away. Says it's urgent."

Standing up, Osric scowled deeply. "Very well. My apologies, ban Wyvald, but one of the first things I learned after I accepted this job from Lord Albin was that, when someone with the prefix 'Sir' has a request, it must be fulfilled immediately. Where are you staying?"

"The Flying Unicorn Inn—it's right next to the Stone Kobold. That was why I was drinking there, in fact."

"Why don't we meet for drinks at the Old Ball and Chain to-morrow night? We can catch up in a more civilized setting."

Torin grinned. "I would like that very much, Captain." Osric tilted his head. "And shave, will you please? Your face looks like a ravaged forest."

As they exited Osric's office, Torin said, "I was thinking of growing a beard, actually."

"Well, make up your mind one way or the other, you look ridiculous."

"Says the man who always has stubble."

Rubbing his slightly hairy chin, Osric said, "Yes, but on me it works."

With that, Osric left through the west-wall door at top speed. Torin made his way toward that door more slowly, but Newcastle grabbed his shoulder.

"Yes?" Torin asked.

Newcastle removed the hand quickly from the shoulder. "You served with the captain?"

Torin nodded.

"Hmp. You should come by more often. He usually ain't that — that *human.*"

# IAIAN

Danthres was striding ahead of Iaian as they walked out of the Stone Kobold. One of the other bartenders recognized the description of the person whom Kort said killed Gava. It was a tall, skinny human with a large, hooked nose. They were now headed to where the bartender thought the man—whose name was Camrin—lived.

At Iaian's muttering, she stopped and turned around to face him. "What's ridiculous?"

"Besides your face?" He added a grin to make it look like he was kidding.

"Iaian, I'm perfectly happy to run you through and claim that some random person did it before I could stop them."

"Look, it's just not fair, okay? When I signed onto the guard thirteen years ago, it was simple. Sure, there was a shit-ton of crime, but it was all committed by morons. Now, though, the morons get caught, and most of 'em don't bother, 'cause the Castle Guard's all for maintaining law and order in the demesne." He said that last with as much sarcasm and bitterness as he could muster—a considerable amount, all things considered, as he was pretty well pissed off at the moment.

Danthres just stared at him with that really ugly face of hers. "And how is this a problem, exactly?"

"Because now the only people committing crimes are really smart people, and they're damn near impossible to catch. Take this murder— used to be, someone wanted to kill a bartender, they'd just kill her in front of everyone. Now, though, everyone's worried about getting caught by us, so they start a brawl to hide and make it damn near impossible to find them. If there hadn't happened to be a wizard in the Kobold, we'd be shit outta luck. Wasn't so bad before, when Brisban was in charge, but now, with Osric? It's impossible to do police work."

"You mean impossible to take bribes."

"I don't know what you're talking about." He started walking again.

"You really think I don't know?" Danthres called after him.

"What I really think is that you're another one of Osric's holier-than-thou shitbrains who think that they're above it all. That's not how this city-state works, and it never has been."

With her ridiculously long legs, Danthres caught up to him quickly. "How city-states work is something that can change rather rapidly. Believe me, I know."

Iaian had no idea what that meant, and didn't care enough to ask. It had to do with whatever Danthres's past was, and Iaian found that that subject was very low on the list of things he cared about.

So he just kept walking.

They arrived at a boarding house where the bartender at the Stone Kobold was fairly certain Camrin lived. After knocking on the door, it opened to reveal a wizened old woman in a battered housecoat and wearing a kerchief over her hair. "Whaddaya want?"

"We're with the Cliff's End Castle Guard, ma'am," Iaian said.

"Yeah, I can *see* that, y'idjit. I ain't blind, y'know. Whaddya *want*?"

"Is there a man named Camrin living here?"

"S'what if there is?"

Iaian sighed. "*If* there is, we need to talk to him."

"An' if he ain't, you don't need t'talk t'him, that it?"

Whirling to give Danthres a "see?" expression, he then said, "Ma'am, if you could just tell us where Camrin is, so we can talk to him."

"That ain't whatcha said. Should say whatcha mean."

Danthres, Iaian noticed, was walking around to the other side of the boarding house. Iaian started trying to figure out how he was going to approach Osric about requesting to be put back with Linder—he'd been in the Guard as long as Iaian, and he knew how the job was done, dammit, including not abandoning your partner while he's questioning a crazy old woman—while he slowly said to the woman, "Look, ma'am, I'm trying to be patient, but if you don't just tell me if Camrin lives here or not, I'm gonna have to arrest you."

"I ain't done nothin'."

"No, you haven't—including answering my question. So tell me, right here right now—"

He was interrupted by a male voice screaming, "Oooof! Let go'a me you crazy bitch! Aaaaaaaaah!"

It was coming from around the corner, where Danthres had wandered to. Running in the direction of the shouting, Iaian turned to see his new partner kneeling on the back of a skinny human with a hook nose, having wrenched his arm behind his back.

Danthres looked up at him. "Want to help me arrest this shitbrain?"

Before Iaian could reply, Camrin cried out, "Whatcha arrestin' me for? I didn't do nothin'!"

"You killed Gava," Danthres said.

"I don't know nobody named Gava!"

She got to her feet, pulling Camrin up as well. "The bartender at the Stone Kobold."

"Ow! Is *that* what that bitch's name was? Huh. Bad enough she wouldn't sleep with me, but then she called me ugly."

Iaian rolled his eyes. "Hate to break this to you, chuckles, but you *are* ugly." Then he looked at Danthres. "How'd you know he'd be back here?"

"The woman had the same type of nose that Kort told us the killer did, so I thought she might be related to him—probably his mother. And she was obviously stalling so he could get away. So while you talked to her, I came around back, and sure enough, our murderer was climbing out a window."

The woman in the housecoat finally came around the corner and started screaming. "That's my boy! Y'can't take my boy away!"

"Shut up, lady," Iaian said, "or we'll keep you together by throwin' you *both* in the hole."

They led Camrin down the road toward Meerka Way. "You know, Iaian," Danthres said, "given that this imbecile just confessed to murder without a thought, and given that you fell for his mother's obvious delaying tactic, perhaps you should consider that the criminals aren't getting smarter, but that you're getting stupider."

Iaian just seethed, more determined than ever to ask for a new partner.

As they turned onto Meerka Way, Dru, a guard from Dragon approached them. "Lieutenants, I'm glad I found you!"

"What is it, Dru?"

"We got a message to find you two—there's been a murder down Alfar's Way. A wizard named Finnert got his throat cut right in front of his shop."

Iaian sighed. "We *got* a case."

Dru grinned. "Yeah, Sergeant Newcastle said you might say that, and he said to tell you that Cap'n Osric wanted you two on it. I can take your prisoner, put him in the hole till you're done."

Danthres practically threw Camrin at Dru. "Take him. C'mon, Iaian."

She strode up Meerka Way toward the intersection with Alfar's. Grumbling, Iaian followed her. "Who put the gargoyle up your ass?"

"It's a *wizard*. We need to solve this one quickly." Danthres sounded almost reverent.

"Have you ever even *met* a wizard?"

That earned Iaian one of Danthres's typical stares of annoyance, thrown over her shoulder as he struggled to catch up with her. "Just the one in the Stone Kobold yesterday. I've never really moved in the same circles," she added with a tone of bitterness.

"Trust me, they ain't exactly the paragons of virtue they pretend to be."

"As if *you'd* know," she said dismissively.

"Fine, ignore my years of experience."

"Gladly."

Iaian sighed again. Danthres had mastered the art of sarcasm, so he knew that she was not employing it just then.

They saw the crowd gathered in front of Finnert's Magick Shop more easily than they could see the shop itself. Iaian noted several guards from Dragon keeping people away from the area right in front of the store.

"What've we got?" Danthres asked.

The oldest of the guards, whom Iaian recognized as a lifer named Mannit, said, "Danthres? Mitre's left thumb, when'd *you* get promoted?"

Danthres then did something Iaian had never seen her do: smile. "Six months back. I see they finally put you on days."

"Yeah, thought I'd see the sun every once in a while. Not that you can see it with all the damn buildings. Anyhow, can you take a look at this stiff so we can get him off the street?"

Iaian had taken advantage of his partner's reminisce to look at the body. It was an older human, thick beard, silver-and-black hair, wearing the usual robes that wizards wore. His neck was sliced open, dried blood near the wound.

"You can get him off the street now," Iaian said. "This ain't the crime scene."

"What?" Danthres asked snappishly.

He pointed at the body. "His throat was cut. There should be blood everywhere, but there isn't. Someone dumped the body here."

Danthres turned to Mannit without even acknowledging that Iaian was right, which pissed him off more than it probably should have. "This is Finnert?"

Mannit nodded. "He owned the place, and his clerk found him just lyin' there on the street when he came out to close up."

"All right. Can you talk to these people, see if any of them saw anything, and get a detail to take the body to the shop? And keep that clerk around."

"Right." Mannit moved off to give instructions to the other guards to take care of that. Iaian didn't envy whoever had to carry Finnert's body to the cave outside the Cliff's End city limits — that was where bodies were kept and generally incinerated, unless someone had specific instructions on how to dispose of their remains otherwise. Visiting there was Iaian's least favorite duty.

Looking over at Danthres, he amended that to second least favorite.

"Let's go inside," she said.

"Why didn't I think of that?"

"Are you always this disagreeable, or only when you have women partners?" Danthres asked.

"You're one to talk."

They went inside the small shop. It was a fairly standard setup: shelves lined with potions and scrolls and such on the walls of either side, a few stands with other items dotting the floor, and a desk in the back behind which the clerk stood. Behind that desk was an entryway to a rear room that probably included offices and storage.

"Surprised the killer left the robes on," Iaian muttered.

"What do you mean?"

"Well, wizards are always wearing those stupid robes."

"They're not stupid," Danthres said defensively. "They wear those robes for the same reason that we wear armor."

Iaian snorted. "We wear armor to protect ourselves from the crazies."

Danthres snarled. "Why we wear *decorated* armor, then. Plain armor would protect us, but our cloaks indicate our rank and the shields on our chests and cloaks signify our assignment. The robes let everyone know that they're wizards."

"Yeah, like going around shooting fireballs and turning people into newts doesn't do the trick." He stared at his partner. "I'm not seeing any sign of a struggle or any blood."

Nodding, Danthres said, "We should check the back."

"No!"

Whirling around at that voice behind them, Iaian saw another older human in blue robes, though he had no beard and darker skin.

"Who the hell are you, and what're you doin' in our crime scene?"

Danthres shot Iaian a look. "Please excuse my partner, sir—he takes himself a little too seriously. I assume you're here as a representative of the Brotherhood of Wizards?"

"Yes. I am Myk Dourti, and you may not enter the rear room of this shop. There are things back there that you are not fit to see."

"One'a yours was killed," Iaian said, "and we gotta find out what happened."

"Actually, you do not. This is now Brotherhood business. You will leave this shop at once, and inform your thugs not to touch Finnert's body."

Danthres moved forward. "I'm sorry, Mr. Dourti, but I'm afraid that, for once, my partner is right. When a body falls in Cliff's End, the Castle Guard's mandate is to investigate."

Dourti folded his arms over his robed chest. "Not when the body belongs to the Brotherhood. You will remove yourself from this site or I will remove you."

"Look," Iaian started—

—and the next thing he knew, there was a bright light, and when it dimmed, he was in the squadroom blinking spots out of his eyes.

Danthres was standing next to him, while Nael and Karistan both dropped the scrolls that they were carrying over to Ep in shock.

Suddenly, Danthres turned a bit green, then doubled over and threw up on the floor.

Osric came in from the kitchen, a pastry in his hand, Newcastle right behind him. "What the hell just happened? I thought you two were on the wizard murder."

"We were," Iaian said, watching with amusement as Danthres wretched. "The Brotherhood took us off it."

"What does that mean, exactly?" Osric asked in a low, dangerous tone.

Iaian just threw his hands up. "Take it up with Myk Dourti. He's the Stupidhood of Wizards rep that teleported us here."

Shaking his head, Osric yelled, "Dammit!"

"Cap'n, can I talk to you for a sec?"

Osric nodded, then turned to Newcastle. "Make Tresyllione some tea, would you, please? Teleport Spells tend to be hard on the stomach. And get someone to clean that up."

"Good thing I've drunk my belly into submission," Iaian said with a grin.

Iaian then followed Osric into his office and closed the door. "What do you want, Iaian?"

"A new partner. Or better yet, my old partner."

"Tresyllione needs someone to work with. Everyone else has quit, or refused to be paired up with her. You're my last resort."

"Fine, then I quit."

Osric regarded Iaian quizzically. "Really? You can barely do *this* job, Iaian, what makes you think you'll be able to do another one at your age?"

"I ain't *that* old." Iaian shook his head. "You're right, I don't want to quit, but I can't take workin' with that bitch. Look, I'll help finish off the Gava murder, but that's it. I'm done with her. I don't know why the hell you promoted her."

"Because if she can get her attitude in check, she'll be the best detective in that squadroom."

"Yeah, well, you must see a lot more with one eye than I can with two, 'cause all I'm seein' is the attitude."

Osric shook his head. "Fine, finish Gava, and then you're back with Linder. With Quane quitting, I need to bring in someone new in any case."

"You partner the new guy with her, they won't stick around much longer'n Quane did, you ask me."

His scowl deepening, Osric said, "I don't recall asking you, Iaian. In fact, what I asked you was to partner with Tresyllione, which you couldn't manage for more than a day."

"Cap'n—"

"Get out of my office." Osric pulled out his dagger and started sharpening it.

Knowing better than to even try talking to the captain when he was in a sharpen-his-dagger mood, Iaian got up and left.

He wondered if he'd be able to stand another twelve years of this shit.

# NEWCASTLE

Bel Newcastle rubbed his jaw, trying to ignore the ache that cut through his mouth. He knew he should have gone to a healer, but it wasn't *that* bad at first, and he figured it would get better in time. Instead, it got worse, and now his wife Rhi was bugging him to see a healer already, but he didn't really have time, and besides, the place would fall apart without him.

At least, that was what he kept telling himself. It wasn't really so much the case anymore. When Brisban was the captain, the office was a disorderly mess, but Osric had brought his military efficiency to the running of the Castle Guard. Newcastle appreciated it, he really did, especially since it made his life easier. He didn't move as fast as he used to since he started having problems with his knees, after all.

Today he'd been busy, processing the paperwork on poor Quane's departure. Newcastle hadn't really expected the boy to be able to handle being a detective, and it had been his considered opinion that it had just been dumb luck that enabled him to figure out who hijacked that boat.

But nobody ever listened to Newcastle's opinions. They just had him handle the paperwork and keep track of assignments and fetch tea for the detectives when wizards hit them with Teleport Spells that made them throw up. He was okay with that.

Besides, two more years, and he could retire with a full pension. Then maybe he could take Rhi on that cruise.

Danthres and Iaian came into the squadroom from one of the interview rooms just as he filed the last of Quane's paperwork with Ep. The poor kid hadn't even been in the Guard long enough to earn any kind of pension, so he was going out into Cliff's End with nothing but whatever he'd saved. He made a mental note to check up on the boy, which he always did when someone left the Guard. Some day, he'd *actually* check up on someone…

"Camrin gave up his accomplices," Danthres said. "He hired a dwarf and a human to start the fight so he could kill Gava." She shook her head. "He wasn't even sorry that he killed her."

"Yeah, well, whaddaya expect? We were at war with the Elf Queen for so long, nobody thinks life means nothin'."

"What a ridiculous statement."

"Kiss my ass."

Newcastle shook his head. "Do you two do nothing but argue?"

Iaian grinned. "Not anymore. As of this confession, I'm done with you, Danthres."

"Except for the paperwork," Newcastle said quickly.

"Yeah, yeah."

Sighing, Newcastle went over to the kitchen to see if there were any pastries left. Rhi was more likely to convince him to go to the healer than Iaian was to get his paperwork done in a timely manner.

Osric then stuck his head out of his office and bellowed, "Newcastle! My office!"

Again, Newcastle sighed. It was never good when the captain bellowed your name followed by "My office!" It usually meant an unpleasant conversation. Of course, at least Osric was good enough to give you fair warning that it was going to be unpleasant. Brisban never gave any indication that he was going to tear you a new one until after you were already in the room.

To Newcastle's relief, Osric didn't close the door, so it wasn't going to be *that* kind of talk. Once he sat down in his chair, and Newcastle parked himself in the guest chair, the captain said, "We need to bring in a new detective."

Newcastle nodded, not sure where Osric was going with this.

"The problem," the captain continued as he took out his dagger, "is that nobody's ready yet. There are some promising guards, but nobody who's as ready as Sergeant Lorenz thought Quane was, and he couldn't handle it, either."

Speaking very tentatively, Newcastle asked, "Can I make a suggestion?"

"That's why I brought you in here, Newcastle." Osric started sharpening his dagger, which did nothing to alter Newcastle's tentativeness.

"I think we should just let Danthres work on her own. She—

"No."

Newcastle frowned. "Sir, she—"

"No. You can't solve crimes by yourself. You let yourself get caught up in a pet theory and pursue it to the detriment of other possibilities. That's too easy to do if you're working alone. Plus, the interviewing of witnesses and suspects takes twice the time with one detective." He shook his head. "Besides, if Danthres has to deal with people by herself, either she or the people she deals with or both will be dead before too long. Someone needs to be a calming influence on her."

"I'm not sure that's entirely possible, sir."

"Yes, but we have to at least—"

Whatever it was they had to do, Newcastle would never know, as they were interrupted by a bright light that heralded the sudden appearance of an older human in their midst, wearing blue robes, and carrying a stern expression. Newcastle had to blink spots away from his eyes after the light burst.

"Captain Osric, the Brotherhood of Wizards requires your assistance."

Osric rose to his feet, pointing his dagger at the wizard. "The Brotherhood of Wizards should keep out of my damned office when I'm having a meeting."

"Your meeting can wait," the wizard said. "I am Myk Dourti, the representative for the Brotherhood for this region."

"I'm glad you're here," Osric said with what Newcastle could tell was utterly false sincerity, "Lord Albin wishes to speak to you about the manner in which you summarily dismissed the officers in his Castle Guard."

"There is no time for such trivialities."

"I doubt, sir," and now Osric was waving the dagger about, "that Lord Albin considers it trivial. I doubt King Marcus and Queen Marta would, either."

"It is trivial by comparison to this: another wizard has been killed. And—against, I might add, my own recommendation—the Brotherhood has requested that your Castle Guard investigate this murder, as it appears to have been committed by the same perpetrator as Finnert. This second wizard also owned a shop, his throat was also cut, and his body was also left in front of it."

"Does that mean you'll permit us to *properly* investigate Finnert's murder as well?"

Dourti let out a very long sigh. "Yes, we will permit your detectives to examine Finnert's shop—however it must be supervised by the new manager, who has purchased the location from the Brotherhood following Finnert's death."

"That's fine. I'll have Lieutenant Tresyllione—"

"No."

Osric scowled. "Excuse me?"

"Neither Lieutenant Tresyllione nor Lieutenant Iaian may be the lead investigator in the case. We have examined their records, and the former is too inexperienced, the latter with a troubling record. We are not enthralled with Lieutenants Karistan or Nael, either, and Lieutenant Linder's casework also leaves quite a bit to be desired."

Newcastle winced. He just listed all the detectives.

"As it happens, we have a new hire in the squad, who is starting tomorrow," Osric said.

Somehow, Newcastle managed to restrain himself from gaping at his captain. Bluffing a wizard could not possibly have been a good idea.

"We will need to examine this man's record."

"He doesn't have one—"

Dourti frowned, and started to speak, but Osric kept going.

"—in Cliff's End. He served with me in the army when we fought the Elf Queen, and he helped me develop the strategy that won the day at the Nemerian Wastes."

At that, Dourti blinked. "He was your aide?"

"Absolutely. The finest soldier who served under me, with one of the keenest minds I've ever encountered. He will handle the investigation."

"What is this guard's name?"

"Lieutenant Torin ban Wyvald."

"From Myverin?"

"Yes."

Dourti nodded approvingly. "Very well. If he's from Myverin, he must be a very thoughtful individual. We have preserved the body and the shop with a Stasis Spell, which will only last a day. It's Kort's Spell Emporium on Boulder Pass."

Newcastle blinked. "The wizard who died is Tam Kort?"

Dourti stared at Newcastle as if only noticing he was even in the room for the first time. "Yes. Why?"

"He was a witness in a recent case we had," Newcastle said quietly. "The murder of a woman named Gava in the Stone Kobold saloon."

A look of distaste came over Dourti at that. "Yes, Kort was fond of—of such establishments. I always thought he'd be killed in one of them. I never imagined he would instead be killed in his own shop." He turned to Osric. "Your Lieutenant ban Wyvald will report to the shop first thing in the morning?"

Osric nodded. "Absolutely."

"Good." With that, Dourti gestured and disappeared in a flash of light.

Before Osric could say anything, Newcastle said, "I'll send someone to fetch Mr. ban Wyvald right away."

"He's staying at the Flying Unicorn."

Newcastle nodded, and got to his feet even as Osric sat back down and went back to sharpening his dagger. He hesitated before moving to the door. "Captain—what if ban Wyvald doesn't take the job?"

"He'll take it." Osric spoke with confidence.

"What if he *does* take it?"

Now Osric frowned. "I beg your pardon?"

"Every detective in here came up through the ranks. They may resent someone being given a lieutenant's cloak without earning it."

Osric stood back up, pointing at Newcastle with his dagger. "Torin ban Wyvald was one of the only reasons why we even *survived* the Nemerian Wastes. I exaggerated to Dourti about his helping with strategy there, but I needed to convince him. But ban Wyvald's quick thinking and observational abilities were a big part of why the 17th lived through that winter. Trust me, he's done his time in the trenches—just not the trenches *here.*"

"I understand, Captain, but—"

After Newcastle's hesitation went on for a second, Osric prompted him: "But what?"

"I'm not the one you have to convince, sir."

Instead of responding, Osric just sat back down and picked up the sharpening stone.

Which, Newcastle figured, was answer enough.

Rubbing his jaw, he went out into the squadroom on aching knees to find someone to fetch their new detective.

# DANTHRES

THE LAST THING DANTHRES EXPECTED TO SEE WHEN SHE WALKED INTO THE squadroom to start her shift was the primary witness in the Gava murder.

She especially didn't expect to see him wearing Guard armor with a gryphon crest and wearing a brown cloak. He was seated at Quane's old desk. Nobody else was in the squadroom, which wasn't much of a surprise. The shift was just starting, and the only detective other than Danthres who had ever come in on time in the past six months was Quane.

Staring at Torin ban Wyvald, she said without preamble, "You do know that impersonating a guard is a crime in this city-state, yes?"

Rising from the chair, ban Wyvald smiled. "A pleasure to see you again as well, Lieutenant Tresyllione."

Osric and Newcastle came in from the former's office. "Ah, good, Tresyllione, you're here. I believe you've already met your new partner."

Danthres's gray eyes widened. She didn't even understand what ban Wyvald was doing in Guard armor, and now she was supposed to be *partnered* with him?

Speaking slowly, she said, "I've met Mr. ban Wyvald, yes, as a witness in a case that hasn't even gone before the magistrate."

"And he still will be." Osric walked toward the two of them. "Only he'll be testifying as a lieutenant in the Castle Guard, which should make him a much more impressive witness."

While Danthres had to concede that the magistrate tended to put more stock in statements made by the Castle Guard and the nobility than he did ordinary citizens of the demesne, it didn't explain what this idiot was doing as a lieutenant. "Is this some kind of joke?"

Osric glared at her with his one good eye. "Have you ever known me to joke, Tresyllione?"

"No, sir," Danthres said. "Your humorlessness is legendary."

That prompted a snort from ban Wyvald.

The captain turned his glare on him, and then said, "You two are to report to Kort's Spell Emporium on Boulder Pass."

Ban Wyvald stood, and immediately winced.

With a grin, Danthres asked, "The boots, right?"

"Yes." He sounded surprised.

"It usually takes at least a month to break the damn things in. Not that I expect you to last that long."

"Your confidence is touching."

"The shop," Osric said, "and Kort's body are being preserved with a Stasis Spell by the Brotherhood until you two arrive."

Both Danthres and her new partner's jaws dropped at that. The latter said, "Kort is dead?"

Nodding, Osric said, "His throat was cut, same as Finnert. This time the Brotherhood has specifically asked for our help."

Danthres couldn't believe it. One wizard being killed by so mundane a manner as having his throat cut was difficult to credit—two was almost impossible.

Then Osric said, "Also, ban Wyvald is to be the lead investigator on this—at least whenever you're in the presence of any mages."

"What!?" Now Danthres was convinced that this *had* to be a joke.

Holding up a hand, Osric sounded aggravated when he explained. "It was the only way to get the Brotherhood to agree to an investigation at all. They were not happy with your behavior at Finnert's murder scene, nor with how much experience—"

"What's wrong with my experience?" Danthres blurted out. She wasn't surprised that a wizard would think poorly of her behavior at the scene, though the Brotherhood should have had more of an issue with Iaian. Then again, at least she was on the case, which Iaian wasn't, so she supposed that counted for something.

"The issue with your experience is that there's not enough of it."

She pointed at ban Wyvald. "It's a year-and-a-half more than he's had."

"She has a point, sir," ban Wyvald said. "I think it would make more sense—"

Osric's scowl was almost glowing. "I can assure both of you that right now I have a very minimal interest in what either of you think. Now get to Boulder Pass."

Danthres was unhappy, but based on Osric's attitude, this was as much politics as anything. However, she did have one last question. "Will we also be able to look at Finnert's shop?"

Nodding, Osric said, "The shop is remaining closed and two guards from Dragon are keeping an eye on it until you get there. But go to Kort's first. Any questions? No? Good." With that, Osric turned to go back into his office.

With a sigh, Danthres turned to leave, not bothering to see if ban Wyvald came with her.

As it happened, he did, though he walked gingerly thanks to his new boots. "I see Osric is still pretending to ask if anyone has any questions without actually allowing time to ask them. He used to do that in the army as well."

Not looking at her partner, she said, "Don't even try to make small talk with me. I don't care to get to know you, and I'm still not sure I entirely trust you."

"Whyever not?" He sounded surprised at that.

Now she did look at him. "You need to ask that? You were my prime suspect in Gava's murder until Camrin confessed, and I'm still not entirely convinced that you didn't have something to do with it."

"Why is that?" he asked defensively.

Smiling wryly as they exited through the portcullis, Danthres said, "Because in the year and a half I've been with the Guard, I have never had a single witness provide as much detail about a crime as you did who wasn't intimately involved with the crime."

Shrugging, ban Wyvald said, "I was trained to be observant."

"In Myverin?"

"Yes."

"I always believed that place to be a myth."

At that, ban Wyvald grinned. "That puts you in company with the vast majority of the people I've met outside Myverin."

Staring at his smile, Danthres shook her head. "On the other hand, it probably is everything people say it is, if you came from there with such perfect teeth."

Laughing, ban Wyvald said, "Indeed. Listen, Lieutenant, I understand that you do not wish me to be here. I must confess to being rather stunned that Osric offered me the job. But I was hardly in a position to decline the opportunity."

"Oh, I don't blame you for taking the job. Worry not, though, I'm sure I'll find plenty to blame you for as we proceed. Which won't be for long."

"That's the second time you've said that. What make you think I won't last?"

"Six months of experience. I'm hoping that, once you — Osric's pet soldier — run screaming from the castle, the captain will finally see the wisdom of allowing me to work alone."

They were proceeding down Meerka Way, moving past the mansions of Unicorn Precinct. "I'm hardly Osric's pet anything," ban Wyvald said. "And you might be underestimating me."

Danthres would have expected him to be more exasperated or annoyed or angry — but no, he was speaking in the same pleasant tone he'd been using every time she talked to him. It was starting to seriously piss her off.

She whirled on him. "You're not a detective. You're not even a member of the Guard. You're a friend of the captain who got lucky, and it is my considered opinion that you'll wash out of here faster than Quane did — and Quane was the biggest idiot I've ever been partnered with. This job is *important*, ban Wyvald — we speak for people who can't speak for themselves."

And then she turned and continued to stride down Meerka Way.

"Interesting," ban Wyvald said. He was able to keep up with her stride, which she found annoying. "I hadn't really thought about the job in that way. But then, I've had very little time to think of it at all, as Osric came to me last night and had me come to the castle and be fitted for this ill-fitting armor."

Danthres couldn't help but smile at that. It had taken Lady Meerka's armorers seven tries to get hers to fit properly.

Ban Wyvald continued: "I came to Cliff's End because I had nowhere else to go. I went to Osric simply because he was someone I knew. I never imagined he'd offer me a job."

For a moment, Danthres was bitterly amused that ban Wyvald came to Cliff's End for the same reason she did. But the moment passed, as most people came here for that reason. They were neither of them unique in that.

They passed Oak Way, and ban Wyvald then asked, "We're now in Dragon Precinct, yes?"

"Yes," Danthres said simply. The conversation was only irritating her more, and she was at the point where she wanted to keep it brief.

They turned onto Boulder Pass. A crowd was gathered near the magick shop, but it was a smaller one than what she saw around Finnert's place. Since Kort's was surrounded by a glowing blue sphere, Danthres couldn't bring herself to be overly shocked that people were gaping.

As soon as they approached, the same wizard who'd kicked them out of Finnert's appeared suddenly in a flash of light. "About time you arrived," he said without preamble. "The spell was only going to last another hour." With a gesture, the blue sphere dissipated, prompting a gasp from the onlookers.

One of them stepped forward, moving close to Dourti. The wizard said, "Ah, good, you're here. This is Yan, he's the manager of the shop. He will handle whatever you need — I have other, more important, business to attend to." With that, he gestured and disappeared in a flash of light.

Danthres had been hoping the wizard would stick around. Disappointed, she turned to Yan, a dwarf wearing a bright yellow tunic that almost blinded Danthres. "Where's the body?"

"It was discovered on the street," the dwarf said, "though we removed it in short order."

She sighed. "You *really* shouldn't have done that. It will be a great deal more difficult to ascertain who killed Kort if his body's been moved."

However, ban Wyvald was peering at the dirt road — while the main thoroughfares of Cliff's End were cobblestone, side streets like this were still glorified pathways — and said, "It doesn't matter. This *isn't* where Kort was killed."

Danthres couldn't believe this. "Excuse me?"

Ignoring her, ban Wyvald looked at Yan, pointing at a spot in the dirt. "This is where you found the body, yes?"

Sounding impressed, Yan said, "Yes, Lieutenant, that is precisely where his body was. How are you aware of that?"

"There's a body-shaped impression in the dirt. The impression is exactly the same size as a person's body, without any variance — which means he didn't fall, as that usually leaves an impression that does not perfectly conform to a person's shape. When people fall, they twitch or thrash about or try to stop their fall, or do something else to pervert the shape of the impression."

After blinking, Danthres stared down at where ban Wyvald was pointing. It just looked like dirt to her.

"Also," he added, "there's only one set of footprints between the door and here, heading to and from, and there's also only a little bit of blood on the ground. The body was placed here after Kort was killed. If, as you say, his throat was cut, had he been murdered on this pass, there would be far more blood."

Now Danthres rolled her eyes. She was almost starting to respect ban Wyvald's observations, but now he was just parroting Iaian. "You don't know that."

"I do, actually. Believe me, I've seen more than my share of cut throats in my time—the blood tends to spray." He turned to Yan. "May we see the inside of the shop, please?"

Yan nodded and walked toward the shop's entrance. "Please come with me." He glanced up at Danthres. "You must feel very fortunate to have so knowledgeable a partner."

Danthres didn't even dignify that with a response. When she caught ban Wyvald smiling, she glowered at him.

However, the inside of the shop told them nothing more than Finnert's did. It had a similar arrangement to the other one, except the desk was along the side wall, running the length of the shop, with a doorway covered in beads leading to the rear storage.

This time, Danthres went into the rear while ban Wyvald continued to look fruitlessly at the main floor.

The back was filled with floor-to-ceiling shelves filled to bursting with boxes, scrolls, jars, and more. She glanced at something in one of the jars that looked really disgusting, and decided not to peer at it too closely.

Besides, the door that went to the area behind the shop caught her eye: it was covered in blood.

Leaning back, she cried out, "Ban Wyvald!"

He came in a moment later. "What is it?"

She pointed at the door.

"Ah. Yes. As I said, cut throats tend to spray blood."

"But everything's in place, neatly on the shelves." Danthres shook her head.

"There's no indication that there was any kind of struggle. I can't imagine that a wizard would just *let* someone cut his throat."

"Indeed." Then ban Wyvald chuckled. "A pity, really."

"What is?" Danthres was confused, as she found nothing humorous about anything that had happened since she walked into the squadroom this morning.

"Under other circumstances, we could ask Kort to cast the Inanimate Residue Spell that would peel back the scene. If Dourti ever deigns to speak to us again, perhaps we can ask him."

"Perhaps." Danthres shuddered at the notion. She'd already dealt with wizards more in the last week than she ever expected to in her entire life. Mages did not consort with the likes of her, after all. But then, wizards didn't usually get killed, either. "I believe we shall speak to him again, but until then, we've learned all we can so far from this scene."

"Have we? I don't see that we've learned much of anything beyond the fact that Kort was killed here and taken outside."

Now Danthres grinned, looking forward to showing this neophyte how detective work was done. "We know that he was killed by someone he knew and trusted. It's not possible for a wizard to be caught unawares by a stranger, so he must have allowed his killer to get very close to him. The killer then wanted everyone to know that he'd killed a wizard, so he left the body outside in front of the wizard's shop where it was guaranteed to be seen in very short order. Our killer is someone who is bold, a friend to both victims, and who has something to gain by their very public deaths."

Nodding, ban Wyvald said, "Yes, I can see that. Thank you."

To Danthres's annoyance, he sounded completely sincere.

Grumbling, she turned on Yan. "We need to investigate the other store, but we may need to come back here, so do not open up just yet." Glancing at ban Wyvald, she said, "We'll need to contact the manager of Finnert's store."

"Oh, that's easy enough," Yan said. "I'm the manager of both stores."

Danthres whirled on him. "Really? When did that happen?"

"Just last week, actually. Why?"

# YAN

YAN HAD BEEN SITTING IN THE INTERVIEW ROOM FOR WHAT SEEMED LIKE hours. He couldn't hear the timechimes in here, and there were no windows, so he had no idea how long it had really been.

All he'd said was that he was the manager of both stores. Then they took him to Finnert's store, and then they had the guards who were watching Finnert's take him back to the castle under arrest!

That wouldn't have been so bad, but then they put him in this damn room. The only illumination came from a lantern providing insufficient light, a table, three stools, and a door, which remained opened just a crack. Yan could hear voices and footfalls, though none of the former were distinct enough to make out actual words.

He dabbed the sweat that was beading off his high forehead. When those two lieutenants came in here, he was going to give them a piece of his mind, you could bet the house on *that*! He had been rehearsing the harangue he would give those two in his head for the last however-bloody-long he'd been in here, and once they showed up...

And then, finally, the pair of them came in, their cloaks swirling imperiously behind them as they walked through the door.

Opening his mouth and holding up a finger, Yan promptly forgot what he was going to say to the two of them.

"Our apologies," said the male detective while Yan sat there stupidly with his mouth open, "but we needed to check on some things before we could speak to you."

"Check on what things?" Yan's voice came out as a croak. He'd been hoping to come across as aggrieved, and instead he sounded like he'd just woken up.

The ugly female detective said, "We needed to confirm a few things with the records office in the castle's other wing and speak to some people."

"What people?" Yan really hoped they didn't talk to his wife.

Unfortunately, the woman didn't answer the question. "Imagine our surprise to learn that you were the one who inherited ownership of *both* shops."

Yan swallowed. "Yeah, I know that. You coulda just asked me."

"Really?" The woman sounded amazed. "You would have volunteered information that gives you an excellent reason to have killed Kort and Finnert?"

"Are you nuts? Why would I want to kill those two?"

The man smiled, showing teeth so nice, Yan thought *he* might be a wizard. "I believe Lieutenant Tresyllione just explained that."

"You see," the woman—Tresyllione—said, "you've gone from being the manager of one shop to the manager of two shops to the owner of two shops. In my experience, the owner makes more money than the manager."

Yan shook his head. "Yeah, well, there's some shit that money can't buy. I'm already lookin' to sell."

Tresyllione blinked. "What?"

"Which shop are you selling?" the red-haired man asked.

"Both." Yan shuddered. "I only been at this a day and I already can't take the nonsense from the damn Brotherhood. They got rules, they got regulations, and for Xinf's sake, have they got paperwork. I can barely *write* in Common, and they're asking me to fill out all these scrolls with requests and permissions and work orders, and I just can't *take* it! Worst thing that ever happened to me was those mages getting killed."

The man shook his head. "It seems I was wrong about him."

After staring daggers at her partner for reasons Yan wasn't too clear on, Tresyllione turned to Yan. "Who are you selling to?"

"I ain't sold it yet," he said with a sigh. "If you know anybody who wants to buy a shop or two, send 'em my way, willya? There's only three stores sellin' those new Bags of Holding, and I own two of 'em."

"You know, it's easy for you to *say* that you wish to sell the stores," Tresyllione said, "but it's been my experience that murderers lie. Besides, we also spoke to your wife."

Yan winced.

Tresyllione continued: "She told us that you weren't home when the murders took place. And—"

The other detective interrupted. "The murders were also committed—" Then he realized what he'd done. "My apologies, Lieutenant, please, go ahead."

"As Lieutenant ban Wyvald began to say," Tresyllione said, sounding a bit exasperated, "the murderers were committed in the shops when they were closed by someone whom the victims knew and trusted."

"That perfectly describes you, doesn't it?" the man—ban Wyvald—said.

After giving another look to her partner, Tresyllione said, "I'm afraid, we'll need to know where you were when the two wizards were killed."

Yan started fidgeting on the desk. He really was hoping to avoid this.

But he couldn't get arrested for murder. That would get him hanged.

"Talk to Suzett," he said with a heavy sigh. "She runs a place on Sandy Brook Way. I been there pretty much every night the last month." He leaned back in his chair. "Myna's gonna kill me."

Ban Wyvald said, "Myna would be your wife?"

"Yeah." Yan frowned. "Hey, wait, you said you talked to her!"

Tresyllione grabbed ban Wyvald by the arm and led him out of the room, muttering, "Next time, keep your damned mouth shut."

Putting his head in his hands, Yan muttered to himself. Myna was *definitely* going to kill him. Still, better that than a death sentence.

Though not by much...

# BONEEN

Boneen stared at the body of his old friend Javy Marta.

In his life, Boneen had only seen two dead wizards before today, and both of them died in their beds. Seeing Javy lying in front of his magick shop on Maple Lane was the most repugnant sight he'd ever seen. His throat cut open, dried blood caked on the wound, and his body just—just *lying* there.

He looked up at the guard from Unicorn Precinct who'd responded initially to the call for help. "Have you ever noticed, young man, the major difference between a dead body and a living one?"

"Erm." The guard frowned, clearly confused. "One's dead and one's alive?"

Boneen sighed. "Dead bodies don't move *at all*. Living bodies move in so many subtle ways. The ironic part is that Javy here is the one who showed me that. His father died a while back. His father wasn't a wizard like we were, so he only lived a normal lifespan." He shook his head. "The funny thing is, I was the only other wizard there. None of the others could be bothered, not even the wizard Javy was apprenticed to. Never understood that. In fact—"

He cut himself off when he heard voices coming down Maple Lane.

"You shouldn't have interrupted me."

"My apologies, but I had no idea you were going to continue speaking."

"And that idiotic 'and that's your wife?' question. I told you when we went in that we were going to lie about the wife."

"Actually, you said no such thing."

"I didn't?"

"No. I thought you *had* spoken to the wife while I was looking up the records."

"I don't believe—"

"Ah, hello," said the man, who had red hair. He and his companion, a hideous woman who was obviously half elf and half human, both wore guard armor with brown cloaks. Boneen had no idea what the cloak symbolized.

"I'm Lieutenant Danthres Tresyllione," the woman said. "We're with the Cliff's End Castle Guard, and we're here to investigate the murder."

After a sidelong glance at Tresyllione, the man said, "I'm Lieutenant Torin ban Wyvald. You found the body?"

"Yes. My name is Boneen. That's Javy Marta, and he and I were friends. We were meeting for lunch."

"You're also a wizard?" ban Wyvald asked.

Boneen nodded. "I didn't realize the Castle Guard had investigators—or that the Brotherhood would permit you to be involved."

"This is the third murder of a wizard in the last few days," ban Wyvald said.

"Hadn't you heard?" Tresyllione asked, sounding suspicious.

Shaking his head, Boneen said, "I've been vacationing in—well, it's hard to explain, exactly, but suffice it to say, I have not been anywhere nearby for the past month. I only came back to Barlin this morning, and used a Teleport Spell to meet up with Javy here in Cliff's End." He snorted. "He mentioned that he had some gossip about two other wizards who also apprenticed with the same..." He trailed off, as something horrible occurred to him. "Tell me, were the other two deaths Finnert and Tam Kort?"

Tresyllione frowned. "You know them?"

"Only by name. Javy, Finnert, and Kort all apprenticed with Myk Dourti about fifty years ago."

That got the two cloaked guards to exchange surprised glances. Tresyllione then looked at Boneen. "You're saying that all three of the victims apprenticed with the local representative of the Brotherhood?"

Boneen made a face. "When did they appoint that idiot to be the local representative?" He shook his head again. "Never mind, nothing those imbeciles do surprises me anymore. In any case, Lieutenants, I wish I could be of more service, but I attempted to cast a spell known as Inanimate Residue on the vicinity."

Nodding, ban Wyvald said, "We're familiar with the spell, yes. In fact, Kort cast one for us on an earlier case."

Tresyllione glared at ban Wyvald. "It wasn't for 'us,' you weren't—Oh, never mind."

"In any event," Boneen said quickly, not knowing nor caring what burr got in this pair's armor, "the spell was inconclusive, which means that some form of magick was involved."

Tresyllione stared at Boneen. "So does that mean a wizard killed him? That's insane!"

"It's *not* insane," Boneen said sadly, "though it's rare, especially these days. But no, that's not necessarily what happened. There are several types of magickal creatures that can affect the spell adversely, as can a store-bought spell."

"All right," Tresyllione said, "we need to look inside. Can you remain here, in case we have more questions?"

"Absolutely. I want to know who killed him." Boneen stomped toward the door, wanting to be there when the lieutenants looked around.

Inside, the shop looked pretty much the same as it did when Boneen had last been here—which was when Javy opened it. He'd rearranged things a bit, giving the potions more prominent shelf space near the desk, and having a door to the rear where there used to be beads.

The two detectives went into the back room while Boneen studied the inventory. All the usual items, including those ridiculous love potions that people kept buying even though they never worked the way the people buying them hoped they would.

He heard the two lieutenants muttering about blood through the door. Ignoring them, he looked around for the display for the Bags of Holding.

Frowning, he didn't see them.

Muttering a quick incantation, he cast a Search Spell to find the bags.

The spell revealed no such item anywhere inside the store—not even in the storage area.

"Lieutenants!" he cried out.

The two detectives poked their heads out from the back room. "What is it?" Tresyllione asked.

"The Bags of Holding aren't here."

They exchanged a look and then walked in. "Bags of Holding?" ban Wyvald asked.

"They're bags that are a portal to another dimension—they enable one to store considerably more than the bag's external capacity. It's only limited by what will fit through the mouth of the bag."

Tresyllione asked, "And Javy sold these?"

"The entire reason he and I were having lunch today was so he could show off the Bags of Holding. The magick required to make them work is incredibly difficult. Javy was very proud that they'd finally found a way to make it work."

"Who's 'they' in this context?" ban Wyvald asked.

"No idea." Boneen shrugged. "Javy just said he was working with other wizards on it. I didn't really care all that much, so I didn't ask. But he said they went on display last week." He opened his arms wide, as if to take in the entire shop. "So where are they?"

# DANTHRES

Danthres stared at Torin ban Wyvald, and tried to come up with a way to get him to not join her in the interview room.

After the disaster with the dwarf, she wanted to just go it alone. While she'd only been a detective for half a year, she had developed a methodology, and ban Wyvald was completely spoiling it with his amateur idiocy.

Newcastle had given Quane's old desk, which was behind Danthres's, to ban Wyvald. He was looking over a scroll, and then turned around.

"Lieutenant Tresyllione, may I make a request?"

She blinked. "I suppose."

"I was wondering if I might interview Mr. Dourti alone."

Unable to help herself, Danthres burst out laughing. "Excuse me?"

"When I was in the army, I was one of the people in charge of interrogating prisoners. Over the years, I developed a methodology, and I'm afraid that your own interrogation methods are spoiling my own. And this amuses you?"

"You really think interrogating suspects is the same as interrogating prisoners of war?"

"Yes, actually. Both are inherently hostile, both are utterly uninterested in telling you anything, and both need to be tricked into revealing things they absolutely do not wish to reveal to someone who has the power of life and death over them."

That brought Danthres up short, as she had no clever retort for it.

From Osric's office came the captain's voice. "You'll both be interrogating Dourti."

With a sidelong glance at her partner, Danthres said to Osric, "That's a mistake, Captain. I hate to admit it, but ban Wyvald's right—except it should be me in there."

"It will be both of you, and that is final." Osric took a breath and walked over to the two of them. "I don't think you two understand the importance of your newfound partnership, so I'll explain it to you. You see, Lord Albin believes very strongly in the Guard, and he took a big risk hiring an outsider like me to run it. As a result, for the past ten months, he has meticulously read every single scroll that has gone through this squadroom to make sure I'm doing as good a job as he had hoped I would do when he hired me to replace Brisban."

Danthres had to resist the urge to spit. There were a lot of people in this world whom Danthres hated with every fibre of her being, but Brisban had always been second from the top of that list, surpassed only by her cousin Sicund. The happiest day of her life since arriving in Cliff's End was the day Brisban died.

Osric continued: "One of the things Lord Albin has noticed is the heavy turnover rate of people whose job description includes being your partner, Tresyllione. So ban Wyvald is your last chance. If you can't make it work with him, you're finished in the Guard."

Swallowing, Danthres said, "Captain, I—"

But Osric wasn't done. He turned his one-eyed gaze upon ban Wyvald. "As for you, you've been granted a very special privilege, bypassing the usual promotion structure because I firmly believe that you're the only person in all of Flingaria who can save this woman's job. And if you can't, you'll be back on the streets with her looking for work."

Nodding, ban Wyvald said, "I understand."

"I don't!" Danthres stood up. "I've done a damn good job of—"

"You've done a decent job, Tresyllione, yes. But close this case? You'll be wearing magick armor. Prior to Finnert's murder, there had been no reported unnatural deaths of a wizard that weren't during a time of war. The people who solve this will be well set, believe me."

Before Danthres could reply to that, a familiar voice sounded from the west-wall doorway. "Excuse me."

Whirling around, Danthres saw Myk Dourti.

"Welcome back, Mr. Dourti," Osric said in what Danthres recognized as his most insincere polite tone.

"I do not feel especially welcome. Why has this castle been warded against Teleport Spells?"

"My apologies," Osric said unapologetically, "but Lord Albin purchased the wards after a wizard presumptuously teleported into his castle unannounced."

Dourti scowled. "I was told you wished to speak to me about the murders. I have better things to do than waste time with the likes of you."

Danthres bridled, while ban Wyvald said, "We understand, sir, truly, but there are questions that we must pose if we are to learn who killed Kort, Javy, and Finnert."

"You yourself told Captain Osric," Danthres added, "that the Brotherhood wanted us to solve these murders."

With a sigh, Dourti said, "Very well. Pose your questions."

Indicating one of the interview rooms with a hand, ban Wyvald said, "If you'll come this way, sir. I believe it would be best if this conversation took place in private."

"That, Lieutenant, is the first thing you've said with which I've completely agreed." The wizard stormed past both detectives and went into the interview room.

Danthres exchanged a look with ban Wyvald, then looked at Osric.

The captain merely said, "Get it done, you two."

After Danthres walked in, ban Wyvald right behind her, she saw Dourti standing at the table. "Where, exactly, am I to sit in this dreadful room?"

Pointing to the stool behind the table, Danthres said, "Right there, Mr. Dourti. We just have a few questions, and I'm sure this will all be resolved very quickly."

"I hope so." Dourti sat in the indicated stool. "I have a great deal of *important* work to be doing."

"Fascinating," ban Wyvald said.

"Excuse me?" Dourti asked archly.

Shaking his head, ban Wyvald replied, "My apologies, but that's far from the first time you've indicated that there's work more important than this. And yet, we've spoken with several other wizards—"

Dourti stood up. "You did *what*?"

"Is there a problem?" Danthres was now leaning against the wall, and at the mage's outburst, she raised an eyebrow. "It is standard procedure for detectives to question people who knew the victim of a homicide."

"You should not have questioned members of the Brotherhood without checking with me first."

"Why?" ban Wyvald asked. "They are all private citizens who are free to speak to whomever they wish. None of them seemed to have an issue with discussing what they knew of Finnert, Kort, and Javy. Indeed, by talking to them, we were able to determine what the three of them have—or, rather, *had* in common."

In fact, aside from Boneen, they all had great reluctance to discuss anything with the two of them. Danthres hadn't realized how incredibly snotty wizards could be. She was glad that ban Wyvald had the good sense to lie to Dourti about that.

"You already *know* what they have in common," Dourti said dismissively as he sat back down, folding his arms over his robed chest. "They all owned shops."

"Yes," ban Wyvald said, "and they were also killed by someone who knew them all well and had access to the back rooms of their shops."

Dourti cocked his head to the side. "Interesting. You suspect Yan, don't you?"

A bit mockingly, Danthres matched his head gesture. "Why do you say that?"

"Do not attempt your tiresome rhetorical trickery on me, Lieutenant. Yan is an obvious candidate for committing these murders, as he fits the criteria you just listed."

"Yes, he does." Danthres came away from the wall. "And indeed, we did interview Yan, only to discover that he can account for his whereabouts during the times that the murders took place."

Rolling his eyes, Dourti said, "I'm not surprised that you just *believed* him."

"Oh, we didn't. But we checked, and there are about half a dozen witnesses at Suzett's on Sandy Brook Way."

Smiling, ban Wyvald added, "Quite helpful, was Suzett."

"He could have paid those concubines off," Dourti said, pointing a finger at Danthres. "He owns the shops now, so he'd be motivated to spend the money."

"Unfortunately, that doesn't *quite* work," Danthres said, "because Yan had no such motivation to commit Javy's murder—and he has an even better alibi for that one, as he was in our holding cell when it happened."

Taking a seat in one of the stools opposite Dourti, ban Wyvald leaned on the table with both elbows. "Besides, we actually were not done enumerating the commonalities among the victims. For example, they were the only three shops in all of Cliff's End that sold Bags of Holding."

"A very popular item," Danthres put in, "especially for people who shop down Jorbin's Way. Much easier to carry multiple items from many stands home if you can put it all in a single container."

"I'm sure they also all sold the same type of love potion." Dourti stood up. "Lieutenants, you are wasting my time, which is far too precious to be wasted on the likes of you. If there's nothing else."

Standing up to face him, ban Wyvald said, "There's just a few more items, sir, please, if you'd sit down."

Declining the invitation to sit, Dourti instead started to pace. "You said you had questions to ask me. Thus far, your only questions have directly related to things I've said rather than the solving of these murders."

"Fine," Danthres said, "here's one. Why didn't you tell us about the most important commonality the three victims had?"

Derisively, Dourti said, "You already knew they all owned shops."

"I meant that they *all* apprenticed under you."

Stopping in mid-pace, Dourti whirled upon Danthres with outrage. "How did you know that? The bond between apprentice and student is *sacred*! Such as you should *never* be privy to such private information!"

"You may wish to speak to your fellow wizards about that," ban Wyvald said. "The information was provided to us without hesitation."

"By whom?"

Before ban Wyvald could respond, Danthres quickly said, "We ask the questions in this room, Mr. Dourti, and right now I would ask you to sit down."

Dourti put his hands on his hips. "I demand to know who provided this intelligence to you! It is a dire breach of protocol!"

Stepping between Dourti and Danthres, ban Wyvald said, "Policing the Brotherhood of Wizards is outside our purview. Our goal is to discover who kill three of your fellows."

"You don't understand —"

Talking over ban Wyvald's shoulder, Danthres said, "No, *you* don't understand. Put your house in order on your own time. You're on ours right now, and we're not done talking to you."

"Please sit down, Mr. Dourti," ban Wyvald said quietly but firmly.

With a snarl, Dourti sat down. "This is ludicrous."

Danthres and ban Wyvald both sat down opposite Dourti. The latter said, "You do not deny that all three victims were your apprentices? Bear in mind that lying to us is an offense within this city-state."

Somehow, Danthres managed not to snort. Nobody who sat in that stool ever worried about that—but then, that was usually because they were arrogant enough to think they wouldn't get caught. In six months, Danthres hadn't seen anyone sit on that stool who was anywhere near as arrogant as this mage.

"Yes, I trained all of them. What of it? I've lived for two centuries, Lieutenants, and I've trained many wizards."

"And you worked with all three of them on creating a Bag of Holding," Danthres said.

"Quite a difficult endeavor, we've been told," ban Wyvald added.

"You never managed it, with any of them."

"Not for lack of trying, certainly."

"No, and yet they managed it without you."

Dourti cried, "They did no such thing! It was *my* research that led to the creation of the Bags! *Mine*! They had *no* right to cut me out of the profits! You think any of those three idiots would have even come close to the right spell without my guidance? And were they grateful?"

"So that's why you killed them?" ban Wyvald asked.

Danthres winced, as asking the direct question always made people stop talking.

But Dourti, still screaming, replied. "Yes! They deserved to die for betraying me like that! I showed them love and affection far more than any other wizard would have! And this is how they thank me?"

Quickly, Danthres stood up. She said formally, "In the name of Lord Albin and Lady Meerka, I hereby place you, Myk Dourti, under arrest for the murders of Finnert, Tam Kort, and Javy Marta. Other charges to be added as necessary."

Dourti scoffed. "I do not recognize your authority to arrest me, mortals." With that, he gestured.

A moment later, tendrils of energy surrounded all four of his limbs, pulling him outward and upward so that he floated several handslengths over the floor, his arms and legs splayed.

His eyes blazing, spit flying from his mouth, Dourti cried out, "What is the meaning of this? I will *not* be restrained in this manner!"

Smiling, ban Wyvald said, "We did warn you that the castle was warded, did we not?"

The door to the interview room opened, and Osric stepped inside, along with Sir Gevlin, Boneen, and another one of the wizards they'd spoken to, Lord Ythran.

Dourti stared right at Boneen. "I should've known. You've never understood the bond between apprentice and student, Boneen. As soon as these two mortal imbeciles told me that I was betrayed—"

Boneen sneered. "Everyone knows who you took on as apprentices, Myk, stop being such a fool."

Ythran stared daggers at Boneen. "You revealed his apprentices?"

"Of course I did," Boneen said, sounding confused as to why it was an issue—a confusion Danthres shared.

"We will discuss that later." Ythran regarded Danthres and her partner. "The Brotherhood of Wizards thanks you for your hard work, Lieutenants. We shall deal with this murderer ourselves."

Sir Gevlin stepped forward, holding up a rune. "I'm afraid not. Mr. Dourti is in our custody now."

He touched the rune while muttered something, and Danthres quickly covered her sensitive eyes. Through her eyelids she could tell that there was a flash of light. When she opened them, Dourti was gone.

Angrily, Ythran asked Gevlin, "Where is he?"

"He is now in our holding facility beneath the castle."

"That was *not* our arrangement." Ythran's dagger-stare was now fixed on Gevlin.

The noble was taken aback. "Er, I'm sorry, My Lord, but I am performing my duties as instructed by Lord Albin and Lady Meerka. I'm afraid that you must register any objection with them."

"Oh, I shall, rest assured." With that, he stormed out.

Biting his lower lip, Gevlin muttered, "I'd best go with him," and ran after the mage.

Danthres noticed that ban Wyvald was shaking his head. "What is it?" she asked.

"It's just sad, is all. You could tell he really cared about those three. He said he gave them love and affection—and they went and created their lucrative product without him."

"Love and affection?" Boneen asked. "He said that about his apprentices?"

"Yes, he did," ban Wyvald said. "Why?"

"The very last things a wizard should show an apprentice are love and affection." He shuddered. "It seems the rumors were true about him."

"What rumors?" Danthres asked.

"Never mind. I'd best follow Sir Gevlin and Lord Ythran. Well done, Lieutenants."

The diminutive wizard waddled out of the interview room, leaving Danthres with her new partner and her captain.

She smiled at Osric. "Magick armor?"

Osric snorted. "If you're lucky. Good work, you two."

As the three of them went out into the squadroom, ban Wyvald said, "I owe you an apology, Lieutenant."

Danthres whirled on him. "Oh, you do, do you?"

He grinned. "Indeed, I do. You're an excellent interrogator. It was a pleasure to partner with you on it."

She sighed. "Much as it pains me to admit it—I feel the same way. Perhaps you'll last a *bit* longer than Quane did."

Speaking over his shoulder as he headed to his office, Osric said, "You'd better hope it's a lot longer!"

Carefully waiting until the captain was out of earshot, Danthres said, "What I hope is that I can work alone. Since that seems to be rather a forlorn hope indeed, I suppose I could do worse than partnering with you, ban Wyvald." She chuckled, looking over at Iaian's desk, currently empty. He and Linder had taken a call earlier. "In fact, I have done worse, quite recently."

"Well, thank you for that, Lieutenant Tresyllione. And please, call me Torin. Being called 'ban Wyvald' reminds me of—of something I'd prefer not to be reminded of."

Frowning, Danthres said, "But that's how Osric refers to you."

Ban Wyvald—or, rather, Torin—smiled ruefully. "Yes, he does. I gave up asking him to call me by my given name after a month."

Danthres chuckled. "Very well—Torin. And you may call me Lieutenant Tresyllione.

Torin's face fell, and Danthres found she couldn't hold in her laughter. She added quickly, "Or Danthres is fine, as well."

They sat down at their respective desks to start filling out the paperwork that would be needed so Dourti could be properly prosecuted. Rather, Danthres filled it out while Torin, who as yet had had no instruction in same, watched and learned how to do it.

By the time Danthres was done, and had finished answering Torin's many — and, she had to admit, intelligent — questions about the procedure, a pageboy entered the squadroom. "L'tenants Tresyllione and Binwid?"

Torin gently corrected him. "That's 'ban Wyvald.' What may we do for you?"

"You two an' Cap'n Osric need t'be comin' wif me. Lord Albin needs t'see you."

# TORIN

Torin found himself to be very impressed with the statuary that lined the corridors of the central area of the castle. The eastern wing where the Castle Guard's squadroom was kept was functional and utilitarian, with only a few bits of decoration—the ugly dragon statue, the pretty unicorn tapestry.

The quality of the sculpture, however, improved tremendously in this section. The pieces displayed on marble stands here were more elegant than anything Torin had seen since leaving Myverin, where he'd been training to replace his father as Chief Artisan. That training was ended abruptly by Torin running away from Myverin as fast as he could go.

He made a mental note to ask someone in the court who the sculptor was, when the opportunity presented itself.

For now, the pageboy led him, Danthres, and Osric toward a set of large wooden double doors.

Leaning over to Danthres, he whispered, "So I'll get to meet the Lord and Lady?"

"We both will," Danthres whispered back, "and just the Lord. Lady Meerka would only be in the meeting if it involves the treasury, from what I've been led to understand."

Torin raised an eyebrow. "You haven't met them yet, either?"

"I'd been hoping to continue to not have done so. The captain's always in a foul mood after he talks with Lord Albin."

Further conversation was ended by the pageboy opening the double doors to reveal an opulent room filled with comfortable furniture—including a large chair and a sofa—more statuary as well as a lovely tapestry on one wall, and a fireplace, currently inactive.

Seated on the sofa were the two wizards, Boneen and Lord Ythran, the former's legs dangling above the floor. A bald man with a thick mustache and a hawk nose that rivaled Torin's own aquiline proboscis for size sat in the large chair. Since the meeting was with Lord Albin, and since the bald man was the only one in the room Torin didn't recognize, he had to be the most powerful man in the demesne. Next to his chair was a small sideboard on which sat a crystal goblet about a third filled with an amber liquid.

"Ah, Captain Osric, thank you for joining us."

Osric inclined his head. "Of course, My Lord."

The captain's words confirmed it, and the lack of a woman in the room besides Danthres confirmed his partner's opinion that Lady Meerka was not present.

"This," Osric continued, indicating the two lieutenants with a gesture, "is Lieutenant ban Wyvald and his partner, Lieutenant Tresyllione. They were the ones who closed the case."

"Welcome to the Castle Guard, Lieutenant ban Wyvald," Lord Albin said jovially. "It seems you had quite the first case."

Testily, Lord Ythran said, "If we may dispense with the tiresome formalities, we need to resolve this immediately."

"I don't see that there's anything to resolve," Albin said equally testily. "You asked us to find the person who killed three wizards. Lieutenants ban Wyvald and Tresyllione did so."

"Yes, and Dourti's apparent guilt—"

"Apparent?" Danthres's parroting of Ythran echoed off the stone walls of the room.

"Yes, 'apparent,' and if the mortal would please be silent," Ythran said with a sneer, "we may continue. Dourti's *apparent* guilt would explain why he was reluctant to involve the Castle Guard in this case. I will admit that it would not have occurred to us to suspect one of our own."

Boneen muttered, "Wouldn't have occurred to *you*, perhaps."

Torin tried not to snort at that. He was mostly successful.

"But Dourti *is* one of ours," Ythran said, "and we must be the ones to dispense justice."

Albin shifted in his chair. "Hardly your place after asking us to step in. The law is crystal clear on this matter. If the case involves magick, it falls within the Brotherhood's jurisdiction, but if you refuse to accept that jurisdiction, it becomes the purview of the Castle Guard. When you requested that my detectives investigate—"

"Yes, I understand that." Ythran waved his arms back and forth dismissively. "But that was before we discovered that the perpetrator—"

"We're going around in circles," Albin said, interrupting the wizard right back. "Lieutenant ban Wyvald, can you confirm that Myk Dourti is the perpetrator of those crimes?"

Torin nodded. "Yes, My Lord. He, in fact, admitted it to Lieutenant Tresyllione and myself, and then attempted to escape arrest."

"And you will both testify to that before the magistrate," Albin asked, "making his guilt a matter of public record?"

Danthres said, "Absolutely, My Lord," while Torin simply nodded.

Now Ythran was squirming, and Torin started to see what the lord of the demesne was getting at.

"We do not wish—" Ythran started, then hesitated.

Boneen rolled his eyes. "Dammit, Ythran, the man killed his apprentices! Over *commerce*!"

Ythran snapped, "And that is not a fact that it would be well for the general public to be aware of."

"Yes, it would be just *terrible* if they knew that we were fallible."

"It would, in fact." Ythran was gesturing like mad as he ranted. "The Brotherhood was formed in part to reassure the people that wizards are very much *in*fallible, that the days of megalomaniacal wizards like Chalmraik the Foul and Mitos are a thing of the past!"

Torin shuddered. He'd never encountered any of the crazed wizards that had tried to take over Flingaria over the decades, though he'd heard quite a bit about them growing up in Myverin. Indeed, one of his father's (many) arguments for why he shouldn't leave the safety of Myverin was that he was far less likely to be enslaved by a mad mage if he stayed home.

Albin leaned forward. "Understand something, Lord Ythran. If you do not allow us to bring Dourti to justice, if you do not allow our magistrate to pass judgment upon someone who killed three of Cliff's End's merchants, then we will let it be known far and wide that the Brotherhood of Wizards is a sham that hides its mendacity behind arrogance and falsehood."

Torin wasn't sure that entirely made sense, but he wasn't about to correct the lord's syntax in this setting. Or ever, truly.

Besides, his words seemed to have an effect on Ythran, who looked as if he'd been asked to swallow a live snake.

Danthres, for her part, looked satisfied. Torin was impressed with her zeal for justice, and he wondered where that came from, exactly. Half elves who lived past the age of three days were almost always from Sorlin, a little colony to the south that was generally considered to be peaceful and orderly. Of course, that very peace and order may have led to her striving for it outside Sorlin's borders. He made a mental note to ask her about it.

"What is it you want, then, Lord Albin?" Every word was practically spit by the wizard.

Albin leaned back in his chair and grabbed the drink off the sideboard. "If you wish to take Dourti into your custody and if you wish the truth of his crime to be kept from the people in order to keep your precious reputation intact, we will require the cooperation of the Brotherhood." He turned to Danthres. "Lieutenant Tresyllione, your report on the murder of that poor young woman who tended bar at the Stone Kobold indicated that a mage was able to cast a spell that revealed the events of the recent past?"

"Uhm—" Danthres swallowed, looking less pleased. "Yes, My Lord. It was a wizard named Kort—he was a witness to Gava's murder before he was killed by Dourti. For that matter, Boneen here cast the same spell on one of the wizard murders, but it was inconclusive due to a mage being the murderer. Magick can apparently interfere with the spell, and that was one of the things that led us to Dourti as a suspect."

"Interesting. Thank you, Lieutenant." Lord Albin turned back to Ythran. "We will keep the Brotherhood's secrets, but only if you provide the Castle Guard with a wizard who can serve as a sort of examiner, who will cast this peel-back spell that Lieutenant Tresyllione described."

Ythran folded his arms. "So it's to be extortion, is it?"

"Simply an acknowledgment that actions have consequences, My Lord."

Torin noted that Lord Albin didn't start referring to Ythran as "My Lord" until he made his request.

For several seconds, Ythran simply sat with his arms folded, before speaking again. "And if I tell you that the Brotherhood does not respond well to extortion, and that your attempt to bargain with us will result in your demesne being sanctioned by the Brotherhood?"

Albin took a sip of his drink before replying. "That would be your prerogative. But considering how much unlicensed magick there is in this city-state, I would think you would jump at the opportunity for one of your own to be part of the process by which it's pursued and stopped. However, if you wish to sanction us, then by all means, do so. We'll put Dourti on trial and reveal his crimes for all to see. And I'm sure there are plenty of merchants who will eagerly jump at the real estate opportunities provided by eighty-three magick shops that will have to close once you sanction Cliff's End. I'm also sure that you will be hard-pressed to replace the lost revenue from the sudden shuttering of those shops, not to mention all the mages who hire themselves out privately." Albin smiled. "It's entirely up to you. And keep in mind that sanctioning Cliff's End for the devastating crime of following the law will not be looked upon favorably by the King and Queen, either."

Putting his head in his hands, Boneen said, "Oh for pity's sake, Ythran, just accept the offer. It's not as if you have a choice."

Witheringly, Ythran said, "There is always a choice, Boneen. If you had simply kept your mouth shut—" He shook his head. "Fine. You believe we have no choice, then *you* may serve as this—this magickal examiner that Lord Albin suggests."

"What?" Boneen rose to his feet, but his diminutive height made him no taller while standing than he was sitting on the couch. "Why am I to perform this ridiculous task?"

Ythran shrugged. "You know Inanimate Residue. You've already proven you can work with the Castle Guard, since you were so *incredibly* cooperative with them."

"But—"

Gesturing, Ythran stood up. "It is done. Boneen shall be your new magickal examiner. I assume you will find accommodations for him here in the castle. In exchange, I expect the wards to release Dourti into my custody."

Sir Gevlin stepped forward. "With My Lord's permission, I will take care of that."

Albin nodded, and Gevlin indicated the door. "Come this way, please, Lord Ythran?"

Torin smirked. Gevlin, it seemed, did not consider Ythran to be "his" Lord.

As soon as Ythran and Gevlin departed, Danthres exploded. "That's *it*?"

"Is there a problem, Lieutenant?" Albin's tone lowered the temperature in the room.

"We can't just let Dourti *go*!"

"On the contrary, Lieutenant, we had little choice in the matter. Wizards are stubborn creatures, and if we attempted to hold Dourti and subject him to our laws, the backlash would have been vicious."

"But what about justice for his victims?"

"They were also wizards." Albin shrugged. "I appreciate your zeal, Lieutenant, but this was the best possible outcome. Trying to keep Dourti here would have started a war between the Brotherhood and King Marcus and Queen Marta. We only just finished fighting the Elf Queen, I doubt that a new conflict would benefit anyone. This way we were able to get a killer out of our city-state, and gain ourselves a valuable asset."

That got a sneer out of Boneen. "How nice to see that, at my age, I'm reduced to being an asset."

"Oh you will be quite the asset, Boneen, believe me. When Sir Gevlin returns, speak to him about what arrangements you require here at the castle." He looked at Torin, Danthres, and Osric. "Thank you, Captain, Lieutenants. You've done *very* well today. That will be all."

Danthres just stood there while Osric and Torin headed out. Gently, Torin touched her shoulder, at which point she shook her head and followed them out.

"I don't know what disgusts me more," she said, not bothering to wait until they were out of earshot of Albin's sitting room, "that the Brotherhood are so much more interested in preserving their image that they'd barter with justice like that, or that Lord Albin would go along with it for his own benefit."

"Our job is to keep the people of Cliff's End safe, Tresyllione," Osric said. "Justice is simply a fortuitous side benefit — and one we didn't get this time. But you caught Dourti and he *will* be punished. I doubt we did him any favors by turning him over to the Brotherhood."

He stopped, turned, and smiled at them. Osric didn't smile very often, and Torin could tell that he wasn't any better at it now than he had been on the front lines.

"I knew I was right to put you two together. You did excellent work. Now go home and take the rest of the day off. First case tomorrow's yours, and I expect you both to close it."

With that, he turned and walked down the corridor.

Danthres still looked aggravated—though, Torin supposed, that was her normal look. "Are you all right, Danthres?"

She let out a very long breath. "I will be. I suppose. But I'm really starting to learn to hate magick."